Libby Purves is the author of eight bestselling novels and many works of non-fiction, and is a familiar Radio 4 broadcaster and *Times* columnist. She lives in Suffolk with her husband Paul Heiney and two children.

Also by Libby Purves

Libby Purves

A Long Walk
in Wintertime

FLAME
Hodder & Stoughton

A CIP catalogue record for this title is
available from the British Library

ISBN 0 340 82931 1

Typeset in Sabon by Palimpsest Book Production Limited,
Polmont, Stirlingshire
Printed and bound in Great Britain by
Clays Ltd, St Ives plc

Hodder & Stoughton
A division of Hodder Headline
338 Euston Road
London NW1 3BH

to Christina Hardyment

AUTHOR'S NOTE

All the characters are entirely fictional. Sad to say, there is no such fair and no such family as the Baileys. However, Carters Steam Fair is a family-run traditional fair based in Berkshire, and it was Anna Carter's painting of their gallopers which sowed the original seed for this novel.

I am grateful to her both for her artistry and her generous technical advice. She is to be thanked for any accuracy this book shows about the traditional fairground world; but not to be blamed for lapses in that accuracy. Like all novelists, I took only as much of the advice as suited my purposes.

None of them would ever forget Alice's thirty-seventh birthday party. For one thing, it began in the Royal Opera House when they had been expecting nothing grander than the pizzeria in Floral Street. They had met outside on the pavement as Daniel had insisted, and stood laughing in their working-day clothes, ready for some ordinary unsurprising surprise party.

But when Daniel came, it was not to lead them into the pizza house. He was brandishing a fan of tickets and announced rudely that their stomachs would have to wait. He marshalled the six of them into the amphitheatre entrance and up the bare back staircase of the Opera House. Daniel always moved fast, and on this occasion he went at such a speed that the friends were panting their protests by the time they reached the top. On the bar, seven drinks stood in a neat row, marked McDONALD; and beside them a bewildered Alice with her ticket still in her hand, waiting perplexedly.

"Danny – what?" she said. "They've put out *seven* whiskies, for God's sake – Oh, you never said!" She had glimpsed Jennifer's fair head and Rod's balding one behind him, and her face softened into delight. "Jenny and Rod coming too – that's fabulous!" Alice slid her round glasses off, waving them, letting the world blur. It was a trick she had, when surprised by something she had seen. In a moment, though, the glasses were on again, for behind the puffing Rod, round the gilded corner of the amphitheatre bar came Yasmin, dark and saturnine, smiling crookedly. Yasmin! Yazz, so hard to get hold of these days, so disdainful of the opera always – yet she had come, had meekly climbed the sixty-seven steps for the first time that Alice could remember.

She started forward, her arms out, warm with happy surprise. "Yazz!"

Finally, giggling and shoving one another with their customary affected camp, came Stevie from the GardenGrow health shop round the corner and Simon from the bar, her daytime crony of canteen lunchtimes. "Busman's holiday, darling," said Simon. "Your *prodigal* husband didn't even ask if we got staff discount. Not that we do. Unless you do, you *office* people?"

"Drinks!" said Stevie, fanning himself. "Bottoms up, as the actress said to the cardinal."

Daniel put an arm round his wife. "I thought we should all come to your poxy opera with you, for once," he said placidly. "See this Argentine crooner you think so highly of."

Alice laughed, shook her head, and took a long draught of her watered whisky. "Dan, you are unspeakable. What a waste of money, bringing this lot to *Stiffelio*. Yasmin hates opera, Stevie and Sime only like ballet . . ."

"Oh, but we *do* like big dark Argy tenors," said Stevie. "And we want to watch you exercise your *unique* talent for empathy with silly libretti." Simon brandished a red booklet. "Very silly, in this case. We read it in the pub. *Aloud*. We shall get great inspiration seeing you cry your eyes out over the travails of a nineteenth-century Protestant evangelist whose wife has been on the tiles. He forgives her, you know. *Bitch!*"

The electric bell rang, incongruously like every schoolbell that sounds through tatty corridors of learning. On a bubble of gaiety, the party swept onward through the bar and down the steep slope between the seats to the open part of the balcony. Daniel had somehow organized seven seats in the very front row of the amphitheatre, close to the gilt and sky-blue extravagances of the ceiling. Leaning forward over the red velvet rail, faces flushed, the party giggled at the dizzying height and the smallness of the stage below. "My favourite place, seat of the gods! We are gods!" said Stevie happily. "Even Rod is Rod the God."

Rod, the only one in that bright row wearing a City suit and tie, coloured slightly. He was never wholly comfortable with the high-spirited camp of some of Alice's friends. But Dan and Alice were OK. Solid. Good parents. And just as well Alice had Jenny as well as this arty crowd. A woman with children needed sensible friends. Important, that. Rod settled his broad bottom into his seat, giving Stevie a brisk tight smile before looking away.

"Party bags. Pass them on." Daniel, still deadpan, handed out plastic sacks with gilt flowers on them, each containing a pair of folding cardboard opera glasses, a tube of throat sweets and a clip-on bow tie. Simon, whose calling required him to don a real one every single night, moaned at the sight of his and affixed it ostentatiously over his left ear in the manner of a small girl's hair ribbon. Alice sat in the centre of the row between Yasmin's silent, ironic smiles and Stevie's exuberance. Further along, Jenny said to Rod under her breath, "Isn't Dan *amazing*!" and Rod shook his head.

"Incredible. I suppose it's one of his jokes. Alice is always complaining that nobody will go to the opera with her even in the cheap seats."

"Well, I would," began Jenny, pulling at her neat white collar and wishing she had been told enough to dress for the occasion. "I do like music. But with the children to think of it seems such a wicked cost—" A ripple of applause from the stalls below cut her off, leaving her "wicked cost" hanging in the air. She sniffed, breathing in the wafts of perfume from the richer balcony seats below as the great room began to darken.

Around the sweeping Victorian galleries, red-shaded lamps glowed briefly like a scattering of bright toadstools, then vanished in turn. Alice was glad of the gloom, even glad for the moment to have these dear friends turned into insubstantial shadows at her side. She leaned forward and breathed the air she loved most, eyes half-closed, tuning herself to the hum of the orchestra in its tiny shining world of brass and varnish and mellow sound.

The overture began in a series of ominous thumps. Alice looked down. The warm light gleaming along the cellos and basses, glancing bravely off the brass, entranced her as it always had. The birthday party forgotten, without effort Mrs Alice McDonald threw off her life, her house, husband and children to drift on the overture's first notes. Rapt, she fell into total empathy. The great spirit of Stiffelio, the agony of faithless Lina, the baritone fury and fear of Stankar the father consumed her. For forty minutes – and then again for eighty, after another convivial row of drinks – Alice sat like a rock, eyes shining, oblivious of the amused, sidelong glances of her friends.

On her left Yasmin was restless, barely tolerating music and plot. When the Act II curtain rose on a desolate graveyard scene where Lina prayed for forgiveness at her mother's grave, Yasmin shook the shaggy black layers of her hair and uttered a barely audible "Doh!" of disgust, raising her eyes in invisible, affected horror to the surtitle board ("Ah, Mother . . . She is so pure . . . but I . . . offer penitent tears as a gift to the Almighty!") Women, in Yasmin's world, did not beg for forgiveness. They rarely, in her view, even needed to apologize. Lina ought to run off with Raffaele and have some fun, not spend the rest of her life apologizing to that old stiff, Stiffelio. Someone should tell her. No, hell, thought Yasmin moodily, picking lint off her neat black lapels. No point even advising her. Bloody woman was past hope, her with her floating drapes and yowling soprano. She could do as she pleased. Anything, just as long as she stopped singing. In the dark, surreptitiously, Yasmin looked down at the luminous dial of her very expensive watch.

Rod and Jenny held hands, not bothering much with the surtitles or the plot. They belonged to Sir Thomas Beecham's great amiable British public which "knows little about music but likes the noise it makes". The sets were marvellous, too. Jenny, a children's book illustrator, took mental notes in the graveyard scene: the way the corner of the church protruded into the foreground might help with her composition for *Bobby's Worrying Ghost*, a text of appalling banality by a celebrity author. Her roughs had to be in by Friday lunchtime.

Simon and Stevie cast more experienced, cynical eyes over the sets. Simon, like Alice, worked for the Opera House and Stevie had spent years as a dresser with the Royal Ballet before retiring in his forties to run the health food shop. But while Alice sank effortlessly into the illusion, detaching herself from the daily mundanities and corporate crises of the place with equal ease, that was not their way. Neither could appreciate front-of-house appearances without being constantly and enjoyably aware of the invisible world below and behind. Alice might weep freely over operatic deaths and dilemmas, soar with the soprano and shiver at the baritone and never once give a thought to the fact that a month earlier she had witnessed some tense, bad-tempered early rehearsal of the same scene when she was on an errand to the auditorium to deliver to the cleaners a fresh supply of chewing-gum remover for the carpets. Indeed, it was more likely that on such an errand the reverse would happen: the illusion would overtake her and she would freeze to the carpet like a piece of chewing gum herself, rapt by the drama, utterly accepting a fiction that even the director was hardly trying to create as yet. "You are," said an exasperated supervisor of her early days, "like one of those hypnotic subjects who are so suggestible they go under at the first swing of the watch. It's not professional, Alice." But Alice had laughed, and not cared.

Stevie and Simon, on the other hand, could not watch the most finished performance except through a ragged cloud of trivial knowledge, from the latest Costume gossip about the understudy for Dorotea and her suspiciously expanding waistline to their gleeful ability to visualize the awkward squeezings and scuttlings that followed each exit into the great stage's notoriously shallow wings. Their acquaintance with the damp black back wall, the antiquated mechanisms in the fly-tower overhead, the roughly chalked stacks of scenery in the old glass market hall alongside the stage, the internal and external rows about the coming redevelopment and the Lottery money excited them as much as Verdi's heartbreaking vision of human frailty. Sometimes, during ballet rehearsals in the old days, Stevie used to desert his post in Wardrobe and creep under the stage to hear the surprisingly loud thumps and scrapings of dancers. He would rock, alone there, in silent thrilled laughter. To him the pleasure lay in the effort that built the illusion, the thud at the end of the balletic leap. Simon had learned this appreciation from him in their nine years together. "It's like watching a drag queen get it together, from pancake to padding," Simon said, when better paid friends asked why he stuck to the Royal Opera House. "Gorgeous old House, gorgeous old whore." Noticing that the spotlight on Lina had wavered and fallen away sideways, he nudged Stevie. The young man and the older one leaned together, companionable, feeling one another's giggles through their thin, elegant shoulders. On Stevie's other side, Alice remained still, concentrated, utterly absorbed.

At last, at the final cry of *"Perdonata!"* she sighed and leaned back in happy satiety, closing her eyes to keep the final image of black-browed pastor Stiffelio at his lectern, forgiving his errant wife in the name of God. *Perdonata!* Perfect. An operatic resolution, a reconciliation made in music.

Daniel, in their early courting days, used to be charmed by the way that Alice kept her eyes shut during curtain calls at the theatre, clapping vigorously but blindly. "I just don't *like* seeing them come back to bow and simper like ordinary people," she would say. "I'm sorry, but he isn't John Gielgud to me. He's still Prospero." It was a source of perennial wonder and amusement to her family that she had kept to this absurd habit despite six years of working in a place where the staff canteen might at any moment be filled with pikemen or nuns in costume from the chorus. "But Mum, you said you'd seen the Egyptian priestesses eating *macaroni cheese*," said Clemmie after a family outing to *Aida* in the days when Alice was still trying to convert her children. "How *can* you believe?"

"I do," said Alice. "I just do." Jamie, two years younger, had muttered, "So do I." But when he tried the closed-eye trick it had not worked. He had still seen the singers, in his imagination, throwing off their magic and bowing like charlatans. Like the magician at his fifth birthday party. Jamie had loitered by the door, still enchanted, while the man packed up. He thought he might see the magic dust, really see it, glittering on the air like Marvo had said. But Marvo had dropped the magic hat so that the false bottom and all the scarves fell out, and he had said "Bugger!" not in a magic voice at all. Alice had thought Jamie was crying because the party was over, and he had never told her about the hat or the rude word. But he flew into a temper with Clemmie, when she scornfully observed that there was no such thing as real magicians, and anyway, Marvo smelt.

Alice sat now, eyes closed, applauding not the human effort but the meaning and the dream. Yasmin glanced at her, grimaced with protective affection then stared down glumly at the stage, hardly bothering to clap even for form's sake. She was not a woman to be intimidated into herd behaviour just by cold glances from the regular patrons. What a bloody waste of time it all was! she thought. Sentimental Victorian religiosity, lollipop music, and an ocean of crappy corporate entertainment clients filling the stalls below with their fat smug bottoms. Hideous. She had never understood what Alice saw in opera, and had been dismayed at her for leaving a proper job as a radio newsroom assistant to be a dogsbody at the Royal Opera House. Six years on, Alice was still here, not even on any visible ladder of seniority. She had wasted her talents in the box office, for God's sake, and the shop; she had drifted between departments in this dated snobbish monstrosity of a building, and when Yasmin questioned her about her responsibilities she always seemed to be doing fatuous things concerned with seat maintenance or telephone lists, or standing in for the person who read the proofs of the programmes. "You're always filling in for someone," accused Yasmin. "You're over thirty. You ought to be running something of your own, yourself." Alice would laugh, and turn the conversation deftly to Yasmin's own successes. She seemed radiantly content with this life, and when seriously pressed, defended it by saying that a low-key career suited Dan and the children better.

Yasmin, ambitious and childless and angry, disliked both the argument and the fact that it was clearly not the whole truth. "You are a groupie," she said. "Admit it." Alice would smile, give Yasmin a sudden brief hug, and play with whichever of her floating, theatrical, red-and-gold scarves she was wearing.

Once, faced with a more than usually exasperated Yasmin who was outraged that she seemed not to care about the forthcoming general election, Alice had tried to explain properly. "I like what I do, Yazz. You like scoops and uproars and setting the political agenda. I never did. If I could sing or play, I'd do that all my life. Since I can't, I just enjoy helping to make space for other people to do it in."

"Then make a proper career of it!" said Yasmin. "Join a smaller company, do opera outreach, be an arts administrator! Be an organ-grinder, not a bloody monkey!"

"No," Alice had said simply. "Don't want to. I just want to be at the very centre, near the very best, and breathe the same air and be a bit useful. You know. Martha and Mary. I do some Martha jobs, but really I'm just Mary, sitting listening and worshipping. It has the advantage that I'm not so essential that I can't get home to Danny and the children. Look at you: you couldn't have children, the hours you work. Not if you were being fair to them."

Yasmin had been really angry then; that conversation had marked the beginning of an unacknowledged but distinct estrangement. She did not want children. Nor, after Alan, did she ever want to waste time on another man. "But I bloody *could* have a baby," she said, "if I wanted. You must stop saying these womany things, always compromising, giving up halfway." Since that day, a coolness had descended between them and Yasmin had been even harder to pin down, even busier in the evenings. Now, with the warm waves of applause around her, she looked at Alice and regretted it. Sweet, bright Alice, who never bore a grudge, stirred something half-buried in Yasmin, who bore many of them. "Must see more of her," thought Yasmin. And then, because sharp thoughts were never far from her rare moments of softness, "It's not fair to leave her stranded with terrible mumsy cabbages like Jenny Pope."

Jenny, pink-faced and enthusiastic, was still clapping, glancing sideways at stout, thin-haired Rod to make sure that he was happy too. She paused to pick a thread from his worsted sleeve. Yasmin looked away.

"Oh, isn't that *lovely*, I forgot they did that," said Jenny suddenly. Far below then on the stage, a footman in red-and-gold livery and a white wig, like an animated playing card, had walked on to the stage with a bouquet for the diva. "Oh, that *is* a nice touch, isn't it?" Four out of the seven gazed down affectionately at the scene onstage; Yasmin looked at the blue ceiling in pointed disgust, and only sharp-eyed Simon glanced sideways to catch a movement from Daniel. From his trouser pocket, Dan drew a short cardboard cylinder and held it upright. Then he cleared his throat, so that with the last fading of the applause all eyes turned to him. Raising his other hand, he pulled sharply on a string hanging from the base of the cylinder. With a soft puffing sound tissue-paper flowers leaped from it, unfolding, waving on the thinnest of green wires, until the paper bouquet was almost as big as the one the singer onstage was holding.

"Didn't know if that would work," he said complacently. "Gas cylinder, lifejacket sort of effect, apparently." And with a bow he handed the enormous, nodding, multicoloured thing to Alice. "Happy birthday."

2

There were no taxis to be had when the party spilled out into the busy, hooting summer night. So, leaving behind the chatter and rock music from the Covent Garden cafés, they walked home to Camden. "Alice likes walking," said Daniel firmly. "And this is her party, so you can just suffer, Rod."

"Do his tum-tum good" said Jenny, patting it maternally. "What a lovely treat."

They walked north from the drifting, vivid life of late-night Covent Garden into the dark dull officeland around Euston, then north again towards the lights and seedier street life of Camden. Simon threw a pound to a young man huddled in a cardboard box, and quickly, deliberately degraded his generous impulse with a camp shrug of, "He was so *pretty*." Jenny pretended not to see or hear this. Daniel and Stevie argued about the moral status of opera, the expensive art, in a country where people slept in boxes.

"Alice would say," said Daniel measuredly, walking fast, "that part of the need this country has is, precisely, for things like opera. To foster a consciousness of transcendence and beauty, which in turn would make our politics and our society better and more mutually responsible. But," he added carefully, "she admits the Royal Opera should go out more and meet people."

"Why didn't she stay in the Education Department, then?" asked Steve.

"She didn't like spending time going round polytechnic halls," said Daniel, dryly. "She said it was the travelling, but actually I'm afraid she just likes breathing the same air as Solti and Domingo."

"Well, the flowers were a great touch."

"Were they not?" Daniel laughed, a little uncomfortably, and changed the subject.

Yasmin walked next to Alice. "Well, did you like that hokum?" she asked. "Woman betrays man, man too holy to do anything about it, preaches sermon, forgives woman?"

"There was more to it than that," said Alice primly. "Ask Danny. He was brought up a Catholic. Very important – confession, forgiveness. Reconciliation. Great Verdi theme."

"Bollocks," said Yasmin. "If you cheated on Dan, would he forgive you?"

"Dunno. Maybe."

"OK, if he cheated on you?"

"I *hope* I would," said Alice. "I hope I would see something – beyond it all . . . Something more beautiful." She was already a little drunk.

Yasmin snorted, not without affection. They walked on past impersonal office blocks. An Irish mist of light drizzle damped their hair and shoulders and momentarily suppressed their spirits, but after half an hour they reached Camden High Street and turned into the broad scruffy road where Alice and Daniel had lived and raised their two children and based their erratic travels for twelve years. The downstairs lights were blazing from the curtainless windows, and Clementine McDonald, aged fourteen, opened the basement door before they reached it. There was a tortoiseshell cat on her shoulder. "Hi. We guessed you'd walk. Mrs Potter's gone back next door, but she said she'd stay awake till I ring and say."

"Better ring her, sweetheart," said Daniel. And to Rod, "Awkward age, they don't want real babysitters but you can't quite bring yourself to leave them. Mrs Potter keeps sort of half an eye."

"Wouldn't know," said Rod heavily, taking off his City coat. "I just live for the day we don't need a bloody au pair." He sniffed the air and favoured Clemmie with a vast bonhomous smile. "Something smells ter-riff-ic, young lady!"

Clemmie gave him a level stare. She had her mother's brown hair, neatly bobbed to shoulder length, and a round face saved from homeliness by a pair of big, exceedingly sharp and intelligent eyes, not as dreamy as her mother's, but of the same grey-green. "Cassoulet. I didn't make it," she said briefly. "Dad did."

"Ah, yes. Of course." Rod cleared his throat.

"See?" said his wife playfully. "Some men can cook! Isn't Alice lucky?"

"Dan, Dan, the very New Man," sang Simon. The subject of his mockery grimaced and vanished towards the kitchen. The friends, all well used to the house, turned into the big living room where a table was laid and James McDonald stood waiting, more stiffly than his sister, to pour wine into a row of glasses.

"Ooh, you *are* up late," said Jenny cosily. "I keep forgetting how big you are now. Twelve, is it?"

"Thirteen at Christmas." The boy was slighter than his sister, thinner in the face, less positive. Jenny's maternal eye swept over him. Nervy. Needed feeding up. Good at art, Alice said.

"Haven't you got school tomorrow? Term has started, hasn't it? Just?"

The child's face darkened. He turned aside to fiddle with the peeling label on the bottle of Rioja and muttered curtly, "It's a Baker day. There isn't any school."

Jenny, impervious to Jamie's reluctance, was inclined to sweep on with her interrogation on a tide of well-meaning and whisky (which, to tell the truth, was working strongly on the empty stomachs of all the party, and making Rod long nervously for the arrival of the cassoulet. Simon and Steven, he noticed, were all but snogging).

"I didn't know they had Baker days at grant-maintained schools," pursued Jenny, brightly, to the child's averted head. "Such a bore, always in the middle of the week just when term's started – and the teachers always say they never learn anything useful at these training session. I am right, aren't I? Finchamgrove is GM now, isn't it? A very good school . . ."

Party politeness has its limits, and Jamie was old enough to judge with finesse the exact stage of tipsiness at which grown-ups could be relied on not to remember mild discourtesies. He deftly filled two glasses with the red wine, thrust one firmly at her and moved across, away from her flow, to a quieter corner. Yasmin was cross-legged by the fireplace stroking the cat, her head forward, her glossy black hair flopping over her face. She shook it back to glance up at the boy when his shadow fell across her. "Hi," she said.

Jamie stopped and smiled his tense half-smile. Better Yazz than Jenny. At least she never asked about school.

"Do you know what your dad did?" said Yasmin conversationally. "He made us all go to the bloody opera."

"I know. 'Cos it's Mum's birthday treat."

"Did *you* give her a treat?"

"Yup. Breakfast in bed and cards and a picture I did, with a proper frame I bought with Dad."

"What's the picture of?"

"Nothing." The boy wriggled, uncomfortable again. "Sometimes my pictures aren't of things. They're sort of patterns."

Jamie slid on again, away from even Yazz. This was getting too close to the Jenny conversation, too close to the problem of school. Jamie's art teacher was impatient at his growing craze for abstract, repeating patterns. "Wallpaper," she called them. She gave him bad reports and made him draw fruit in bowls while the others laughed at him, even the ones who couldn't draw for toffee. Alice and Daniel always said they were entirely on his side, that patterns were as valid as still lifes, and that Mrs Davis obviously adhered to the Heinrich Himmler school of art.

But they laughed while they said it. They didn't do anything. They didn't care. One day, he was going to get out of Finchamgrove. Out of school entirely. It certainly couldn't wait until he was sixteen, or he would die. It was different for Clemmie. She had organized her own escape to that batty sport school. Meanwhile, he wished grown-ups wouldn't spoil his free time by talking about it. If he went to the kitchen, pretending to do something with the bottle, he could get away for a moment. Then the food would be served and he could go to bed, and shut his eyes and see patterns.

He glanced across at Simon, whom he liked; Simon had a friend in the expensive end of the fabric business who gave him wild and wonderful swatches of pattern. When Simon remembered, he always brought some in his shoulder bag for Jamie to copy. No sign of any this time. Jamie sighed.

On the way to the kitchen, he met his father and Clemmie coming back, Daniel with a vast earthernware pot wrapped in an oven cloth, Clemmie with a Victorian china wash-basin full of Caesar salad and two baguettes under one arm. "Get them to table, Jamie, before they're too pissed. Quick!" said his sister. Relieved, he ran ahead with the message. The adults heaved themselves from floor and sofas, groped around for glasses, and lumbered to the heavy oak table in the bay window. Jamie carefully lit the candles while his father went back for the potatoes, and stood aside to let the adults through. There were only seven chairs.

"You not eating with us, children?" asked Rod, lowering himself on to a creaking chair.

"No," said Alice. "We had our family party at breakfast. They really do have to go to bed sometime, you know. Even McDonald children. It was sweet of them to get every-thing ready."

She smiled at Clemmie, who made a jaunty thumbs-up with the baguette, deposited it and went to the door. "G'night. Happy birthday. We'll wash up if you get too drunk."

Jamie was by his mother's chair; she pulled her son to her, arm round his waist, and rested her forehead momentarily on his chest. "Mmm. All right, squirrel?"

"Yep. Happy birthday, Mum." He made no move. Alice threw her head back to look up at him. " 'Night, Jamie. Thanks. Lovely party, lovely birthday. Lovely picture, I love it. Sleep nice."

The child disengaged himself, raised an uncertain hand in greeting to the company, and vanished. Alice's eyes fol-lowed him for a moment, an incongruous flicker of worry in her face. For a moment, it seemed that she might fol-low him, but she turned instead to Daniel, oblivious of her guests. "Dan, we've been so tied up with Clem's thing, and he's been terribly quiet – do you think he's OK at that school?"

Daniel flinched slightly. She never had been a woman to hold back on family worries just because it was the mid-dle of a party. Thoughts sprang to her lips with no kind of social filter at all. He muttered something, and leaned away from her to lift the lid from the cassoulet. Fragrant steam rose, and murmurs of greed: *"Famished* . . . wonderful . . . um, spicy sausage . . . Dan, what a man . . . Alice, you are *lucky,* ducky, he'd make somebody a wonderful little wife . . ."

And on went the supper, as so many late, convivial suppers had done before in this untidy room among the sagging bookshelves and threadbare beautiful rugs from shoestring holidays. There was always, thought Yasmin with a twinge of envy, something studentish about Dan and Alice's entertaining. They were carefree, the plates never matched, and a level of rowdy enjoyment developed so fast that gossip and repartee and blackly enjoyable jokes were being exchanged before the guests had got their coats off. It had never even mattered that the food used to be so terrible in the days before Dan took over the cooking. Neither Alice's gluey risotto nor her notorious Irish stout stew served with burnt baked potatoes could dampen the good humour of those evenings. The wine helped, too; in the McDonalds' frequent financial crises, the drink had somehow never stopped flowing. It had, Yasmin reflected with a faint shudder, often got pretty bad, but always it was plentiful. Tonight it was good. Daniel's career was flourishing. He had gone up a grade at the university.

Yasmin's talents did not lie in such convivial directions. Child of a tidy South London home, schooled to orderliness and hard work by her lonely mother, rarely seeing her Palestinian banker father, she had lived at home through her time at the London School of Economics and moved to her neat, bare flat off Portland Place only when her career was established. Her rare entertaining was precise, the wine good, the food light and elegant. "Very Manhattan," Dan used to say, approvingly. "Look, Allie, Pink Fir Apple. Designer potatoes." Yasmin did not like Dan much.

Right now, as he ladled out the cassoulet, she tried to see him through Alice's eyes. Tall, hawk-featured, loose-limbed – God, the pace he had set on that walk through London! He seemed to think all women wore flatties like Alice. He was attractive. *Undeniably* attractive, she thought; and that weasel word carried the usual implication that she would have liked, very much, to deny it. That fluffy blonde moron Jenny was clearly basking in his attraction, holding up her plate coyly with little squeaks of anticipation, her pink-faced banker husband beaming stupidly, not seeing the flirtation at all. Simon and Stevie were already spearing lumps of Toulouse sausage and nibbling at the best bits of the salad.

Alice had apparently forgotten her momentary anxiety about Jamie and was dipping bread in her gravy and talking, bright-eyed, to Rod. "Turkey? Oh, you'll love it. You really shouldn't get uptight about bugs and things, there's a lovely clean wind on the coast. We took Clemmie to Kalkan when she was two and I was hugely pregnant with Jamie, and there weren't any real hotels built even, but they're so wonderful to children, and the rock tombs are worth anything to see. Timmy could climb up – he's four, isn't he? Clem had a haircut in a Turkish beard-trimming shop . . ." Yasmin saw Jenny's *moue* of distaste. This particular hygienic little family, she thought sourly, would end up going to Disneyland instead.

The evening rollicked on; midnight struck – at about twelve fifteen – on the erratic mantelpiece clock that Dan had rescued from a skip years ago, running up the street doubled up with laughter as it chimed crazily from under his coat. Later, at Stevie's noisy insistence, Simon sang "Diamonds are a girl's best friend" and, goaded by Alice's demands that he provide a macho counterweight, Rod sang his old school song, a sub-Etonian number with rowing seen as a metaphor for life.

Stevie recited "Dangerous Dan McGrew", then sang "The Ould Triangle" with a spoon and a wrought-iron candlestick. Neither Jenny nor Yasmin sang, but Alice had by that time drunk enough to be chivvied into playing Trilby in a rendering of "Ben Bolt", with Stevie in a burnt-cork goatee beard as Svengali hypnotizing her. Then Daniel sang "The Parting Glass", and a maudlin, late-night hush fell over the table.

Daniel had a melodious tenor voice. He had always sung his young children to sleep – given his darling Clementine her name, in fact, as he sang besottedly to her in the delivery room. It had charmed him and Alice out of several difficult situations on their travels. It was one of their shared assets, Dan's voice. Alice smiled as he began. He sang straight, without emotional tricks, but noticeably favoured the poignant songs.

> *Oh, all the money that ever I had,*
> *I spent it in good company*

The company watched, and smiled, and turned their glowing red glasses in their hands. Daniel, his dark hair ruffled, sang on in the flickering candlelight, almost abstracted, giving the words no emphasis or expression beyond what the tune gave.

> *And all the harm that ever I did*
> *Alas, it was to none but me*

Softly, leaning towards Simon's thin shoulder, Stevie began to hum the tune behind Daniel's warm, beautiful notes.

> *And all I've done for want of wit*
> *To memory now I can't recall*

Suddenly Dan looked towards his wife, and seemed to falter, but only for a moment.

> *Come, fill to me a parting glass*
> *Goodnight and God be with you all.*

"Which is a hint," Daniel concluded briskly, dropping with crude suddenness into a conversational tone. "Go home, good people. Spread the word and Prepare for Power."

All in all, it was a memorable party. In later years, Alice was to find it ironic that her thirty-seventh, her best ever celebration, should in the event have left her for the rest of her life with a nagging dread of birthdays.

Indeed, although by no means all went ill during that second half of her life, it was noticeable that Alice McDonald never celebrated her own birthday; and grew quite snappish when others tried to make her.

3 ∫

When the guests had obediently gone, Daniel and Alice began stacking plates and dishes and carrying them through to the kitchen. Alice leaned on a worktop, pushed her hair back off her forehead, and said, "Thanks, sweetheart. That was a brilliant party. What a daft idea, though, honestly. Taking the whole lot to the opera. Did you see Yazz's face at the first interval?"

Daniel did not reply. His back was to her as he loaded the dishwasher. Alice scraped plates and passed them to him, continuing, "I was so thrilled to see Yazz. I don't know how you dragged her out for the evening. She's so high-powered now, she's running the whole pitch for taking Independent News Services into Europe on satellite, or something. It's amazing."

Daniel remained silent, went on loading. Alice sensed something wrong and stopped prattling.

"Danny, you OK?"

With an abrupt clatter he stood up and slowly turned to face her. "Allie," he said. "It's no good. I didn't want to tell you till today was over . . ."

"What?" It must, she thought confusedly through the wine, be work. University lecturers were no longer as secure as they used to be, but they would manage, whatever. He had tenure.

"Allie," said Daniel, "it didn't mean anything."

She stared at him. "Dan, come on. You sound like a television play. *What* didn't mean anything?"

"I had an affair," he went on desperately. "Ages ago. I mean, in the summer term. A fling. It's finished. It's been finished for ages. She was very . . ."

Alice could not look at him. She twisted the tea towel in her hand.

"Very what?"

Daniel did not answer.

"Very pretty? Very young?"

"Young, yes."

"What was her name?"

"Look, that's the last thing that matters. She was a student. In my Year Two group. Called Lisha. It was stupid – that's why I didn't want you to know. Because it was stupid. I felt ashamed."

Primitive, wounded, desperate, Alice's mind raced through the past summer. How had Dan been in June and July? Fine, normal, cheerful? Yes. Surely. They had made love? During that time? Must have done. Although, after all these years of marriage, it got less frequent . . . did for everybody . . . but she would have noticed if it had been not at all.

She stared at the tea towel, thinking. He said it was finished in the summer term. So, July . . . summer holidays. What happened? A July week in Norfolk, camping in Godgran's great overgrown garden, Daniel had been definitely edgy, refusing even his one annual trip to Mass with his godmother. Then, August: London for weeks, and yes, he was bad-tempered. But it was so bloody hot, they were all bad-tempered. All the business about Clemmie's school. No, he was good over that. Jamie wanting to go and play laser battle games every day, Dan snappish with him. Jamie hating Finchamgrove, asking need he go back. Dan saying yes . . .

Then all four of them in Greece, borrowing Rod and Jenny's rich friends' house on Levkas with the frogs in the swimming pool. Normal? Yes. It was better by then; Dan was light-hearted, made love, shared novels with her. Thinking of this Lisha, writing to her, all that time? No. He said it had ended.

"Why did it stop?" she asked at last.

"Because it was an awful mistake."

"And is she going to be at college? This term? You've been back for that meeting."

"She's not in my tutorial group."

"Have you seen her since last term?"

Daniel looked miserably down into the open dishwasher. He had known this would be hard but had not expected the terrible inconsequential, illogical, emotionally driven flow of questions from Alice. He had thought he could make a narrative of it on his own terms. The rest was going to be harder. And on Allie's birthday. Oh Christ. What a bastard. Somewhere in him a small treacherous flame was lit, a flame of resentment that she, in her innocent, blind, questioning, should make him feel such a bastard.

"No. But there was a letter from her at college. That's why—"

"You mean you only told *me* because you thought I'd find it out from her?" Alice was angry now, her anger helping to assuage the grief and insult. "You've been bounced into this, Dan, haven't you? Really, haven't you?"

Daniel tried again to recover control over the scene. "Allie, there are some things we need to talk about. Not just our own feelings, I know that's going to take ages, I know what I've done. But there are practical things I have to tell you. Come through. Let's sit down. Get it over."

Numbly, she let him take her hand, lead her to the sitting room and the tattered armchair by the fire. On the table, the pathetic detritus of the dinner party reproached them with its pointless conviviality: Yasmin's lipsticked cigarette ends; Simon's paper bow tie carefully fixed round the inverted pudding bowl with a chocolate mousse smile daubed above it; Rod's cardboard opera glasses folded into an unlikely aeroplane; a wine cork, its end burnt in the candle so that Simon could draw a curling moustache and goatee beard on Stevie for his Svengali role.

Alice sat in the chair. Daniel knelt back on his heels in front of her, no longer touching, his eyes on her pale face. She had taken off her glasses and let the world blur.

"Alice, let me start at the beginning. I had this fling. She was – she wasn't very old. It went on all last term." He paused.

"And?" Alice wanted to ask a hundred questions: where, why, how often? Did they ever think about her?

"And . . ." He could not look at her, and turned away, and looked at the fire irons. "She got pregnant."

Frozen with horror, Alice had a sudden vision of Jamie. Would this – Lisha's – baby look like Jamie? With the hair that wouldn't lie flat, the dark hawk looks, the double crown like Daniel's?

Daniel continued, monotone, relentless, trying only to get the narrative done with. "She – and I – we agreed, in July, that it was a mistake, the thing was to make a break, make a new start. So the best thing was a . . ."

He was silent for a second. Alice heard her voice, small and shocked. "An abortion?"

"A termination," said Daniel. "She absolutely agreed—"

"What do you mean, agreed? You mean it was your idea?"

"It's an idea everybody has when something like that happens," said Daniel, with a momentary return of his usual spirit. "I certainly didn't talk her into it, if that's what you think."

Alice remained silent, looking at him.

"Anyway," said Dan. "She went to have it done. And I thought that would be the end of it all."

"And if the baby was good and dead, you wouldn't have to tell me?"

Daniel looked at her now, with – if she could only have seen it – considerable love and compassion. "Yes. I suppose. That was the idea."

"So," said Alice slowly, "why are you telling me now?" *He's going to leave me*, she thought, bile rising in her throat, his undigested cooking tasting suddenly, nastily, in her mouth. *She didn't have the abortion at all. He's going to leave me for a teenager. Leave Clemmie, and Jamie, and me.* She gave a long, shuddering breath and repeated, "Why are you telling me now?"

"Because I might be going to lose my job," he answered flatly and, drawing in his breath hard, began suddenly and horribly to weep. "Allie, I can't tell you how terrible—"

Alice had seen him cry before, just once, when his mother Niamh died suddenly on holiday and the news had reached Daniel through a bald telephone call from the tour company. It was, he had said, the shock as much as anything.

This time, she thought flatly, it couldn't be shock; whatever this was, he had lived with it. But fifteen years of loving habit made her stretch out a hand. He took it and let himself be drawn a few inches closer, shuffling on his knees on the carpet, his other arm in front of his eyes. Men crying, thought Alice. Why is it so uncomfortable? We tell them to get in touch with their emotions, to weep freely, but we hate it like hell when they do. Our world rocks. She looked down, helplessly, at the dark, jerkily moving head.

"Daniel, tell me everything. Now. It's the least you can do."

So Daniel told her.

Lisha – stupid name, thought Alice with sudden vindictiveness, stupid baby-doll name – had had the abortion at the end of July, ten weeks into the pregnancy. Despite her determination she had, as Daniel put it, "taken it very badly". He shook a little as he recounted the outline of these events to Alice, kneeling at her feet by the dying fire on that birthday evening.

He had had no idea she would be so much affected. In all their conversations on the subject, Lisha had seemed as brittle and worldly as a woman twice her age. It had, in truth, rather shocked him. Accustomed to Alice's dreamy idealism, maternal softness and generous affection, Daniel was rattled by the cynical way in which Lisha's contemporaries seemed to speak of these things, and felt old and vulnerable and very glad the affair was over. The girl had shrugged her slender shoulders at his solicitude, flicked back her hair, and said, "It's something and nothing. For fuck's sake, eight weeks, it's as big as a cashew nut. Mariella's had three termies, you're out by lunchtime."

But, waking in the clinic from the light, brief anaesthetic, Lisha had screamed and wept and hyperventilated and called for Daniel by name. Sedated, she fell into heavy helpless nightmares and awoke far worse, with a high fever. Alarmed by the power of her reaction, the matron had telephoned her parents, listed as next of kin on her registration form, and delivered the double bombshell: that their nineteen-year-old daughter was in an abortion clinic and that her mental condition was giving concern.

The Danforths had come directly, to find their daughter babbling of Daniel McDonald and dead babies. They took her home. All Dan knew, after that, was contained in a brief letter he had found in his pigeonhole when he returned to college for the pre-term meeting.

"What did it say?"

Daniel hesitated, then crossed to the untidy bureau in the

corner which was his private domain. He pulled out a plain cream envelope, much folded and handled, containing a single sheet, and gave it to his wife.

Alice looked at it as though it was a snake. Reluctantly, at last she pulled it from his fingers, took out the sheet, unfolded it with an unsteady hand and read.

Daniel,

I am not in your tute group this term so we won't meet. Probably it's best. I think you ought to know that my parents know about everything because I freaked a bit in the clinic and they got called in. I've told them to stay cool, but they want to write to college and if the Dean won't listen, then they say they're going to the newspapers. I just wanted you to know it isn't me that wants all the bloody fuss.

L

Alice let the paper fall and shaded her eyes for a moment. "Daniel, how old is she?"

"Nineteen."

"Five years older than Clemmie. And you made her kill her baby, and she still doesn't want to hurt you." As layer upon layer of foggy horror rolled in across the mist of an evening's drinking, the clouds of swirling, buffeting emotion disabled her and made her too weak even to sit up. She moaned. Daniel moved swiftly to kneel beside her, his hand hovering uncertainly over her arm. He read her thoughts too easily and babbled the only reassurance he could.

"Allie, oh Allie, I've told you it all. That's all. There isn't any more. You know the lot now. As much as I do. And I didn't blarney her into having the abortion, believe me. I wanted it all over with, yes, I admit that, I was terrified, because of you and the children. But I stood back while she decided, I really did . . ."

Alice hardly heard. The phrases of the letter – "I told them to stay cool . . . it isn't me that wants the fuss" – burned in her mind. She would have written like that once, a teenager too fiercely proud to rebuke the man who wronged her. No, not wronged, that was old fashioned; the man who had been, rather, her partner in disaster. Clemmie might write such a letter, one day; might be weakly heroic in the face of catastrophe. The hurt which rose from the letter mingled with her own barely comprehended private hurt and disillusion, almost choking her. Daniel knelt quietly, saying nothing. They stayed like that for maybe half an hour, while the crazy clock struck two; then, as an afterthought, four. It was twenty-five past two. At last Alice said, in a quite different, forcedly bright voice, "If her parents do go to the Dean, will you lose your job?"

"Probably," said Daniel flatly. "Especially if they threaten to go to the press and claim I made her have the abortion. Think about it. What is it that I teach?"

Alice looked at him, and gave a terrible, joyless giggle, high-pitched, out of control. "Moral philosophy," she said. And, as if from a great distance, heard herself laugh again.

4 ∫

Alice woke in the morning with a headache and a sour metallic taste in her mouth. It was not until she sat up, groping round for her glass of water, that she remembered everything and shrank back, appalled, into the pillows. Daniel's side of the bed was flat and empty; for a terrible moment she thought him gone for ever, then remembered the conclusion of last night. Wordless and exhausted, they had gone to their broad bed, picked up the duvet kicked carelessly to the floor in the birthday morning's waking, and by silent consent had lain side by side, not touching, under its shared accustomed warmth.

Besides, she could hear Clemmie in the hallway talking to Daniel in the kitchen and his replies, indistinct but as level as usual. Clemmie was talking about school kit.

"Tell you what, if you give me a lift when you go to college, I could do the socks and stuff at John Lewis without Mum. That'd save time, and when she gets out of work we could have a burger instead of more shopping." Clementine had a genius for time management; her reception class teacher used to complain that if she set a group to do cutting and sticking, they would always finish early because Clemmie, a natural forewoman, had organized two of her small contemporaries to do all the cutting, two to fill in the colours, and the rest to stick the fish in the cardboard pond. She herself would supervise. The educational value, said the teacher rather sourly, was reduced to virtually nil. Except of course for Clementine.

Alice smiled, in spite of herself. It sounded as if Clemmie was at it again; she had already completed most of her trunk in preparation for her new school adventure.

"So OK, Dad? Is Mum up? She's doing early work today, isn't she? So you stay home for Jamie's Baker day and go into the college meeting tonight. I could take Jay to John Lewis if I have to."

Daniel, further from the stairwell, was saying something. Then it was Clementine again. "Oh, OK, I'll take it up."

Footsteps clumped up the stairs, and the door creaked open. "Hi, Mum. Tea up."

Alice raised herself on her elbow, mumbled thanks, and reached for the mug, which said, in mock-Gothic characters over a rag-week cartoon, *COGITO ERGO SODDIT*. The tea was hot and strong, balm to her dry, aching throat. The world, clearly, had not ended. Clemmie plumped herself down on the end of the bed and surveyed her mother with a critical eye.

"Hangover? Poor Mum."

"Yes . . . a bit. Clem, I will come to John Lewis with you, I can get the afternoon off."

"No need. It's only socks and stuff. We did the rest."

"*You* did the rest, sweetheart. You've been amazing."

"Well, it was all my idea."

Clementine, two years into her apparently smooth schooldays at the grant-maintained comprehensive of Finchamgrove, had dropped the bombshell two months back that she wished – nay, intended – to go to boarding school in Berkshire. A new boarding school, something quite different, just about to open up. She had read about it in the Sunday paper. The British College for Sporting Excellence, or BCSE, as it was known, was a governmental triumph, a feather in the Education Secretary's cap. It was to be funded largely by an international sports foundation and geared for girls with a particular athletic or sporting talent. It would, Clementine insouciantly told her astonished parents, cost very little because she intended to get a riding scholarship. And this on the strength of a few lessons on holiday in Norfolk and two summer fortnights at pony camps in Wales.

"The instructors there said I've got real talent. It's what I want to do. Besides, you switch sports if it isn't working. I could be a sprinter. There's a fitness test, which is why I've been in the gym so much. Can I try, Dad? Please?"

It was Alice who had been doubtful: should they allow Clemmie even to dream of such a life, a boarding school, a sporting hothouse, a life which would be hopelessly unaffordable if she failed the competitive scholarship test? Should she board anyway? Unlike some of their richer friends, the McDonalds had never even considered sending the children away. They had manoeuvred both, with difficulty enough ("Middle-class backflips," said Daniel in disgust) into the excellent, clandestinely selective Finchamgrove and were already discussing Clemmie's GCSE subjects with its brisk, achievement-minded staff. Besides, was a sports career something any child should be encouraged into?

Daniel had been tickled and delighted that his darling Clementine should show such initiative and said that she must at least do the test, if only to learn about the gap between aspiration and achievement. "Let her take it, Allie. Who knows?"

So Clemmie had sat an academic entrance exam, passed with flying colours and been offered a conditional fifty percent scholarship on the strength of that. "You see," she explained to her parents, "they want a reputation for producing bright sports stars, not dim ones. So you pay less fees if you aren't dim." Subsequently, she had gone down to the new campus in Berkshire for a weekend of intensive riding. "You have to trot, canter and jump with folded arms, without stirrups, and bareback. It was brilliant." She had come back covered in bruises and been recalled the following weekend for a running and swimming test and a medical. During this latter, Alice sat in horrified fascination while her daughter was examined more thoroughly than ever she thought likely this side of the SAS ("Or the white slave trade," said Daniel). "It's like vetting a horse," explained Clemmie, although she herself was a little shaken by the Dutch doctor's thoroughness.

Finally, she had been offered a full scholarship. The head of the new institution, a handsome soldierly woman called Felicity Frere who had been an international dinghy champion in the 1970s, reassured the McDonalds.

"I know it seems extraordinary, a new concept, but think of it as like a city tech or a stage school. Fostering special talent. She'll get her A levels, don't you worry, but she'll get a proper grounding in her sport as well. We're here to treat serious talent seriously. If riding isn't her true sport, there are others. I think she could be a useful swimmer. She says sprinter, but the bones are wrong."

"She always was keen on games," Alice had said lamely. "But we didn't think . . ."

"No," agreed Miss Frere. "People don't. City children waste most of their physical gifts slouching around street corners." Daniel looked offended, as if he was about to speak; but Alice babbled quickly to cover a sudden guilty image of Jamie spending yet another afternoon at LaserQuest with his pasty-faced friends. "It would be a crime," said Miss Frere, reading her mind, "to keep a child like Clementine walled up in a Camden comprehensive, you know. You must let us have her."

Clemmie agreed. "I know I never said so, Mum, but I do hate living in London all the time. I only come to life when we go to Norfolk to see Godgran. I like the idea of space." And then, because of something in her mother's look, "I'll be home in the holidays. They have really long holidays, ten weeks in summer, four at Christmas and four at Easter."

Daniel had taken revenge on Miss Frere by checking up, with painstaking thoroughness, on every qualification of every teacher and conducting an analysis of the academic curriculum. He could find no serious fault with it. So Clemmie was going. Now, sitting on the end of her mother's bed, alive with well-organized enthusiasm, she glowed. "Two more days, Mum."

Alice, sucking weakly at her tea, was forced to smile at her daughter. Deep within her numb misery some small part was still ticking, bleeping, calculating, and it said, *That's good. Whatever happens to us now, Clemmie's on her own track, she'll have something to hold on to.* Aloud, she said, "Jamie's going to miss you at school."

Clementine frowned, her excitement blighted for a moment. "Yep. I know. But I think he'll be all right." She did not sound entirely convinced. Alice drank more tea in silence and tried not to listen to the small voice within. *Jamie's not going to take it well at all if Dan and I split up, or if Dan loses his job and the house has to go. Jamie's only just hanging on as it is, and without Clemmie at home . . .* Aloud, she said, "Yes, I'm sure he will." Then, with an effort to sound normal, "Is Dad around?"

"Yep. Having breakfast. Jamie's asleep. Baker day, remember?

Dad's going to drop us near John Lewis for the school stuff, then we'll all have a burger when you get out of work. Aren't you going to be late?"

Horrified, Alice looked at the clock for the first time, and precipitated herself out of bed and into the bathroom. Alone there, she leaned on the basin while a wave of nausea swept over her, and wondered whether she could, in fact, go in to work. But if Daniel was at home, work was clearly the place to be. They would have to talk. But not today. Not with Jamie at home. She cleaned her teeth with vigour, threw cold water over her face, pulled on a black velvet jumpsuit and long, tatty red-and-gold waistcoat from Camden Market, wound on a blue-and-gold floating scarf, and looked around for her pirate boots. It was a chilly September, and winter clothes had always suited Alice's temperament and colouring. Pulling on the first velvet jackets and swashbuckling boots of winter was always a pleasure to her. She revelled in it, just as dainty summer birds like Jenny revelled in the first warm days of spring when they could go sleeveless in broderie anglaise and bare-legged in neat blue shorts.

As she came out of the bedroom she found Clemmie playing with the paper bouquet, the exploding folding flowers Daniel had presented to her last night. The child looked up entranced. "Amazing, Mum. Paper roses, like in the song. Did Dad give it to you?"

"Yes," said Alice.

"Where on earth did he find them? Dad is amazing, isn't he?"

Alice, turning her face away, forced out the semblance of a laugh and made great play of her hurry. With Jamie asleep, it would be quite possible, she thought, to get downstairs and out of the house without speaking to anybody, especially Daniel. If she needed breakfast to counteract the waves of hangover, she could get a croissant in Covent Garden. Cautiously, she came downstairs, collected her shoulderbag from the living room and tried to get down past the kitchen door in silence. Daniel was too quick for her. Emerging, he blocked her way to the front door. Clemmie could be heard upstairs, dragging cases around.

"Allie, are you OK? To go to work?"

"Yes, of course." She averted her face, as if it was she who had somehow been shamed by the night's terrible conversation. "I'm late. I must go."

"I'm taking Clem and Jamie to John Lewis this afternoon. Clem thought we could all meet up at six for a burger somewhere. Planet Hollywood, even?"

"OK – yes, OK. Why not? Fine."

"You and I can talk this evening."

"If we must."

Alice pushed past him, pulled both door locks with clumsy urgency and, head down, hurried outside into the dank autumn morning. Something, not her own self, was heard to say "'Bye". Sighing, Daniel watched her half-running down the road, then closed the door and turned towards the kitchen. A scrap of red on the first landing caught the corner of his eye, and he looked up. A small figure was sitting on the stairs, looking at him.

"Jamie? You up already?"

"Yup. What was it you had to talk to Mum about specially this evening?"

"Never you mind."

"Is it about me and school? Are you going to make me go to boarding school like Clemmie?"

"Jamie, we've been through that. Clemmie chose to go. It's because of all her sport, and riding. It's a special school. We couldn't afford to send you boarding anyway."

"School's bad enough, without having to sleep there."

"Well, never mind," said Daniel unhelpfully. "There's no school today anyway. What do you want to do?"

"LaserQuest," said the boy unhesitatingly. "With Darren and Tim."

"No," said Daniel. "Not on a weekday, not in term. Do you want to go to a museum?"

Jamie brightened. "V and A?"

"OK. Then John Lewis, then a burger. This morning, do your room, all right? I've got lecture notes to work on."

"All right."

Sighing, Daniel went into the kitchen to clear up his own and Clementine's breakfast dishes, and the detritus of the night before.

●　●　●

Alice, on the Underground, suddenly found the numbness of the morning dissolving, and painful, constructive thoughts beginning to form. So, Daniel had a fling with a young girl. A lot of men did that when they got near forty. For all she knew, the girl Lisha was a hard case, not a victim. Dan was sorry; had ended it, he said, and did not want to leave home. They had shared a bed, albeit stiffly, last night.

The messy aftermath of his fling was not something he could have foreseen. He said he had not urged the abortion on his – on the girl. The girl sounded all right now, anyway, self-possessed enough according to her letter. Daniel was in a difficult position through his own fault, but plenty of men did worse and ended up in less difficulty. There was an element of bad luck in all this. The horribleness was not all of Daniel's making.

Crushed up against the other passengers, wrapped in private thought, Alice swayed from Camden Town to Mornington Crescent and on to Euston. Breathe deeply, begin again, keep it calm and rational. Daniel had had a sexual adventure; regretted it, ended it, panicked over the consequences, at last confessed to her without excuses. He wanted to stay. Wanted his family. These things she must hold on to with her rational mind. If she were to survive it she must suppress the other part of her, the part still wincing from the horror, the betrayal, the humiliation, the darkly incestuous idea of Daniel the good father screwing a teenage girl, fathering a baby and wanting it dead—

No. Not those words and images. Not that. Alice pressed her head against the cold steel bar she was holding on to. Those thoughts were not helpful. She must be positive. The children must be central – the living children – not the dead one.

Hugging the bar, Alice found tears running down her face. The London Underground is no bad place to cry. Strangers, forced physically together from neck to knee, throw up psychic barriers of extraordinary power. A black woman next to her did not look at her tears, nor did a large man in a dark suit, on whose chest she was effectively weeping.

Oh, why? Why must everything change? Why must the scenery of her life be pushed over, revealed as fragile laths and torn canvas, and leave her alone on this desolate stage without a script? She had no idea of what to do, or whether to do anything. Dread of the future, consciousness of age, gripped her for the first time. Down a spinning, tear-filled tunnel she saw herself as a divorcee, a single mother pushing forty, earning just enough to eat, with troubled, aggressive children, alone and without laughter in a mean and claustrophobic council flat.

The train jerked to a halt and Alice let herself be borne out and along the platform by the press of bodies. Outside, she dashed her velvet sleeve across her eyes and walked rapidly down the accustomed streets towards the Opera House. The open air and the familiar route calmed her; she seemed to have left some of the dread and panic behind with the noise of engines in the subterranean tunnel. Her bright cloth bag slung carelessly on her shoulder, Alice McDonald walked towards the pulsing life of Covent Garden, deep in thought.

Daniel McDonald was thinking too. Alone in the tidy kitchen with the children banging around overhead, he made himself a cup of coffee and sat at the table. It was a 1960s Formica one which Alice and Jamie had covered with an eclectic collage of scraps from magazines and family photographs, glued down and varnished several times to make a bright, rather headachey design which did not repel spills and heat marks quite as well as they had hoped. Daniel put his mug down on the face of Mikhail Gorbachev, out of whose ear a tiny motorcyclist appeared to be riding and across whose chin a baby Clemmie crawled. He felt sick.

Last night, the relief of confession had buoyed him up, and the fact that Alice had slept in the same bed with him seemed an unlooked-for blessing. He could not fully enter into her feelings, did not want to throw his imagination that far; it was too much. But she had not rejected him entirely. She had not shouted and roused the house, not locked him out, shredded his clothes or broadcast his terrible behaviour to his children. Daniel realized with a small shock of surprise that he feared that last unveiling more than almost anything. The focus on Alice, telling Alice, had been so intense these past few days that he had had no time to let himself think about the horror of the children's knowing. Clemmie, especially.

Ah, no. Face that when, if, it happened. The first thing was to discover whether the anger of Lisha's parents was going to cost him his lectureship. That much he must force himself to confront. Immoral behaviour, seduction of a pupil, bringing disgrace on the good name of the university – these things could technically bring him down. The mention of the press in Lisha's letter sent shudders through him. DIRTY DON WRECKED MY LIFE in the tabloids, MORAL PHILOSOPHER'S DISGRACE in the broadsheets. Lisha would not want to co-operate with such things, but her parents could provide everything the papers needed. Names, details, photographs. If they were angry enough.

But would they do that to their daughter? Expose her affair, her rejection, her abortion and breakdown? Daniel could not imagine doing such a thing to Clemmie; but nastier exposures were printed every week. And he did not know the Danforths, could not estimate whether their vengeful pride and anger would for a while outweigh their solicitude. To sacrifice him, they might be willing, for a while, to sacrifice Lisha.

Slowly, a new realization formed in Daniel's mind. He was not a pawn in all this. He had a duty, too, which went beyond his selfish duty to his family. If Lisha's parents would not protect her, he must. He could go to them, and tell them he was leaving anyway and applying for another job, They would see that he was paying the price, sacrificing his own comfort for hers and theirs. The heroism of it pleased him. A thought ran through his head that in giving up his job he would also be making a sacrifice on behalf of his own family, but he pushed that aside. It was obviously better for them not to be involved in a public fuss. Better for the children never to know. Daniel picked up his mug and took it to the sink, rinsing and rubbing it clean with small, precise movements. He had not enjoyed feeling like a callous, birthday-wrecking bastard the night before. But if he were a secret hero, if he cut the knot and left of his own accord . . . he smiled, and sent a jet of hot clear water hard into the steel sink.

Alice was smiling too; a reflex response to a tall black roller-blader who cut across her path with a cheeky thumbs-up as she crossed the Piazza towards Floral Street. She, too, had thought of a way to be heroic, to solve everything. She was aware, beneath the surface, of blacker and more nihilistic feelings but pushed them violently down. Alice had had an idea.

Her scarf streamed triumphant as a banner behind her, blue and gold, as she broke into a run towards the great white wedding-cake building she loved.

5

The rendezvous at Planet Hollywood went as well as could be expected. Daniel joked with Clemmie about her school's righteous insistence on seventy per cent cotton-mix socks and a personal supply of foot powder. Jamie was quiet, aware of the looming certainty of school the next day, but not as restless and unsociable as he sometimes was. He talked to his father about the newest laser-battle technology which had just arrived in yet another boarded-up former pub some streets away from home. "They've got net walkways, and pretend ruins to shoot round, and the guns are much lighter. You ought to come and see. Me and Barney went . . ." Daniel listened abstractedly.

Alice talked mainly to her daughter, referring to Daniel only in the third person, as "Dad". They walked home, and the children vanished to their bedrooms, Clemmie to fine-tune her school packing and Jamie to drag off his clothes, don pyjama trousers and flop on the bed with his latest science-fantasy paperback.

Alone together, Alice and Daniel roamed nervously round the sitting room, avoiding one another's eyes, closing curtains and straightening cushions to put off the moment of engagement. Finally, they both turned simultaneously and spoke.

"Allie, I've been thinking—"

"Dan, we have to talk—"

They laughed awkwardly, then Alice gestured at Daniel to speak first. She sat down, and began playing concentratedly with one of the many frayed corners of upholstery on the arm of the sofa. Daniel began.

"I think we ought to make a clean break out of all this."

The words "clean break" cut into Alice like a knife. She gasped.

Seeing her white face, Daniel at once cursed himself for a clumsy fool, and suppressed a small jet of triumph that she minded so much.

"No, sorry, I didn't mean that. Allie, never that. But the situation. The Danforths – Lisha's parents. They could make things terrible for us. Publicity, the children – and I'd lose my job in the end anyway. You know how sensitive the university is about all this harassment stuff. They'd have me out, one way or another. So I was thinking, why not pre-empt all that? Tell them they don't need to kick up a stink because I'm leaving London University?"

"But you're *not* leaving," said Alice stupidly.

"I spent this afternoon chasing up some things," said Daniel. "Rang Alan, and G-T, and Raj. There's at least one job I could probably have for the asking. They haven't filled a lectureship at UEA—"

"UCL?" said Alice, still puzzled. "But—"

"No, UEA," said Daniel. He felt faint anger. This was not easy for him either, and she kept interrupting, not understanding. "University of East Anglia. In Norwich."

"What?" said Alice. "Commute up? Like Frank, on that train to Cambridge all term?"

Daniel sighed, and walked over to the window, feeling more and more that his immense and heroic sacrifice was not being properly applauded.

"Frank," he said, "has a visiting professorship they begged him to take. Frank is a telly don. Frank can afford to live in Hampstead and commute out. I'm talking about a move, Allie. A family move. All of us. A new start."

Alice looked down at the piece of upholstery in her hand, hardly seeing that she had pulled the piping right off in an untidy, unrolling sausage of threadbare chintz. She said nothing.

Daniel continued, "It's not the end of the world. You like Norfolk anyway."

"I like Norfolk," said Alice, evenly, "for holidays. I like camping in Godgran's field. That doesn't mean I want to live all year in Norwich. I like going to the Aldeburgh Festival, come to that, but it doesn't mean I want you to get a job at Ipswich Poly."

"There aren't any polys," said Daniel automatically, pacing up and down the floor. "They're universities now. Anyway, UEA is a real university. I mean, it was one before all the changes. The job would be OK. Not my first choice, but OK. A lot of teaching."

Alice raised her head and stared at him. "And what about my job? Have you thought of that? And the children?"

"Clemmie would be fine, now, wouldn't she? And Jamie hates Finchamgrove anyway. Norfolk schools are meant to be really good."

"*And my job*?" said Alice, dangerously.

"I said, I'm only suggesting," said Daniel, "one way for us all to get out of this thing I've done to us." He sat down suddenly, tired and as white as Alice. "Allie, it's one way. I don't know any other ways. I'm sorry."

Alice looked at him with reviving love. "OK. You've had your turn. Now do you want to hear what I've been thinking?"

He nodded.

"The thing is," said Alice, "I don't want these people going to newspapers or to the university either. But I think they might not actually do it. And I think that if I went to see them – "

Daniel was staring now, aghast at the very suggestion, but with a wild, mad, dangerous hope rising within him. Alice stumbled on.

"– they might see that it was just a one-off, just one of those things. That you weren't like that. That it's only fair to give your own family a chance. She – Lisha – doesn't have to see you much anyway, this year, does she?"

"Not at all," said Daniel. "The bit of her course that I teach is over. But Allie, you can't do that!"

They talked it over, to and fro, increasingly at ease with one another; discussed whether it would look as though Daniel was hiding behind a woman's skirts, and whether he would in fact be doing just that; whether a visit from Alice might not inflame the Danforths still more, and form part of their story for the newspapers. They evaluated what the university would think if such a plea came out.

Daniel, at last, quelled the daft hope that had risen in him and came down strongly against the idea. Alice remained adamant that a plea from her might touch the hearts and consciences of the problematical Mr and Mrs Danforth. She shone with conviction, gesturing excitedly, desperate to persuade Daniel. His hesitancy seemed crazy, cowardly. They argued on, moving further apart again.

"Allie, it'd look terrible. It would *be* terrible. It's my responsibility."

"But I'm involved. If they saw that it was my life, the children's life . . . that it would put us all into exile . . ."

It must be remembered that everything, for Alice, was heightened just then to the point of madness. Black anger had been artificially and suddenly suppressed under a thick woolly veil of liberal reasonableness; and, moreover, her emotional life had been led, for the past six years, at least half through the medium of Italian tragic opera. Here, self-immolating soprano innocents do, at times, plead so heartbreakingly and bravely that they bring vengeful baritones to melting forgiveness. Daniel could have seen the condition she was in, and guessed what she would do; but, in his own continuing shock, he did not.

In the end no agreement was reached by bedtime; and again, wife and husband shared a duvet without touching so much as an accidental hand or foot. Alice woke before Daniel, padded cautiously across to the cluttered dressing table, and drew from his wallet the much-folded letter from Lisha which she had seen him put there two nights earlier. With a blunt eyebrow pencil, on the back of a packet of Rennies, she scribbled down the printed address and telephone number from the letterhead and slid the letter back. Only because, so she persuaded herself, Dan might throw the letter away and regret it.

Daniel, knowing nothing of this, departed for college and went through the motions of a day's work, tormented at every turn of the corridor by the need to search his colleagues' faces for any indication that the scandal had begun. Jamie went, reluctantly, to face Finchamgrove. He dawdled in the doorway, his lip quivering, but his mother for once did not notice. And Clemmie went to her friend Anita's to celebrate her last day of sophisticated London teenage freedom with a pizza, a video and a long giggling mooch around Camden lock market.

Alice left the Opera House in her lunch break and found the privacy of a telephone box. Behind its glass panes tourists and buskers, roller-bladers and happy lunchtime tipplers flowed past;

inside, she dialled the number she had written on the Rennies packet. The 0181 for outer London was obvious, but beyond that the eye pencil had smudged; a 4 could be a 2, a 7 could be a 1; a small, sensible part of Alice hoped it would be wrong. "Sorry," the precise Telecom voice would say, "the number you have dialled has not been recognized. Please check and try again." That would be best. Undoubtedly.

But it did ring, and not into a silent unhearing house. Alice always said she could tell "by the echo" when a house was empty. This was not. After three double rings, some distant hand picked up the receiver and a cool prim voice said, "Three eight one. Adrienne Danforth speaking." Alice braced her back against the wall of the kiosk and spoke in turn.

"Mrs Danforth? I am Alice McDonald. My husband is Daniel McDonald."

This was, as she had judged, enough to begin with. After a charged pause, the voice said, "I can't understand what you could possibly want from my family, Mrs McDonald. There has been enough—"

"Yes, enough distress," broke in Alice, with desperate eagerness. "Quite. And to me too. But I would be grateful if I could come and see you. And your husband."

Another pause. Then, as a statement not a question, the voice said, "Not my daughter."

"No . . . no, of course not," said Alice. "I do, please believe me, I do realize what a difficult time—"

"We prefer not to discuss family matters with outsiders," said Mrs Danforth frigidly. "But my husband and I will see you if you wish. Not your husband."

"No, obviously . . ." Alice collected her wits enough to take the directions and agree that she would call at the Blackheath house at five thirty sharp. It would mean leaving work two hours early. Needs must.

She put down the receiver, wiped her clammy hands down her sides, and walked back. Inside the Opera House the warmth of familiar work enveloped her, and she made for the canteen under the auditorium. At the top of the stairs she paused, and suddenly knew that she could not face either food or human company. Instead she passed to the new building, took the lift, and spent the last twenty minutes of her lunch break leaning on the wall outside the chorus rehearsal room, drinking in the deep, grand, resounding calls for peace in *Simon Boccanegra*. Peace, reconciliation. The sorrow of exile, the painful joy of return. She was right and Dan was wrong to be cautious and untrustful. She must try. Light-headed, for she had not eaten, Alice returned to the box-office. On the stairs she met Simon who whooped with pleasure.

"Fabulous birthday party. Did the folding flowers last?"

"Yes . . . yes," said Alice vaguely. "I think so."

"I'm going to get some for Stevie's forty-fifth, don't you think so? Have them presented by a *tiny tot*, as if he was the Queen Mother." Simon blew a kiss and hurried by, blithe as a butterfly. Everyone assumed, thought Alice irrelevantly, that an opera and ballet theatre would be full of young men like Simon. In fact, there were hardly any; these days they stood out quite startlingly among the serious, arty, horn-rimmed types and efficient bristling women. Stevie had once said, in a bitchy moment, that Simon was the only man to flunk a career as a ballet dancer by being too camp. It could almost be true.

Alice went back to the cramped office she shared for the moment, to begin the process of swapping and bargaining for her four thirty departure. She was dimly aware of an unease in herself, a false note; too much was being hidden, too much suppressed. Yesterday it was black anger she pushed beneath the surface; today it was the small mocking voice of restraint, the voice which said, "Confronting your husband's mistress, fine, that's got a history, there's an etiquette for that. But confronting his ex-mistress's parents? There's not a lot of precedent for that . . ."

Resolutely, Alice ignored such warnings and left the Opera House at four thirty to walk rapidly southward in her dashing boots towards Charing Cross station. Trains to Greenwich ran every twenty minutes; she missed one, and fretted around on the station, slopping a nasty cup of coffee down her scarf, looking unseeingly at the bookshop display of tired summer paperbacks.

•   •   •

While his mother was so employed, Jamie left school. Shoulders hunched in his usual school posture of defeat and dread, he crossed the playground, skirting groups of his fellows. At the staff-room window his form mistress, normally the most unobservant of indiviuals and concerned only with registering her charges in and out at either end of the day, noticed for once and said casually to the head of year, "Look at Jamie McDonald. Strange child, always sulking." And the head of year said, "Well, you often get that with clever parents. Overshadowed, poor little rat."

They turned back into the room and forgot him without much difficulty. No trouble, young Jamie. Not a sparkling child, but not a disruptive influence either. Neutral, really; human wallpaper. Not that they would have said that aloud, or even articulated the thought inwardly; but nonetheless, it was there. They were teachers, but tired ones. Bright, responsive children could still light a spark of enthusiasm in them and both women would have said they "loved their job". Jamie lit nothing in his teachers. Unheeded, he hunched down the road towards his bus stop. The bus was not there. He rested his briefcase on the litter bin strapped to the post and pulled out a picture he had done in art, and been castigated for – "Try and see things bigger, Jamie, anyone would think it was a mouse's drawing!" Laughter, not kind laughter, from his peers.

After a long, sad look, he deliberately ripped the sheet in half, pulled the briefcase off the litter bin, and pushed the paper in, shoving it deep. Then the bus came, and Jamie boarded it, heading alone for home.

6

There was no suggestion that Alice, who had walked across Blackheath rapidly and was out of breath, should sit down in the Danforths' immaculate front room. Adrienne Danforth did not sit either but, having ushered Alice in merely stood in a pool of frigid composure, eyebrows raised in polite enquiry. She was a small woman, almost unnaturally neat and conventional in her tweed skirt, cream linen blouse and cashmere cardigan. Her eye rested disdainfully on Alice's spiritedly exotic velvets and grubby Indian scarf.

"My husband," she said, "will be one moment. I think he had better hear whatever it is you have come to say."

Alice nodded acquiescence, and glanced around as she would have done in any friend's house, reading the room. A cold look from Mrs Danforth made her abruptly stop. In certain circles, she remembered, it might still be considered vulgar to "notice people's things". The atmosphere of the room, in any case, dismayed and intimidated Alice. She had grown up in warm, book-lined cramped chaos in North London, and by the time her parents died was leading a married life with Daniel in various cosily bohemian quarters. One or two of their friends had achieved what they privately referred to as "grown-up houses", and Jenny and Rod in particular were rapidly moving that way; but most of the homes the McDonalds met and ate in were either downright scruffy, bookishly untidy, or at best furnished with nostalgic or imaginative tat in the style Dan called haute clutter. Simon and Stevie, at one point, had a cut-out Captain Kirk from *Star Trek* in the front window and in the hall a stuffed polar bear wearing an apron and feather duster.

This cheerless, immaculate Blackheath parlour was very grown-up indeed. Its polished brown furniture, its coffee-table natural history books by the unscuffed leather sofa, and its potpourri somehow forcibly brought home to Alice the absurdity of her mission. She wished Daniel knew and approved of her being here. She wondered whether it was too late to run away.

But as she looked towards the door Mr Danforth, a distinguished, balding figure rather older and far taller than his wife, materialized in the doorway and said, "Ah."

"She's here," said Mrs Danforth, unnecessarily.

"Perhaps we had better hear what Mrs McDonald has to say to us," said her husband. "And then we need not keep her from, er . . ."

He had a pleasant voice, deep, bass baritone even, with a faint northern burr behind the executive manner. Alice saw that she would have to begin. She had entertained fantasies, on the train to Greenwich, of helpful openings, of a distressed but human mother who would, if not fall on her neck exactly, talk to her of grief and worry, giving her somehow an opening to say that yes, she too had bled inwardly for the waste, the sadness, the sordid futility of the abortion. That she had a daughter too, that they were sisters . . .

This clearly was out of the question. Adrienne Danforth was looking at her with icy distaste, her husband contemplating the wall with studied detachment. She saw that she would need all her calm, all her resolution, all that quiet shining conviction which had buoyed her up since yesterday. She must throw herself across this gulf, trusting that an honest appeal from one human heart to another could not and would not fail.

"Look," began Alice, "I came because I know, through your daughter's communication to my husband, that you are deeply upset about what happened between him and her, and that you intend to take some kind of action—"

"Do you blame us?" asked little Mrs Danforth, her pale cheeks colouring slightly. "Your husband seduced our daughter, a child who was in his care—"

"Steady, Adrienne," interposed her husband. "The girl's nineteen now. I'm sure there were faults—"

"And then," swept on his wife, not pausing, "he forced her into an abortion clinic, where she nearly died."

Another protesting sound from her husband. Alice began to warm to Mr Danforth. Although she had said and thought worse to herself over the preceding days, she was more affected by this bald recitation of Daniel's sins than she had expected. She flinched a little, and raised a hand as if to protect herself.

"Given all this – this abuse, it seems to me," continued the small, neat woman flatly, "that your coming here at all is an impertinence."

"I know," said Alice. "I came rather selfishly to ask you not to wreck our family life by exposing us and losing Daniel his job. But I can see there isn't much point. We aren't equally wounded parties. You have more right to be angry than I do."

"Yes. You are quite right. We do," said Mrs Danforth. "I am aware that you were not to blame, which is why Peter and I agreed to see you. But there is no question of our having any consideration for your husband. What he did to Alicia—"

"Alicia?" said Alice stupidly. "Who . . .?"

Mrs Danforth stared, coldly offended.

"Our daughter," said Mr Danforth. "Alicia." He stared. This woman with the tousled hair and hippy clothes looked pale suddenly, green even. He hoped she wasn't going to faint. Momentarily uncertain of himself, the big man picked up a silver frame from the mantelpiece and thrust it at her, saying the name louder, as if she were deaf. "Alicia."

Alice looked at the great ham hand in front of her, and the small delicate frame it clutched. At first she thought the face looking up at her from between the pudgy finger and thumb was Clemmie's. No, it was less round, less healthy than Clemmie's. None of Dan's Irish peasant blood there. With a shock that jolted her visibly, so that Mrs Danforth started away in fright, Alice saw that it was her own face.

Her old, student face: pale, piquant, with full half-smiling lips and big amused grey eyes, the whole framed in a careless cloud of brown hair. Alicia Danforth. Lisha. Lisha looked like her. Lisha looked like the Alice of twenty years ago. She even had her name, the old pet name that Daniel used to groan on her shoulder in the velvet southern nights, the year when

they hitchhiked to Venice and everything was new. "A-li-cia
... bellissima ..."

She never remembered afterwards how she left the Blackheath
house, nor what was said after that moment. Something formu-
laic, meaninglessly polite; some apology for having come. She
was on Greenwich station before she knew it, leaning on a dirty
wall, sheets of tears running down her face, telling a concerned
young guard that she was quite all right.

She spent a long dark hour waiting for Daniel to get back
from delivering Clementine to Surrey. He found her in the
kitchen, tearing and chipping pieces from the silly decorated
table with her fingernails, throwing flakes of family life to the
floor, weeping. She shouted at Daniel then, not able to care that
Jamie stood visible and aghast on the stairway.

"You bastard, you bastard, time-travelling shit. Is that all you
wanted? More of the same, a new model? Christ, I could kill you,
I *will* kill you, and I hope the Danforths do go to the papers, I
hope they fucking ruin you!"

She wept and stormed, and Daniel stood white and rigid
and helpless before this terrible new Alice. Jamie withdrew
silently up the stairs, heading for Clemmie's bedroom and the
brisk robust comfort of his sister. He was standing in its open
doorway, whimpering slightly, before he saw the stripped bed,
and remembered.

7

"They all do that," said Yasmin, passing Alice a cup of green Chinese tea. "You only have to look at the papers, that cabinet minister's moll is *exactly* like his wife. Sort of compliment, really."

"Insult," said Alice, cupping her cold hands round the tea. They were cold all the time now. She could not eat and did not sleep, alone in Clemmie's abandoned bedroom with only the occasional condescending visit of the tortoiseshell cat to assuage her solitude. "It's as if he was saying look, what I wanted was a young woman with that hair and that face and even that name . . . and it was time to chuck away the old one."

She had said this so many times in the past hour that Yasmin, pouring her own tea, decided on confrontation.

"To be fair," she said coolly, "he didn't chuck you away, did he? He told you he wanted to stay. And you said that originally, before you went to see these people, you'd forgiven him. More or less."

"I had," said Alice. "I was all ready to be – big – about it. I don't feel big any more. I feel small and vicious. Like a weasel. A dried-up old weasel."

Yasmin crossed to the sofa and gently, deliberately, put her arms round Alice. The stiffness of her friend's shoulders touched her, and she hugged tighter. "Allie. You're not small or vicious or anything. It's all right. Maybe you're right, maybe it's over with Daniel. It happens to a lot of marriages. It doesn't have to be a failure."

"What the hell do you know about marriage?" said Alice. Yasmin took her arms away, drank her tea, and thought to herself how lucky it was that she had an all-absorbing job, money, prestige, and a new male secretary whose puppyish hero worship did much to eclipse the memory of Alan's treachery. Otherwise, Alice could find herself losing friends with lines like that. Pity had its limits.

"Sorry," said Alice after a moment.

"Don't think twice about it," said Yasmin. "Biscuit?"

It was not her only visit. Alice's night of rage, and the days of sullen, wary domestic politeness which had dragged by since then, had left her tired and irritable but hectically talkative. Clemmie's first and second weekly letters home from school had been passed between her and Daniel, but only talked over with Jamie. The decencies of communication were restored, carefully, in front of the child; otherwise Daniel worked at his desk and Alice sat and read at the ruined kitchen table or lying on Clementine's bed. Or else she went out and toured her friends, talking about it, always talking, often crying.

Simon and Stevie made her laugh, called Dan a devious bitch, offered to cut the crotch out of his trousers for her, and tempted her with tiny parcels of smoked salmon or feta and basil vol-au-vents from the GardenGrow deli counter. After an hour with the pair of them and a whisky bottle, Alice felt brighter and stronger. Sometimes she even remembered to pick up and take home the crazily patterned swatches which Simon had pinched for Jamie from his friend's studio, laughing at the parrot beaks and cupids and intricate Gauguin jungle prints. "Go on," said Simon, "go wild. Have a jungle sofa. James would love it, that's a plus; Danny would hate it, that's another." But the new strength faded on the walk home to Camden, and she would go to bed more despairing than ever. One night after work, she dropped into the flat above GardenGrow and found only Stevie there. He pulled her in, closed the door and went through a pantomime of locking and barring it.

"Simon's working. I have things to say to you, sweetie. Sit." Alice sat on the sofa, covered with half an old theatre curtain, and pulled her feet up under her. Stevie, without Simon, suddenly looked his age and oddly formidable, his hair streaked grey like a badger's, his face animated by sharp, pale blue eyes.

"Alice, dear sweet thing. You have had your time of grieving. Are you speaking to Daniel yet? Properly?"

"No," said Alice. "I can't."

"Can, too," said Stevie. "If you don't, he'll bugger off. Do you want that?"

"No," said Alice again. "I mean, yes. No. Oh, sod it. The thing is, Steve, that girl he took – it was me, me twenty years ago. Only not me, a sort of version of me, and," she was crying again, as she cried every time she talked about it, "it means it wasn't ever me, not the real me, just some *doll* in his head that he wanted, and I thought we were something else. Friends . . ."

Stevie turned his back on her. When she had finished, he said dryly, "Bollocks. None of that matters a fish's tit, does it, sweetie? What matters is, do you still want him or not?"

"How can you say it doesn't matter? Infidelity—"

"Is everywhere," said Stevie. "Do you suppose pretty Simon keeps his little bits and pieces just for him and me? Hmm? Do you suppose that for *one minute*?"

Alice stared. Stevie turned round to her again, and for the first time she saw how lined his face was, and how many of the lines, if he were not for ever smiling, would lead downwards. He would look very, very sad, she thought, if he did not laugh so much.

"But I love Simon, don't I? So when he goes I create, and when he comes back I tell him what a little tart he is, how much I hate him, and how much I love him. And that's it."

"How long . . ." began Alice, and stopped, laughing embarrassedly.

"How long do I give him a hard time? Oh, Allie, listen to me when I say that a week is enough. More than enough. Amnesty sets in on the following Saturday, seven o'clock sharp. Dan has served his time."

Different for you, thought Alice silently, different if you don't have children, if you aren't properly married, if you are gay. She was momentarily shocked at herself for thinking such illiberal thoughts, and looked up guiltily at him.

"Not different," said Stevie, reading her mind. "Not different. All love is much the same, ducky. Painful as piles."

The first time she saw Jenny after the birthday party was on a Saturday afternoon, while Daniel took Jamie to the cinema and

Rod played squash with his business partner and the au pair was at her language club. But Jenny was not alone to be confided in; she had a visitor, a bouncing, animated old schoolfriend called Lucinda with a velvet hairband and noisy two-year-old twins. Alice drank tea impatiently while Lucinda rattled on about her holiday in Ireland.

". . . cottage near Ballydehob, just gorgeous. We got this babysitter one night, couldn't understand a word she said but she was sweet, terribly Ryan's daughter."

"Did she cope all right?" asked Jenny, hefting her baby on to the couch and peering up the leg of its plastic nappy.

"Yah, totally. So we got a night out. Jonno found this amazing restaurant at Toormoore, called the Bard at Bay – all done up in olde Irish style with spinning wheels, and only candlelight. The hoot of it was, this real Essex girl runs it, called Della, only she's got a weird old boy with long grey hair and a bardic robe who spouts poems all through dinner, stuff about Deirdre of the Sorrows – just too atmospheric – but the old boy got seriously pissed off and kept trying to stop reciting and have a drink at the bar, only she'd shoo him back to his wooden stool. It was hilarious, Jonno nearly died laughing – you really ought to go to Ireland, Jen."

"Isn't it awfully dangerous, with the IRA?" said Jenny, turning from the baby to wipe her daughter's nose with a firm, ruthless hand.

"Of course not," said Alice crossly, breaking in for the first time. "That's such a stereotypical English thing – anyway, the ceasefire—"

"Well, nobody bombed us. Did they, poosy woosy possums?" said Lucinda, picking up a twin. "Anyway, Jen, I'll tell you about the cottage hire place if you want to. Must dash. 'Byee!"

Alice wondered whether her arrival had chased the bouncing Lucinda away early. Such thoughts often came to her now; she knew herself to be a brooding, unwelcome presence, a cloud of black unhappiness over any company. Looking at Jenny, complacent between her baby and her four-year-old daughter, she felt as though a wall separated their lives, a wall of children's maturity. Rod wouldn't stray, not with his babies so small. Daniel would never have looked away either in those nursery days. But now their children were well grown, and even Jamie was capable of getting himself up, getting reasonably clean clothes on, his cereal eaten and himself on the bus to Finchamgrove. It was far easier to have children so old and capable, but oddly enough it also seemed to make marriage more difficult to keep up. Maybe a natural force eased couples apart when their peak responsibility began to fade. As soon as the door slammed behind Lucinda and her double buggy, Alice began quietly to cry.

"What's the *matter*?" asked pink-faced Jenny, all concern, tugging at her broderie collar and readjusting the baby on her shoulder. "Poor you. Feeling down?"

Alice fleetingly thought how much she disliked Jenny in this capable, mumsy mood. Jenny had been fun once, back at college. Before banker Rod and the grown-up house with its ruffled Austrian blinds.

"Yes," she snapped. "Daniel has been screwing – er, seeing another girl. Woman." She paused, waiting for the avalanche of sympathy which was surely her due.

Jenny only said, with oddly little warmth, "Poor you. Is it over? Is that how you know about it?"

"Yes. He says so."

"Poor you," said Jenny again, but she was looking at the baby, fussing with some strap or popper. "Good that it's over."

"I don't know whether to leave him," blurted Alice, surprising herself with her frankness. "I really feel like it sometimes."

"Oh, don't do *that*," said Jenny, still with that strange coldness. "Divorce is no fun. Not with children. Lucinda and Jonno nearly did when she found out about his secretary. Imagine, with the twins and everything."

"She sounded keen enough on him just now," said Alice.

"She's got her head screwed on," said Jenny firmly. "Men do these things, you know. Our mothers knew that. They just coped with it. They're weaker than us, you know. Men. They are."

"Jenny, of all the stupid, sloppy, dated things to say—"

"I'm very sorry, but it's how I feel." The soft prim voice cut her off. "I don't believe in all this flouncing out on marriage vows. Do you want more tea?"

So Alice left, with a feeling of finality.

•   •   •

Daniel heard none of the hectic talking. He saw his wife silent, snappishly withdrawn, going through her day like a zombie, pretending he was not there. He tried, many times, to talk. Alice would not or could not respond. After the first outbreak, she never shouted or reproached him, but left any room he was in, sometimes with a small hopeless shrug that went straight to his heart. One evening at the beginning of the third week he confronted her, blocking her way out of the kitchen.

"Jamie's sleeping round at Gavin's," he said. "We can talk."

"About what?" said Alice. But she sat down, and looked up at him. "Not about Lisha. A-li-ci-a. I don't want to think about it."

"Not about Lisha," agreed Daniel. "About the Dean."

For the call had, at last, come. The Danforths' letter to the college had been laid in front of him, and questions asked. He had answered them all calmly, and agreed that it would be most undesirable for any publicity to come of it. Still calmly, he had agreed that his resignation would be best for all parties. He had intimated that in any case he was in talks with the University of East Anglia concerning a lectureship.

The Dean had unbent, then, only allowing himself a brief remonstrance over Daniel's earlier silence, and a snide comment about how extraordinarily lucky he was to find another university post so quickly. Daniel, maintaining calm dignity, had made a form of apology. Then he had left the office and run down the corridor to the gents' lavatory, to be violently sick. He knelt by the pedestal, sobbing and retching. Then, again calmly, he went to his office, opened a certain drawer, pulled out a letter, and dialled a Norwich number.

"About the Dean," he said now.

"What about him?" asked Alice, and a small demon made her add, "Is *he* having her now, then?"

Daniel ignored that. "I have lost my job. The Danforths wrote. I resigned. There won't be any newspaper stuff. They said there wouldn't be if I resigned."

"Better for the children," said Alice automatically. "Are you on the dole then?"

"No," said Daniel. "I'm paid to the end of this term, but they say they would rather I wasn't around. Tim will cover my seminars and I'll just do two standard lectures. Then after Christmas I start full-time at UEA. I'll have to go up first and do some groundwork. Allie," there was an appeal in his voice, "Allie, we do have to talk about it. There's a lot to plan. The house—"

"You want to sell it?"

"We ought to sell it. Buy in Norfolk. The prices there aren't at all bad. We could probably wipe out the last bit of the mortgage even. I got some brochures, Savills and Strutt and Parker—"

"Can't you live in?" said Alice. "Aren't there bachelor chambers, room things?"

"Well, the family—"

"The family is here," said Alice. "You can come home at weekends, can't you? I work here, there's Jamie's school, Clemmie's friends in the holidays. We *live* here." Yawning, she stood up. "I'm for bed. Goodnight."

Daniel shouted then. "It's half-past bloody eight! Bloody talk to me! Do you mean you want a separation, or what? Allie, we can't go on like this!"

"That's the whole point," said Alice. "We won't. It's best you do go. In the week, anyway. Best thing that could have happened."

"Do you know what it's like," said Daniel, more quietly, "to go into the place where you've worked for ten years and be told you aren't welcome any more?"

"No," said Alice, yawning again.

"Well, I hope one day you bloody find out," said her husband.

Pushing past him, she walked upstairs to Clemmie's room and, falling on the bed, cried as if her heart would break. Daniel heard her as he passed ten minutes later on his way to their own room but did not come in. Hearing his footsteps pass the door without one hesitant step, Alice raised her head, paused a moment, then fell back to weeping.

Daniel's hope was fulfilled. Alice did find out what it was like to lose a job. The next morning, arriving at the Opera House with the customary lift of her spirits, she had barely time to unwind her tattered green-and-gold velvet shawl and drape it on the office hatstand before the internal phone rang, summoning her to the personnel director's office. "Not you *too*," said Henrietta, who worked opposite. "That's the third. Maxie and Hugh already today. No, I don't know what's going on." She lied. She did know. Maxie had left in tears, and Hugh was closeted with the union rep.

Half an hour later, white as a sheet, Alice returned. Henrietta, who was ten years younger with a degree in arts administration, looked at her with concern.

"Problems?"

"My husband's dream," said Alice harshly, "just came true. I have one month's notice. We are down-sizing. We are rationalizing, in advance of the coming closure for renovation. My post does not exist beyond October the thirty-first."

"Well," said Henrietta, who had become something of a confidante of the older woman during these past weeks, "rotten luck. There's been a lot of rumours about it. I suppose we should have known. At least it solves the problem about moving to Norfolk. You can look for something there. Theatre Royal, Norwich?" Alice did not answer.

Yasmin took a different line. "Don't even think of going to Norfolk," she said. "Let him stew. You've a teeny mortgage, haven't you? Stay." She put her arm round Alice again, and this time there was no stiffening. The dark-brown head slumped against her, hopeless. "There are so many jobs," said Yasmin. "In our outfit, the European radio thing is really coming together, and you were a *good* news assistant back at the Beeb. I could talk to Ronnie – no, straight to Alan would be better."

"I don't want to be a news assistant," said Alice. "I want to be . . ." she sniffed.

"What?" said Yasmin, letting her go with a small, exasperated shake. "An opera gopher? Look, you even used to sell icecream, some nights. You told me."

"I liked it," said Alice. "You get to see most of the act from the back of the balcony if you're quick getting down to the freezer. I saw *Turandot* three times, free. Oh God, I want my job back. Oh Yazz, isn't there anything I can do?"

"To get yesterday back?" said Yasmin. "It won't ever come, you know."

"Just don't give me fucking *advice*!" shouted Alice. "Or cracker mottoes. Everyone's giving me some bloody line! Jenny, Stevie, you, Daniel."

"Well," said Yazz levelly, "you do keep asking."

"I can run my own life, thank you," said Alice, and soon afterwards left.

"You're too miserable to run your own life," said Stevie, sharply, looking at her sunken eyes and lank hair. "You aren't fit to decide anything at all. Get some therapy."

So Alice went twice to a grey house in Marylebone, where a woman with straggling grey hair and round glasses asked her about her father, mother, lack of siblings, sex life in marriage and ability to express anger. "The source of the anger," said the therapist, "is less important than its quality. Anger stands alone. It is a fact. Its trigger is irrelevant."

"That," said Alice coarsely, "is like saying that snot is more important than the nose it came out of. I don't want to stare at the snot, I want to cure the cold."

The therapist smiled with such knowing benignity that Alice at last expressed her anger violently, throwing a brass ashtray hard across the room. The therapist rang a small unnoticed bell on the arm of her chair and the receptionist came in to usher Alice to an empty waiting room. A few moments later a note was delivered by a brisk secretary, suggesting that she seek "mainstream medical and psychiatric help" through her GP.

When Jamie was not at Finchamgrove, haunting the science-fiction bay of the library through breaks and lunch hours and scraping dismally through any homework that was likely to be checked, he came alive in the dark labyrinths of the laser-gun battle game centres which at that time were taking over derelict shops and small business premises across London. PhaserForce and LaserQuest, Futurefight and Battlezone, he knew them all intimately.

Battlezone was the newest, and cheapest: £1 for twenty minutes, with the incentive of free repeat games for top scorers. Its guns were light but its electrical battle packs reassuringly heavy and chunky across his shoulders. Running crouched along its black alleys, firing suddenly at the flickering circles of light that were unseen enemies, Jamie felt a fierce warm surge of capableness. His aim was good, he was fast and flexible, he could handle himself.

Outside, a cardboard figure of a 21st-century warrior with a sub-machine-gun loomed behind the counter, a grubby bubble over its head saying "Yo! Time to earn some respect!" The young assistant handed each sweating contestant a computer printout of the score. Jamie saw with satisfaction that he, Deathstorm, had wiped out Terminator, Mad Dog, Klingon, and Antichrist, and had only been shot 12 times to Klingon's 47. "Deathstorm rules," he murmured to himself. "Deathstorm is King. More respect." Sometimes he would have said it to Gavin, or Tim. But they were not with him. Jamie McDonald went war-gaming far, far more than any of his friends and therefore often went without them.

8

Daniel left home in the last week of October, as soon as half-term had ended. It was, considering everything, a strangely satisfactory half-term. For Alice, the fog of anger and depression seemed to grow thinner, almost to lift at times as the family reassembled. On the Friday she emptied her desk at the Royal Opera House for the last time, trying not to look at particularly cherished programmes. She had crossed the road with her carrier bags and braved a farewell drink with her few closest colleagues. All of them pretended that there was not already a distance between them, a gap which had been growing silently ever since her sentence was pronounced. They forecast new, extravagantly successful careers for Alice, drank to her and decried the stuffy old House she was "escaping". It was a good performance, and Alice appreciated it. Leaving the group in the pub, she walked at last through Covent Garden Piazza, glancing at familiar shops, smiling at familiar buskers, wondering whether she would ever be able to come to this cheerful, crowded little corner of London again. At last, weighed down by her carrier bags, she gave up walking, hailed a taxi and came straight home.

Home was transformed. Instead of Daniel's questioning silence and the slight, uncommunicative figure of Jamie flitting like a shadow from fridge to bedroom, she stepped into the house and became aware straightaway of the warm riot of Clementine, back from boarding school in tearing high spirits. The hall was full of garish coloured bags, and no sooner had Alice dropped her own sad relics of work among them than Clemmie stampeded down the stairs and flung herself like a tornado on her mother, hugging and laughing and telling her news like a reporter from another, more vivid country.

"BCSE is *ace*, and boarding is amazing, Jamie, you ought to try it. Seriously."

"No way," said Jamie. "No, no, way. I got ninety-two in Battlezone yesterday, Gavin only ever got sixty-four at his best."

"Warrior! He-man!" said Clemmie generously. "Mum, I'm in the first swimming, second dressage and jumping – there might be an event – we're going on a school trip to Olympia, in the hols, only the brilliant thing is that ten of us can be assistant grooms as well as watching, and I got chosen – I did ten three seven in the sprint, on really bad going."

"Are you fitting in any academic studies, might I ask?" said Daniel, emerging from the living room with a smile Alice barely remembered. "GCSE courses, that sort of optional extra?"

"Ten subject choices, Dad. Sorted. They said you could consult, but I said don't sweat, man, we'd discussed it all."

"And they believed you?"

"They're writing. But four sciences, two languages, come on, Dad, what more do you want? Mum, terrible news about the Royal Offal. What are you going to do?"

Alice, laughing and crying, hugged the solid healthy body of her daughter, burying her head in the clean soft neck.

"Oh, something. Doesn't matter." Nothing had been said to either child about Daniel's move. Half-term, they had coldly agreed with one another, was the best time to discuss it properly. When they were all, Alice said with a delicate shudder, "relaxed".

And half-term, strangely, did bring relaxation. With neither parent working and the family wagon rolling along evenly on all four wheels again, both home life and outings regained something of their old spirit. Clementine talked incessantly, particularly to Jamie; Daniel teased her about the sporting life, and Alice joked with the children. It never became too obvious – so they thought – that between Alice and Daniel nothing passed at all. They mingled families with friends, mixing and matching, swapping children, coming together again in large uproarious parties to fly kites or skim down swimming-pool flumes. The cracks hardly showed.

Alice began to see how in the days before easy divorce, dead and hollow marriages used somehow to endure for years, for the sake of children or just of respectability. The thought filled her with cold dismay. She had moved out of Clemmie's room and was sleeping in the double bed again. She bought a single duvet, and rolled herself in it on her side of the bed so that the two of them slept cocooned as chastely and separately as explorers in some Arctic tent.

Only once did a flare of anger light the greyness between them. Clementine and Jamie were watching television after a day-long party at a friend's house, and both parents were invited for a drink afterwards. Adam and Sue were both university colleagues of Daniel's, and an acquaintance who had just won an Oxford professorship was staying with them for a night at the theatre. The subject of Daniel's move came up. Adam, pouring a Dutch beer, said jovially, "You'll find the travelling a bore, I daresay, but the trains are supposed to be good".

Alice waited to see how Daniel would react.

"Oh, it's a full move, not a commute," said Daniel airily. "Eventually, anyway. Better to be on the spot, part of the university."

"Right!" said John Dadgen, the Oxford man, enthusiastically. "You're so right. You can't be part of the place if you spend your life on the M11."

Alice stared. "We hardly ever do the M11 to Norfolk," she said. "It's a much nicer drive on the A12–A14."

"Norfolk?" Dadgen and Adam looked at her. "But . . ."

Daniel had slipped out of the room and was talking animatedly to Sue in the hall.

"Dan's new job," said Alice remorselessly. "Norwich. University of East Anglia."

Dadgen, quick off the mark, covered the moment with a neat piece of campery. "Oh, all the same to me, my dears. As far as I'm concerned these days, everything the far side of Magdalen Bridge is *Bosnia*."

"I take it," said Adam, "that your fellowship is not in geography, then?" The moment passed in laughter.

Later, Alice said to Daniel in the car, "What's all this about the M11? Have you been telling people you've got a job at Cambridge?"

"No," said Daniel sulkily. Then, "I may have said something about the Fens."

"Norwich isn't in the Fens. It's on the Broads," said Alice. "You've been bullshitting. That's pathetic."

It was the first direct hostility she had shown him since the night she got home from the Danforths. Daniel met it with aloofness.

"Anyway," he said, stabbing the clutch, "M11's best for Norwich. You're just paranoid about motorways. M11, turn off at Newmarket." She did not reply.

Clemmie was due back at school on the Saturday, and on the morning she left she drew Alice upstairs on the pretext of needing help with some name tapes in her bedroom. Once there, she kicked the door shut and sat on the bed, making no move towards her packing.

"What's going on?" she asked baldly.

"What do you mean? About Dad changing jobs?"

"No. Got that. Don't think much of it, but got it. I mean about Jamie."

Alice was momentarily at a loss. Soothing, prepared lines of explanation about herself and Daniel "giving each other space" had suddenly become irrelevant. Jamie? What about Jamie?

"Did you know," said Clemmie, popping and clicking the fasteners on her duvet cover, "that he's bunking off school?"

Alice stared at her daughter. "That's nonsense."

"Not nonsense. He is. He registers in, then skips at break and goes to Battlezone. And PhaserForce. On his own. Ginnie told me. Gavin's sister. *Gavin's* even getting worried."

"The school hasn't said anything," began Alice, a wave of hot guilt almost choking her.

"The school," said Clemmie, "is not concentrating. It never did. It couldn't find its own arse with both hands."

Alice let the coarseness go, feeling her own stance on the moral high ground to be precarious. "But you were all right there!"

"I was all right because I run my own life, I know my way round. I know what I want. I can spot the limitations of clapped-out knackered teachers. They're robots, Mum. They really are. Jamie's different. He needs someone to take care of him. He hates Fincham and nobody even notices because he doesn't break windows and get sent to the school shrink."

"You never said any of this," said Alice.

"I couldn't have put it into words till I went to another school," said Clementine judicially. "But Jamie – there's nothing at Fincham for him. It's fine for self-starters and it's fine for remedial morons, but he's in the middle. He's not one of their precious A level superstars and he's not a heartwarming triumph of reclamation either. So they ignore him. They ignored me, till I started winning prizes."

Alice sat next to her daughter on the bed. "Oh Clem," she said hopelessly. "I wish you weren't away." Even as she said it, guilt flowed over her in another disabling wave. There was a silence. Clementine looked consideringly at her mother, then at the wall, and in a small, tight, blank voice quite different from her earlier eloquence, said, "Do you think I ought to come back? Go to Fincham and give Jamie a hand?"

"No!" cried Alice. "No. For God's sake. Live your life, you're good at it. Jamie's our job. We ought to have known all this was going on."

"Not your fault," said Clemmie. "Not really. He obviously does it quite cleverly. Poor old Jay."

When she had seen Clemmie off from Paddington on the school train, Alice drove home and confronted Daniel. Jamie was upstairs banging on his computer keyboard, and Daniel found himself for the first time in weeks deliberately sought out by his wife. He raised a haggard face from the chest of books he was packing, and tentatively smiled at her approach.

"Jamie's skipping school," said Alice, without preamble. "Clem found out."

Daniel sat back on his heels, looking at her. "Little sod," he said. "How does he do that without anybody noticing? Whatever happened to the truant officer? Where does he go?"

"War-game places. You know. Battlezone."

Daniel put down the heavy book he held and stood up. "Do you think it's us?"

"You mean he's upset over your going to Norwich?"

"I meant the whole thing. Us. Not speaking."

"We do speak," said Alice.

Daniel looked at her, then turned and picked up his book again. "I'll talk to him."

Alice went upstairs and stood in the doorway of Jamie's room. It was, she noticed, tidier than it used to be. Jamie sat at his desk, his schoolbag slumped on the floor next to him, fiddling with the computer.

"Hello," she said.

"'Lo, Mum," he said, not turning. "I can't make this one boot up. It's Tim's."

Alice looked around the room, eyes sharpened by worry, searching for clues. Suddenly, with a small shock, she realized why the room looked tidier. There were no pictures. Blobs of Blu-Tack clung despondently to the walls, but Jamie's vivid patterns and swirls of colour were gone.

"Sweetheart, where are your pictures?"

"Threw them out. Last week."

"All of them? Oh, Jay, I would have loved to keep some."

Jamie swivelled on his chair, to and fro, not looking at her.

"Will you do me some more?"

"Don't know," said Jamie. "Did Clemmie get her train?"

"Yes," said Alice. "Boarding school's really suiting her. Look, Jamie, your father's going to talk to you about this, but I wanted to say something privately first. Are you unhappy at Finchamgrove?"

He looked at his mother for the first time, something like hope in his eyes. If Alice had paused, then, given him a moment to respond, many things might never have happened. But she ploughed on, over-brightly.

"Because we do want you to be happy. And there are other schools – not just in London, but different kinds of schools." She meant in Norfolk. At that moment, with her child's pale face before her and her heart still pounding from Clementine's revelation that the supposedly safe school hours were being spent in the darkness and the rattle of fantasy massacres, Norfolk seemed for the first time a positive solution rather than a bitter capitulation. For Jamie's sake, for the sake of some pleasant rural day school far from laser battles, she could face exile and subordination. Plenty of women had done the same.

With – she was surprised to find herself thinking – far worse husbands.

"We could look around," she went on. But Jamie's face was set and stubborn.

She means boarding school, he thought. *Now that Clemmie's doing it, they want me to. Then they can get divorced in peace.* The only school he knew was Finchamgrove. To be in such a place all day and night, to live there, to be cut off from the sanctuary of his own bedroom, to have that bedroom maybe sold and emptied while he was away filled him with immeasurable dread. These things happened, half his class were children of divorce. They happened before you knew it.

"No," he said. "I really like Fincham. I'd rather stay there." He swivelled back to his screen.

Alice decided to leave the question of bunking off for Daniel to handle. "What are you doing?" she asked neutrally.

Jamie knew of only one way to make an importunate mother go away and leave you in peace. Either pretend to do homework, or, "I'm writing to Godgran," he said innocently. "Saying thanks for the half-term fiver."

Alice, as she was meant to do, left the room. That night, Daniel talked to Jamie who, forewarned by his mother's new concern, lied fluently. Gavin, he explained, was exaggerating. He had only sagged off school twice, both times in a group and to avoid double art. He promised not to do it again. Daniel was relieved, and unwilling to make his last evening at home into an inquisition. He and Jamie watched *Deep Space Nine* together, and at dawn he left, taking a suitcase full of books and a briefcase full of clothes.

At breakfast, Jamie looked at his father's place by the stove and at the kitchen chair he had painted for Clemmie's twelfth birthday. He said, in a weary small voice, "This family is *shrinking*."

9

One set of lies was enough; to cancel the other lie of the day, Jamie did write to Godgran after all. Daniel's godmother had been an honorary granny to him for longer than he could remember and always remembered to send a tenner for birthdays and – her own eccentricity – a fiver for half-term. She sent holy pictures too, of Jesus and Mary, which as a little boy he had kept reverently in a special box. Now he threw them embarrassedly into the same box without looking too closely. Clemmie lost hers every time, but then she always had.

He had never written to anyone on the computer before. It was only a month since he swapped a carton of computer games for the old dot-matrix printer which fitted his obsolescent BBC machine. Godgran might like a bit of new technology, being so old. At bedtime, swivelling on his chair in Terminator pyjamas, he called up the primitive word-processing programme and typed:

> Dear Godgran,
>   Thank you for the five pounds. It was really ewsful. I have got a printer now so I am doing this on the computer. Clemmie spent all hafterm raving about her schol.

He was tired. The effort of lying to his father made him a little sick and dizzy. "School" came out as "SchooK", and in correcting it he lost the second o, without noticing. He could finish soon. Jamie leaned his head forward, eyes too close to the green shimmering screen, and rested his forehead on the cold glass. He must finish and lie down. With an effort, he began typing again, thinking carefully about the spellings.

I am doing OK at mine but I tor up all my pictures. Dad is gowing –

Suddenly, he was sweating, typing faster than he knew he could, eyes on the keys, ignoring the screen, shaken as if by the chilly wind that rattled the branches of the ailing Camden trees outside his room.

– is gowing away. Mum says its just becaus of his work but she is lying they are always angry and they pretned they have their old room agen but they have 2 duveys I saw. I think they are going to divorse and Mum is angry and she didnt put my picture up that I did for her birthday and I saw it under the bed and someone trod on the glass and she dusnt like it so perhaps school is right that I cant do art properly.

He sat up suddenly from his crouched position, rubbed his eyes and shook his head. So tired. Away to his left, the dark shape of the doorway might be the beginning of a tunnel, a Battlezone tunnel, and he had no gun or pack on. Must finish. In a panic, he moved the pale blinking cursor on to "PRINT" and pushed the "F10" button. The screen went blank, and the printer chattered self-importantly. Pulling the letter out, neither reading it nor remembering to sign it, Jamie stuffed it in one of the ready-addressed envelopes his mother thoughtfully provided: Miss Violet Lancing, Moss Cottage, Wetheringham, Norfolk. He sealed it, threw it on the desk and climbed into bed. As he closed his eyes, the reassuring weight of the battle pack fell round his shoulders, and a gun was in his hands. Down the dark tunnel a ring of lights moved, and Jamie aimed, fired and slept.

Without Clemmie, Daniel, or a job to go to, Alice found her days disconcertingly long and pointless. She could not listen to music without weeping, and she was bored with constant weeping. No book seemed to engage her. She cleaned recesses of the house that had not seen a duster in ten years, and took bags of outgrown children's clothes to the charity shop. She cooked for herself and Jamie, but the badness of her cooking made her think of the merits of Daniel's, and drove her back to tinned soup. She shopped, slowly and carefully, looking at the prices of food more closely than she had for years. The shedding of her habitual busyness, her gaily frantic working-mother rush, made her see more and fear more. Around her, from the once anonymous mass of fellow shoppers, emerged other slow, meticulous, worried figures, bending over to read special offers and checking bargain tins for dents.

Once, her hand went out to such a tin of red salmon and touched the thin hand of another woman; looking up, she saw the starveling pallor, the smoker's skin and the cheap skimpy clothes of the woman opposite and snatched back her hand as if from a nettle. Another time, she stood in the queue at the small supermarket with two other women and a man, and realized with a small shock that all of them were pensioners. Daniel had enjoined her, in their brief dawn parting, to use the joint account for everything. But his bedsitter in Norwich was costing £85 a week; she knew, because she had seen the letter of agreement on his desk.

He did not come home for the first weekend, pleading that he had people to see; she was as much disappointed as relieved. Jamie, told of this, grew even quieter than before. He was very tractable just now; did everything he was told, got his own breakfast and often his own sandwich for supper, and had even written to Godgran of his own accord.

On the day she touched the hand of the woman in the supermarket, Alice came to a decision. That evening, she rang Yasmin's answering machine. Two days later, Yazz rang back, brisk at eight thirty in the morning, from her desk.

"Hi. Sorry I didn't get back to you sooner. How's things?"

"Not wonderful. Dan's in Norwich mostly. Can I talk to you about work?"

"You found something?"

"No."

"Half past six? At the Grape Alarm, the wine bar in Covent Garden?"

Alice found herself unable to decide what to wear, an absurdity considering it was only Yazz. She settled on a long green crushed-velvet skirt, green blouse with trailing New Age streamers of mock ivy falling from the shoulders, and a gold waistcoat. Looking in the mirror, the words "ageing hippy" floated across her mind, and the streaks of grey in the front of her hair seemed more noticeable than ever before. She looked away. As she was checking for her key by the front door, Jamie walked in.

"Jayjay, I thought you were going to be all evening at Gavin's," said Alice, in a tone of slight dismay that was not lost on him.

"Gavin's a dickhead," said Jamie. He made to push past her, but Alice put out an arm and held him.

"Why?"

"He says things that aren't true, to wind me up."

"What?"

Jamie would far rather have escaped, but suddenly rage shook him, shattering his careful tractability. Why shouldn't his mother know? Why should he protect her from what everybody thought?

"He says my dad's gone for good and that you aren't telling me because I'm a baby."

Alice sat on the second step, still keeping hold of Jamie's shoulders. It was six o'clock, still time to get to the wine bar.

"Sweetheart, that is not true. Dad's got a job in Norwich. We've got a house here. It happens to lots of families for a bit. It'll be all the more fun to tell him your news every weekend."

"Every weekend? Every weekend?" said Jamie nastily. "Like last weekend. He doesn't even have a *phone number*."

"He's in a bedsitter, darling. Honestly. He'll get a phone, and you can ring him every night. Or, tell you what, next time he rings we'll fix for you to go up on the train and see him. Camp out in his room. You used to like trains."

Jamie wriggled from her grasp. "I'm going back to Gavin's anyway," he said. "His dad's taking us to the cinema to see *Apollo 13*. I came back for some money."

Alice gave it to him and walked him down the road to Gavin's house, which was barely a hundred yards from theirs.

"'Bye, sweetheart. Have a lovely film. I'll be back by eight, waiting for you. Get Gavin's dad to walk you back, will you?"

"Course," said Jamie, and sauntered towards the familiar house. Alice glanced at her watch. Six fifteen. Damn, it would have to be a taxi. Blowing her boy a kiss and picking up her green skirts, she ran for Camden High Street where a yellow taxi light was just visible, cruising through the traffic.

Jamie watched her go, then turned his back on the lighted windows of Gavin's house to walk in the other direction, jingling his money in his pocket, heading for Battlezone. Bigger boys played in the evenings. Men, sometimes. Some of them used to be real soldiers; once, he'd got shown a Falklands medal.

Yazz sat alone at a far table in the Grape Alarm, eating stuffed olives with moody concentration, an opened bottle and two glasses in front of her. She motioned Alice to a chair with a wave of her olivestick.

"Late. Did you get away with being late at the Opera House?"

"Sorry. Jamie had something, and with Dan not home, it's awkward."

"You look a bloody sight better since he went," said Yazz.

"Do I?" Alice did not feel better.

"Yes. I would say you were getting into injury time, before you made the break. You'll pick up. Once you're working. Trust Yazz, the Woman Who Knows About Heartbreak."

Alice laughed, wondering how it was that Yasmin's dark, positive face, crooked smile and cynical manner always made her feel both invigorated and at the same time oddly protective. She had often, in the past, wanted to hug Yazz properly, the way she hugged her daughter. She had held off because her friend's brittleness seemed not to invite any such contact. Now, fresh from her own shock, she looked at Yazz with different eyes, remembering the fiasco of her long partnership with Alan, who had thought marriage laughably unnecessary and children undesirable. Alan, who one morning had told Yasmin – at work – that he was marrying the well-born Caroline. The well-born, pregnant Caroline. Alice could see now how the brittleness had grown on her friend since then, together with a faint but definite hostility to Alice's own family life.

"Anyway," Yasmin was saying, "you have a job, if you want one. NA at Euradio, special reference arts and music. Same news assistant job you did at the Beeb, only better paid and newer technology. You edit tape on computer screens."

Alice was taken aback. "Yazz, you're doing too much – that's incredible – I mean, I didn't want you to swing me a job, that's not fair. It's your area, your people – I couldn't take it."

Yasmin drained her glass and looked at Alice with impatience.

"For Christ's sake. Do you think jobs come easy? If you've got the contacts, use them. Everybody does. I spoke to Alan, that's all."

"You spoke to *Alan*? Alan Halliday?"

"Yes, yes. He is still MD of Euradio. I do see him at meetings. Brave little me, were you going to say?"

"No, but . . ."

Yasmin filled Alice's glass. "This may come as a shock to you, little mother, but some of us have to go on working with our exes. Doing big deals with them, for money. Screwing favours out of them, even. Anyway, Alan jumped at the idea of getting someone certifiably bright, and with an in at the Royal Opera House just as things get exciting."

"But I haven't . . . I never was that important, and anyway," Alice continued foolishly, "I can't edit tape on computer screens."

Yasmin had a way of staring at fatuous comments which made even her oldest friends cringe. "Euradio is not on the air until June," she said. "The job would start more or less now. Six months' training, planning and dry runs. Hell, you might even get to sleep with Alan. Bring round one of your ballet dancers and do a Lytton Strachey threesome, why don't you?"

"I am a married woman, you forget," said Alice, with prim frivolity as the wine began to work.

"You *were* a married woman," said Yasmin, and she was not laughing. Neither, after a moment's thought, was Alice.

"One more thing," said Yasmin. "You can spend the time between now and starting work by finding some proper clothes.

The Age of Aquarius has been over for fifteen years." Her smile was crookedly devastating enough to soften the insult, and Alice only smiled, and shrugged, and turned her palms up in a gesture of surrender.

10

Hearing the postman's van chugging to a standstill at the next cottage, Violet Lancing moved stiffly across her cluttered living room towards the front door which gave straight on to the lane. Well, not quite straight; three worn stone steps led down the grass bank, with deep, treacherous gullies of nettles on either side. The *social worker* who had called – Violet always shuddered and deployed mental italics when she spoke of the woman – had been very alarmed by the gullies. "Suppose you missed your footing on the steps?" she said. "You could fall right out of sight, down those ditches."

"They are drains," said Violet. "And I have not missed my footing in fifty years. Nor has the Colonel, and he has only half a left arm to balance himself with. My number three godson is the only person who ever fell in there, and serve him right. He was drunk." The social worker looked up, sharply, her pencil poised to note further indications that this elderly person was At Risk. Violet saw this and scornfully added, "He was eighteen at the time. He is now thirty-nine, married with two children, and teaches moral philosophy. He can hold his drink very well." The social worker smiled placatingly, and observed that Miss Lancing must be thrilled to have godchildren, "having no family". A blue basilisk glare greeted this remark, as the old lady cleared away the visitor's coffee cup with a hint of finality.

"Thrilled? What strange ideas you young people have. There are thrills in life. War. Explosions. Lovemaking. The high mountains. Storms at sea. Wagner. Religious visions. Those are thrilling. Godchildren, however, are not thrilling. They are interesting and sometimes pleasant, but always a responsibility. First and foremost. A duty."

"Do they all live a long way off?" asked the social worker.

"All three in London. None of them models of faith. But I do have family, as you put it. I have a sister in Kenya, in the Heart of Mary Order."

Soon afterwards the social worker left. She had done her job, checked on an elderly person living alone. Back in Norwich she put on file the observation "independent, capable" and after a moment's hesitation put a negative cross against the query "Signs of mental confusion".

Now, Violet opened the door and looked down the steps between the drains as the post van drew up.

"Yew always know, gal!" said the postman, leaning out of the window on his elbow. "Beat me if I know how."

"Instinct and mental discipline," said Violet. "Just like I used to tell you at school, Luke Feaveryear. Not that it did much good. Besides, at our age one has regular habits. There is always a letter from Kenya on Fridays."

The postman pulled out his bundle, frowned at the top envelope and said, "Kenya it is. 'Nother one, too, gal."

"A bonus. How delightful. Thank you." The old woman descended two steps, reached towards the van window and took them.

"I thenk yow," said the postman, let in his clutch and drove off down the damp lane, his exhaust mingling with the morning fog.

Violet climbed back into the cottage, ignoring the milk bottle on the bottom step and followed by her draggled black cat with a mouse between his jaws. She stooped to remove the mouse, threw it accurately out of the crack she always left open at the top of the sash window for just this purpose, and crossed to the walnut bureau opposite the window, above which hung a very beautiful gilt icon of the Blessed Virgin. With a wickedly sharp Second World War commando dagger (the social worker had hated that too), the old woman slit the two envelopes before settling down in a high-backed chair much tattered around the corners by the black cat.

From Mombasa came the usual gentle account of Olivia's life:

of the mission school and the spring planting, the local politics and the problem of the bigger boys attached to the Mission being ogled by the women sex tourists ("Harpies on heat," Olivia called them in un-nunly style). They were a frequent subject of complaint in her letters, the European women who sat by the seashore luring the beach boys with their bleached hair and immodest clothing and mesmerizing, undreamed-of wads of money. Sister Olivia had confronted one of them, a German lady, after two of "her" boys spent a week in the hotel neglecting their studies and their immortal souls. Violet smiled. The thought of pale, meek-looking Olivia taking on a rampant escaped Hausfrau was irresistible.

"After all," wrote her sister, "it seems unfair just to rebuke the boys, when so much of the power and the fault is on the side of these women." True, thought Violet. Women cannot for ever claim the privilege of being victims. In the village, out on the bleak farms around her, there definitely were female victims. But I never was one, she thought proudly. My godsons' wives do not look like victims either. Women were well able to take responsibility, take one another on if necessary as her dauntless sister took on the German seductress. She looked down at Olivia's neat italics with affection, folded the letter and laid it on the arm of her chair.

She picked up the second letter, slit by the dagger, from her lap. The writing she knew: it was young Alice McDonald's. It was Alice's familiar – and in Violet's view over-careful – habit to provide ready-addressed envelopes for her children even now that they had grown large and capable of writing legibly enough for any sorting office. This would be a bread-and-butter letter from Clementine or James. With pleasure, she pulled out the typed sheet. It was typed, but there was something odd about its appearance. Her mind skimmed over that, and she began reading.

Dear Godgran,
   Thank you for the five pounds. It was really ewsful. I have got a printer now so I am doing this on the computer.

Ha! thought Violet. How long since it was considered rude to type personal letters? But how silly, come to think of it, that interdict always was. She continued:

Clemmie spent all hafterm raving about her schol. I am doing OK at mine but I tor up all my pictures.

An uneasiness gripped the old woman as she read. Her blue-veined hand shook slightly. She realized, as her eye travelled further down the page, what it was that had seemed odd about the letter. Not only was there no signature, but at this point, during the "tor up all my pictures", the typing changed, becoming suddenly as erratic and irregular as any handwriting. First there was a long blank, and then the words, a few to a line and erratically spaced, began to form a crazy, spiky, desperate pattern, jerking unevenly along the page, gappy and misspelt. It looked wrong. It was wrong. More, she thought, than just mechanically wrong. She had seen nothing like it since – her mind faltered, rejecting the comparison.

She forced herself to think it through. The last time a letter gave her a thrill of alarm like this was in the war. Even without the dreadful words, the look of the page and the memories it stirred would have alarmed her seriously. The words only confirmed the trouble.

Dad is gowing away. Mum says its just becaus of his work but she is lying they are always angry and they pretned they have their old room agen but they have 2 duveys I saw.

They do see, thought Violet angrily. Oh yes, the children do see. Olivia and I saw perfectly well how it was between our parents as early as 1927, when I was seven and she was five. Only in those days parents did little about incompatibility. They just stayed incompatible. Especially Catholic parents.

I think they are going to divorse and Mum is angry and she didnt put my picture up that I did for her birthday and I saw it under the bed and someone trod on the glass and she dusnt like it so perhaps school is right that I cant do art properly.

The letter ended with too many ys, a row of them, and then silence, as if the writer had been too tired or overcome to continue. Violet looked at it for a long time, immobile. She was still sitting with the letter on her lap when the door opened and, without knocking, the Colonel entered.

"What ho on the Rialto," he said, as usual. Violet, unusually, did not reply. "All right, old girl? Brought the milk in."

The old man was, indeed, carrying a bottle of milk. To open the door with his one hand, he had wedged the bottle under the stump of his left arm, using what was obviously a well-accustomed trick of applying enough pressure from his shoulder to keep a heavy object in place. Now he drew it out from the folds of his tweed jacket with a flourish, and parked it on the polished table.

"In the *kitchen*," said Violet irritably. "Don't be useless, Geoffrey."

The old man stroked his yellowing moustache, ignoring the damp bottle on the table. He looked carefully at Violet, the hand that clutched the letter on her lap, the unfamiliar mistiness in the sharp pale-blue eyes. He was of a generation that knew much about letters and bad news, and if ever there was a tableau suggesting an unwelcome letter it was this. More gently, he said, "Bad news, old girl?"

She roused herself, reaching out to put the letter on the low table, and moving the milk bottle so that it stood on yesterday's newspaper.

"I believe it is. Look."

Between these two, for fifty years, there had been few secrets. Fewer, perhaps, than if they had been married. Geoffrey picked up the letter, sat in the chair opposite, and read. After a moment, he said, "Godgran? Do they still call you that?"

"Their father is my godson. It appears logical. He is only twelve."

She knew him well enough to accept that the first question was always going to be pointless and peripheral. The Colonel, in the authentic spirit of reconnaissance, liked to circle a problem from some distance before homing in.

Sure enough, after a moment more he said, "That jerking around. That's not just the computer, is it?"

"And no signature."

"Probably," said the Colonel, "doesn't know he wrote it. Or

what he wrote." He too had spent time among the shell-shocked. "Remember McAdam?"

Violet nodded. Fifty-three years ago, on the bleak shingle of Orford Ness, Captain Geoffrey Gordon had been in Ballistics, supervising researchers who spent their day shooting up captured Junkers 88s and Dorniers on the dunes and measuring the holes. Violet Lancing was a civilian secretary in Instrumentation, a few huts away. McAdam was a maverick, brought to Orford Ness because of his civilian record in demolition explosives. His CO gave him, Geoffrey always said in retrospect, "rather too free a hand". McAdam blew off both legs one day in a private and unauthorized experiment. It was afterwards that he wrote the letters, strange letters peppered with capitals and predictions, concerning great birds and apocalyptic Beasts. McAdam wrote to the Minister of War, to his mother, to his estranged wife in Scotland. Invalided in a cottage over the river at Orford while he was debriefed about progress in his legitimate work, he would send these letters to Violet to be typed. She and Geoffrey had conferred, and decided never to type or send them. But they both remembered the awful disjointed look of the letters, and staring down silently at Jamie's, printed though it was, they recognized it.

"Well," said Violet at last. "What do I do?"

"Ring the parents?" said Geoffrey.

"Would it be a breach of confidence?" asked Violet. "Maybe I should write to Jamie. Or Clementine."

"But he doesn't know he wrote it. I'm sure of that. The more I think."

The old pair conferred, their grey heads inclined towards one another over the low table, the letter lying between them.

Daniel, to his surprise, was exhilarated by Norwich. At first, the modern campus and its concrete walkways dismayed him, and the ebb and flow of unfamiliar faces made him remember the time when his parents first brought him to London from County Clare at twelve years old. But before the first week had passed, he realized with something that was almost exultation that the conversation here, the thought, the vigour and the energy of the students were equal to those in the community he had left. London was not after all the whole world. He realized, too, that clean winds from the sea and the rivers blew over it all, that the air sparkled and the great curve of Norfolk sky gave him new, illimitable thoughts. He could, he thought, at last write his book here. He would not be distracted by the dieselly, soupy, torrid sexiness, the subterranean beat of London. The Norwich girl students, pretty as they were, did not move him particularly and certainly did not disturb him. Such an idea seemed impossible in this clear air. Indeed, he began to see for the first time that girl students had been an unacknowledged problem to him well before Lisha. For years, maybe; a drag on the edge of his consciousness, a dark chasm.

By day, this new clean energy supported him. But in his bedsitting room at night, Daniel longed unbearably for his family, and for the rich earthy clutter of the Camden house. His bedsit was a neat room at the front of a featureless brick house ten minutes down the bypass from the UEA campus. Outside the window he could see the top of the curly iron signpost saying "B & B. Long Stay Arrangements Considered. No Students", and the flowing traffic beneath the trees beyond. There was sprigged mock-Morris wallpaper in pale creams and pinks, a flounced pale-blue valance round the bed, a blue candlewick bedspread patterned with Prince of Wales feathers, a washbasin in the corner modestly panelled in plywood and white emulsion, and a picture of a chubby-cheeked shepherdess which Daniel longed to remove and put face down under the bed. He did not do it only because it might hurt Mrs Hammond's feelings.

Daniel seemed to himself, these days, to be constantly afraid of hurting feelings. The weeks of living with Alice's open emotional wound left him so afraid of hurting that he was unable even to take down a picture that Alice herself would have turned to the wall within seconds of seeing it. Even at work, he found himself preternaturally careful of students' feelings, and as he moved through his day was for ever standing back in doorways, clearing other people's plates in the cafeteria, and listening patiently to bores of all ages rather than talk them down or take refuge in a book. Only alone in the bleakly chi-chi little room could he relax, lying on the bed in his trousers and socks, jeering at political broadcasts on the television, reading and making notes. Sometimes, to his distaste, he found himself buying a pack of cigarettes on the way home and reviving his old smoking habit. "It's that or go mad," he said apologetically to David, the one colleague with whom he spoke of such things. "That room smells of potpourri, and I can't find where she's hidden the bloody stuff, to throw it out."

"Try the back of the wardrobe," said David, himself a divorcé with wide experience of bed-and-breakfast houses. "They hang little bag things from the coat hangers." So Daniel searched, and sure enough the source of the sickly smell was a little muslin bag. He wrapped it in two layers of plastic and Sellotaped it up, and after that managed to do without cigarettes.

He rang home once or twice, but Alice seemed distant and unconcerned, and Jamie monosyllabic. Ringing Clemmie at school was difficult, but on the third attempt a housemistress got her to the telephone and for ten minutes he warmed himself at her lively conversational flame, basking in his child's optimistic energy. Clemmie was blithe and teasing and full of her own news; clearly, she had no idea that he had been two weekends away from home. When he put the telephone down, Daniel leaned against the panes of the booth, his cheeks wet with tears. He was floating away from home, without an anchor, in a terrible capsule of candlewick and potpourri.

In the third week, walking home from the university to his room at lunchtime to collect a book, an idea occurred to him. He rang Violet Lancing.

"Godma?" he said. "Daniel. I'm in Norwich."

The familiar voice, which had always sounded old but never sounded any older, crackled briskly down the line. "Why? Why Norwich?"

"I'm getting bedded in for a new job here, next term. Doing a few seminars. We didn't tell you yet, because we haven't found a house."

"No. You wouldn't have, would you?" There was a dryness in her voice which he could not understand. It was not likely that Alice would have contacted his godmother with dire and personal news; although as a family they saw her every Christmas holiday and camped in her garden for a week or so every summer, ownership in Violet Lancing rested, it was always understood, firmly with Daniel. Alice made the children write thank you letters, and treated Violet with the same polite deference she would have shown a mother-in-law, but there the relationship ended. "The Catholic bit", as Alice referred to it, created a barrier between them. Daniel did not practise in London, but went to Mass in Norfolk with his godmother and even took his unbaptised children. Alice had never quite liked that but could not decide why. Violet wished Alice would come right out with her objections to religion, and slightly despised her for her reticence. The result was an unacknowledged coolness, which never grew worse or better with succeeding years. Definitely, Alice would not have rung. Yet Violet seemed to know something. That "You wouldn't have" held a meaning. Daniel carried on.

"Thought I might come up to see you. On Friday night, perhaps. Since I'm here. We could drive up to the coast at the weekend. Bring the Colonel, if you like."

"I am not a geriatric patient requiring outings," said Violet. "And neither is the Colonel. We can take a taxi any time we like. There is no need for you to neglect your family for my sake."

She was fencing now, but Daniel had a lifetime's experience of his godmother's tactics. She had been his mother's closest friend, a formidable visitor to their house. He laughed, albeit forcedly.

"No, no, they're busy elsewhere. I'm the neglected one. Come on, let me come and see you. I miss you."

There was a brief silence.

"I would be happier," said Violet, "to think that you were seeing your son on Friday. Whether in Norwich or London. He will not be too busy for that. Then you can come and see me, and I will tell you something. But see him first."

"Well, soon, then," said Daniel.

"It would be pleasant. All of you, perhaps, could come for a visit together," said Violet. "Goodbye then, for the moment." The line went dead. Daniel stared into the receiver for a minute, then clicked it down before picking it up to dial Alice's number. His own number.

"Isn't that lovely, darling?" said Alice brightly in the direction of Jamie's back and the computer screen beyond. "Dad wants you and him to have a boys' weekend, looking round Norfolk."

Cold dismay settled on the child's stomach. This sounded to him very much like Access. He knew about Access, even though he would probably have spelt it Axis. Boys in his class often took trains, even planes, on certain weekends to spend time with distant fathers. Generally they said it was really good, because you got spoilt by your dad and then spoilt by your mum when you got home. He knew they didn't mean it. Sometimes, if he was stupid enough to mention something he had done with "Mum and Dad" over the weekend, those same boys would throw a punch, or kick his bag over so that his books fell out.

"You can get the train," said Alice. "I'll put you on it, on Friday evening, and Dad can send you back on Sunday."

Jamie punched a key savagely, and the screen before him filled with monsters.

On Wednesday, Violet and the Colonel generally took a taxi into town, to shop. Charlie the driver knew the routine: pick up Miss L. at Moss Cottage, down the road to the Flats for the Colonel, into town, park outside the supermarket, wait, load their stuff, wait again reading the newspaper while they drank coffee in the Square and did fiddling, shoe-mending errands. Then back, and up those terrible steps of Miss Lancing's with the bags. The Colonel, since he ate most of his meals with the old lady, hardly took any shopping home. Charlie often wondered, as he sat with his *Mirror* at the wheel or stared insolently at the circling traffic warden on the double yellow lines by the supermarket, whether his own old age would provide such a cosy arrangement.

Like the Colonel, but twenty years younger, Charlie was a widower. He had found no female consolations of his own, and he did wonder about those two – go on, never, not at their age! – but something other than their wrinkles made him regretfully decide that there was nothing loverlike in the relationship. Not only because she was such a Catholic, down the church twice every Sunday, making the Walsingham pilgrimage with all those screwballs at Easter, but because the two of them were almost too close to be anything like a man and wife. They finished one another's sentences, leaned on one another when they got a bit wobbly, and argued with the amiable viciousness of brother and sister, and there never seemed to be any tension. Miss Lancing had once told him that they "went through the war together", so he supposed that might bind people together in a different way to the usual.

On this Wednesday, they seemed to dawdle over their coffee,

and arrived back at Moss Cottage just as the telephone started to ring. Miss L. was up the steps with her key and across the room with an alacrity that struck Charlie as something just a shade unusual. He heard her on the telephone. Something about not being a geriatric, and a taxi – that was why he listened – and "seeing your son". Then she came to the door again and paid him, and drew the Colonel inside as if she wanted to speak to him. Been yakking all morning, thought Charlie admiringly. They obviously have enough to talk about.

"I have spoken to Daniel," said Violet. "Jamie's father."

"D'you tell him?"

"No. I told him to see his son this weekend. Then I will talk to him. Better if the boy himself—"

"—lets his father know," finished the Colonel. "Quite. Wish I'd had a son," he added suddenly.

Violet looked at him, a look so loving that it might have made Charlie revise all his views had he not been already half a mile away and phlegmatically queuing behind a flock of sheep.

"You'd have been a good father. You should have had a son."

"*We* should," said Geoffrey, unloading a bag of vegetables into Violet's cracked plastic rack and using his single hand to sort them with military neatness, all the carrot points facing outwards.

"You and Celia should," said Violet calmly, stacking packets of rice and pasta. "You were married."

"*We* could have been married. After Celia died," said Geoffrey. "You were still young enough. For a son. Or daughter." He added the last words hastily, like a man who senses feminism always lying in ambush. "Would have liked a daughter, too."

"You know why we didn't," said Violet, closing the cupboard door with a snap.

The old man sighed and straightened up, eyeing his carrot parade narrowly. "Yes," he said. "Yes. Oh yes." The vegetable rack seemed to dissolve until he saw only a waste of shingle and the twinkling lights of huts in the distance, along the Ness. He heard the distant sucking of the sea and the nearer rippling of Stony Creek as he sat beside it, Violet's young head heavy on his shoulder, his heart full of guilty joy.

The old man gave a longer, shuddering sigh. If it hadn't been for Stony Creek and that long Suffolk summer . . . if it hadn't been for the quiet hour before the last boat home to Orford, and the flowering of what Violet saw as the sin between them. If it had not been for that, they would be married now. Maybe with a son. And daughter. But he couldn't have known that Celia would die in 1950, burnt to death in the officers' quarters. Nor that Violet would then take this strange, tortured, Catholic line of punishing herself for once eating forbidden fruit by turning down the unforbidden kind ten years later. He picked up an onion in his one hand, and squeezed its hardness. Violet spoke again, more gently.

"Don't think about it, Geoffrey. You haven't for years."

"Have, actually."

"We've got to where we would have been, by now, haven't we? Maybe it's a better way to be."

"I paid my price," said the Colonel gruffly. "I paid my dues." Violet came over to him, and stroked his left arm, his stump, with tenderness. "You did," she said. "You got her out, you nearly saved her life. Don't think about it. Don't start the bad dreams again."

"All the time," the old man said, his voice shaky, "I was thinking about you. All the time in the smoke, all the time in that hospital."

"Well, I found you in the end," said Violet briskly, letting go of his shoulder. "Why are we talking like this now? I've kept you off the subject for years." She smiled, taking all sting out of the words.

"Because of the boy," said Geoffrey, flatly. "Poor bloody little boy. *Two duvets*. We'd not have got to that stage, Violet. Not ever."

On Thursday, Alice ransacked her cupboards and finally found a short, straight black skirt, unadorned cream blouse, and relatively sober waistcoat. Yazz's line about the Age of Aquarius had stung her more than she would admit, but if she had to see Alan she had better dress up as a businessperson. An office dweller. The sleeves of the blouse, she saw in the mirror with her new post-Aquarian eyes, were perhaps a little too flamboyantly full, more d'Artagnan than Armani; the waistcoat's tiny embroidered suns and moons no longer reminded her of the set for *Götterdämmerung* but of some ludicrous old trout with straggly grey hair, the kind you might meet in a fortune-telling booth or a New Age market. Angrily, she pulled her hair back from her face and quelled it with a severe black velvet clip. Shoes were a problem; desperately, she went to Clemmie's room and borrowed some black pumps with short thin heels, which made her feel precarious and silly.

At Euradio's offices, she was shown in to Alan Halliday's office with flatteringly little delay.

"Welcome aboard," he said expansively. "Sit down, do." He was bigger, sleeker, smoother even than she remembered. Alice perched on a leather chair. The big cat purred, "Yazz tells me you're thinking of coming back into broadcasting."

"Well," said Alice, "I need a job. And I used to be a news assistant. But I'm out of date. Technically."

"Doesn't matter," said Alan, turning his head sideways and making as if to pull something from a drawer. Since he didn't, in the event, pull anything out, Alice concluded that his real motive was to show his Greek profile to her at its most beautiful, dipped slant. "He wants every woman on earth to be panting for him," Yazz had said. "That means you. Don't even think of taking it personally."

"I'm not sure—" began Alice.

"I am," said Alan, this time giving her the full benefit of his big green eyes and fine teeth. "You'll fit in here. We have two vacancies. There are a hundred and eighty-three applications, filtered to twenty interviews. I'm interviewing all day Monday." Alice got his message, and flushed with angry embarrassment. He smiled at her, beautifully, and spelled it out.

"If you say yes, then my twenty applicants are fighting over one job. If you say no, they each have twice the chance."

"Then why aren't you interviewing me?" said Alice. "Ask why I want the job, why I can do it, all that. It's only fair."

Alan smiled even wider. "Because I know we want you. Not just Yasmin. I do." His eyes glittered briefly over her exposed legs and black pumps. "There is such a thing as quality. Background. It takes precedence over the usual forms."

She left him still uncommitted, promising to telephone before Friday night. Yasmin passed her in the corridor and raised a dark eyebrow in question. Alice only smiled tightly, said "See you" and, lying to her friend, tumbled out the words, "Must rush, I have to get Jay from school." She hurried on in her annoyingly tight black skirt and crippling shoes.

On Friday, Finchamgrove broke up at lunchtime because of a teachers' union meeting. Jamie had not thought this worth mentioning to his mother and instead went to Battlezone. Here the computer display over the paybooth told him he would find Tyson, Terminator, Ghost, Beelzebub and OJ starting Kruel Kombat in 1 minute 30 seconds. Tapping in his signature as DEATHSTORM, he slipped on a pack and picked up the gun, its weight comfortingly familiar. Sighting along the barrel, he lined up on the teenage attendant.

"'Nuff o'that, kid. No aiming till you're in. Bad habit," said the youth. Jamie crouched aggressively, still aiming, a grin widening on his face. The youth moved towards him, threatening. "Any more and you're out."

Jamie pulled the trigger. He knew nothing would happen, that it was not switched on, that not even the feeble red beam would emerge; but he had not reckoned with the attendant's irritation.

"I warned you!" said the boy and roughly pulled off Jamie's battle pack. "Out!"

"But I paid," said Jamie furiously. "I paid! I'm on the computer! I'm Deathstorm!"

The woman from the pay booth, her face pale and tired from long windowless hours indoors, came over. "Darren, let the kid go."

"He's arsing about," said Darren. "Boss said not to put up with it."

"Yeah, you're right. But just this once. He's a good customer." And to the child, "You behave!" Sulkily, still shocked by his own defiance and the attendant's reaction, Jamie put his pack on and ran through the dangling black ribbons over the entrance.

It was darker than usual inside. The plywood walls, painted like distressed and ruined brickwork, daubed with aggressive graffiti, seemed to rise higher than usual too. Running forward, Jamie missed his usual side tunnel and paused, uncertain. He heard

footsteps to his right, and swerved down the alley opening to
the left of him. He pushed through a hanging khaki net and
swung to point his gun at a wavering circle of red lights. The
t-t-t-teow! sound of fire from behind him was followed by a buzz
from his own pack. He was hit. He fired again, but no answering
teow! bzz signified success. There was harsh breathing near him,
behind him, too close; he swung round but nobody was there.
Ghost! he thought. Ghost, on the list outside. He had never seen
that name. It couldn't be a real—

The breathing continued, and abruptly the walls around him
reared ten, twenty, thirty feet higher, clashed together and began
to tumble on him, crushing him. From somewhere very close now
came more fast breathing, then a thin, high scream and a burst of
sobbing. Outside, the attendant threw a switch and the whole
Battlezone was bathed in bland neon light and revealed as the
tatty plywood stage set that it was.

Tyson, Terminator, OJ, Ghost and the others trooped out
complaining. "Aw, c'mon, what's goin' on?" Mild enough
teenagers, all of them, their young moon faces incongruous
above the camouflage canvas of the stylish battle packs. The
attendant found Jamie alone, silent, still crouched. "C'mon,
kid, out. Nothing to fuss about. How old are you, anyway?"
The woman in the pay booth shot a worried glance at the small
boy's set, dazed expression as he walked back into the lobby.

"You all right, love? Feeling sick?"

"I'm fine," said Jamie. "Someone screamed at me."

The attendant glanced at the other boys who shook their
heads silently. One pointed at Jamie's back, then grinned and
shrugged.

"Well, you get on home. OK?" said the woman.

Jamie left, muttering, "Someone *did* scream." He walked by the
Regent's Canal for a while, filling in until his normal coming-home
time on a schoolday, then turned back towards Camden High
Street. Fitting his key in the door, he walked into the house and
brushed past Alice in the hall without speaking, then turned on
the halfway landing and said in reply to her remark about the
train to Norwich, "Yup, I know. I'm packing. Five minutes." He
was pleased to find that his voice sounded normal.

"Looking forward to it? You'll have fun, you and Dad," said

Alice brightly. She was halfway down the basement stairs, with Clemmie's unsociable tortoiseshell cat mewling at her heels, wanting its supper. "It'll be lovely, won't it?"

"Yup."

While he threw night things into his rucksack, Alice rang Alan Halliday. Jamie heard her voice floating up the stairs. "Definitely. I've thought it over. Monday, then. And Alan – I'm grateful. It'll be a new life. Perhaps I needed something completely different." Jamie stopped, a grimy pyjama jacket in his hand, and shivered.

In Norwich, Daniel left the university with a lighter heart than he had had for weeks. He had rented the room next to his own for two nights, and picked up its key from Mrs Hammond. Surveying it, he hoped that Jamie would not find its clean, blandly chi-chi decor as chilling as he did. He did what he could; put a wad of comics and computer magazines on the bed, reached deep into the wardrobe and suppressed the potpourri. Jamie was coming. Whatever happened, his children were his for ever. Maybe, out of the difficult Camden atmosphere, Jamie and he could even talk about that damn awful school and what was to be done. It would have surprised Jamie, and indeed Alice, to know how much Daniel saw of the hidden, festering trouble within his son, and how much time he spent thinking about it.

At five thirty, after two changes on the Underground, Alice put Jamie on the Norwich train (with a wad of comics and computer magazines) and enjoyed a sense of reviving hope. Some time with his father would do the boy good. An old-fashioned instinct in her felt there was something right about such a colloquy. A couple of days alone might do her no harm, either. Jamie grew harder and harder to understand: surly, uncommunicative, like a teenager three years older. It would almost be a relief to be free of the responsibility after their weeks of solitude together.

As Jamie stepped on to the train, though, he turned his pale face back towards her, the lock of black hair falling over his eye in a heartbreaking likeness of Daniel's, and looked very much younger. She suddenly wished that she were going with him. A fragment of poetry crossed her mind, disturbing. What was it? The boy on the train? "What past can be yours, O journeying boy, towards a world unknown . . ." Browning, was it? No, Hardy. There was something terrible about the boy on the train in the poem, something momentous, something about *all at stake*. The words curled round her consciousness as she looked at him. A door slammed, a whistle blew.

"'Bye, Mum."

"'Bye, sweetheart. Sure you're OK on your own? Got your ticket?"

"Course. I went to Scout camp on the train, didn't I?"

"Well, remember, stay on till Norwich. Ipswich, Stowmarket, Diss, Norwich. Dad'll be there right on the platform. See you at ten to seven on Sunday. Dad knows the right train. I'll be here. Love you. Go careful." She was walking now, alongside the train.

"Go careful too," said Jamie. As the train outpaced her, she could see him hefting his nylon rucksack and vanishing into the second-class carriage whose windows were already misting up with the breath of weekend travellers. She stopped and stood on the platform watching the train go out, then turned towards the Underground. Yazz had rung straight after her call to Alan, demanding that she come out for a celebration drink. Alice took off her glasses, letting the station fade into a soft, warm blur. She stood a moment, polishing them on her sleeve; then with a swift movement put them back on and walked forwards into the sharp-edged world.

The train was full, but Jamie found a seat by the aisle and, dumping his rucksack behind it, sat down and laid his magazines in front of him. Next to him sat a weary-looking man in a business suit with an unopened laptop computer on the table. Opposite were two women, one grey-haired in a cardigan and one young in a tight, skimpy top, and with bleached hair. Jamie looked at them and their magazines without interest, and then turned back to examine the laptop out of the corner of his eye. Perhaps the man would work at it. He might get to see if it was Windows 3.11 or Windows 95. One day, he would have Windows, and the ArtExplosion design software, £79.99. You could make shapes and then rotate them. Animate them, if you had enough RAM.

He sighed. There was not really much chance of the man being a designer he could watch. It would be all boring figures and typing. He turned to his magazines and, with half his attention, began to leaf through them as the train smoothly picked up speed and ran past tower blocks and dereliction, out into the Essex dark.

Daniel stood with a group of students in the lighted doorway of the building. The group scattered into the November evening gloom, vanishing one by one down the pathways under the lamps. Dave, from the department, came out and clapped Daniel on the shoulder with his customary matiness. Why, thought Daniel irritably, do divorced men always touch you so much? He stifled the uncharitable thought. Hell, he might be heading that way himself, reduced to laddish grumbling in the pub about "my ex". Dave was saying something.

". . . to the Goat and Boots? Quick one?"

"I've got to pick up my son," said Daniel. "The train gets in at seven thirty. I'd better go straight there, in case I get held up."

"My digs are near the station," said Dave enthusiastically. "Lovely little local. Go there?"

Daniel sighed. "OK. Want a lift? Car's here."

"Thought you'd never ask," said Dave. "Mine's still in dock. Costing a fortune. How she thinks I can live, with the money she takes off me . . ."

Daniel walked rapidly towards the car park, shutting out the litany of complaint. Dave was in some respects a find, a predominantly amusing and cheerful companion. Here in a new place where he knew nobody, he was lucky at his age to find an acquaintance who was not knit into a family with first call on all his leisure. Dave and Daniel had spent several evenings together, with an ease that Daniel could not just now have felt in another man's cluttered family home. But it was undeniable that towards the end of the day Dave grew annoyingly voluble about his ex-wife and grown-up children. Daniel unlocked the car, threw a pile of books and files from the front passenger seat on to the back, and motioned Dave in. He wished he knew Dave well enough to tell him to shut up about his marriage.

The pub was pleasant enough, though, and Daniel drank a cautious half-pint and relaxed a little. Dave was all right. He had, in any case, now given up on the marriage theme and was delivering scabrous, bitingly accurate portraits of his colleagues, which made Daniel laugh and cap them with memories of his own.

". . . twenty-six memos about not wasting departmental notepaper!"

"Eric used to do that at King's. Why I left, partly. Fifteen memos about abuse of noticeboards. Displacement activity. Anything to avoid coming to the point."

"Was that Eric Hantley, who used to be a junior fellow of Magdalen?"

"That's right! Do you know him?"

"Ran into him at a grisly seminar once. Nottingham or somewhere. Red hair, especially in his nose. Sort of chap who wished he had been born soon enough to be in the Inklings."

At twenty past seven, Daniel left the pub and went on to the station concourse. Dave, rather to his annoyance, came too. "Have the other half in the station bar. Keep you company if the train's late." Now he was in the bar, just visible from where Daniel stood under the indicator watching for news of the train. The black bars rustled discreetly, informing him that the 7.30 arrival from London Liverpool Street was fifteen minutes late. Daniel hesitated, then crossed to the bar. Another half-pint wouldn't hurt.

In the Grape Alarm, Yasmin bought Alice a second large Scotch and praised her appearance.

"You may not wish me to say this, but you do look good in proper clothes."

"I shopped," said Alice. "Once I had decided, I went out and spent one hundred and fifty pounds on respectable office clothes and these boring shoes. I shall probably be back to beads and boots within a month, but I'll break Euradio in gently."

Yasmin, who rarely spent less than ten times that amount on a clothes shopping trip, nodded approvingly and wriggled a little, complacently, inside her narrow black jacket.

"Good girl. Welcome back to the human race. Still miss the Opera House?"

It was the first time it had been mentioned between them since the day Alice left. Alice looked up at her friend gratefully, glad of the chance to talk it out.

"Yes. I can't walk past it. I was nervous about coming here tonight, it's so close. I can't listen to opera CDs at home, either. Even Classic FM sometimes makes me lonely for it."

"But?" said Yasmin, watching her closely.

"But," echoed Alice, "I'm fine, actually. Really I am. Perhaps Daniel being in Norwich made everything so different anyway that, well . . ."

"That you're ready to come out of the chrysalis," said Yasmin. "Like I said, welcome to the human race. Talking of which, have you seen your friend, the almost-human Jenny?"

"Not since the first time I went round after – it all blew up," said Alice. "She seemed rather cross with me for not understanding all and forgiving all."

"For the sake of the children, motherhood, family values and apple pie?"

"More or less." Alice giggled. "But to be fair, Stevie told me to as well. He says he always lets Simon off with a warning. Oh, for God's sake. What a mess." The whisky warmed her. "How am I supposed to get through it all without regular blasts of *Nabucco* from the chorus room and little sneaks into the back of the auditorium to look at the battlements from *Tosca* during orchestra rehearsals?"

"It was bad for you," said Yasmin. "You need the real world. Sharpen you up."

"My round," said Alice, and got up a little unsteadily to make her way to the bar.

Ipswich, Stowmarket, Diss; three stops, and in between them nothing but darkness, cut by the train's fast rattle and the streak of its warm-lit windows through the blackness. Jamie sat with his elbows on the table and watched droplets of rain jiggling on the window, beyond the man who now slept, arms folded protectively on his laptop computer. He tried to imagine how it would be if you were a fieldmouse, out there on an Essex, Suffolk, Norfolk field. He had found a baby fieldmouse once, when they were camping at Godgran's. It was tinier than he could possibly have thought a mammal could be, brown and hunched over in its shiny fur like an old lady, and it nibbled a piece of sweetcorn he pushed towards it. Dad had wanted to kill it or at least throw it out of the house, but Godgran wouldn't let him. She said it was God's creature and as welcome in the house as out, as long as it kept off her Wensleydale cheese.

The mouse might be out there now, crouching in the rain, watching the train. The pattern of words fitted the pattern of noise: *crouch in the rain – watching the train – crouch in the rain.* He felt suddenly sleepy. The train was a noisy monster millions of times as big as a mouse, wailing along at a hundred miles an hour, a Tyrannosaurus Rex. How pleased the mouse must be, thought Jamie, when the train at last was gone and it found itself still safe, in the same wet ditch.

As he fell asleep, some jerk of his relaxing body woke him, and a wave of panic broke. He was being sent, posted, from Mum in

London to Dad in Norfolk. This was it: divorce, access, Clemmie away for most of the time at school, nothing ever the same again. He crossed his arms, holding his shoulders and pressing down, which was a trick he had in moments of panic at school, to make himself feel as if he was again a powerful and competent creature who wore a battle pack and carried a gun and scored high. But then the memory of his scream and disgrace came back, and he kicked out his feet in an involuntary squirm and flushed red, so red that the older lady opposite glanced at him and smiled.

Old ladies! They thought you were a sweet little kid. The bright light in the carriage troubled him now, reminding him of when the neon snapped on in Battlezone and he was on the floor, curled down. He wished, now, that he was out there in the dark with the fieldmouse, not imprisoned on this train which would now for ever and ever shuttle him from Mum to Dad, alone.

Yasmin and Alice left the bar and went out into the throbbing London night. An open-topped bus came down the street full of late tourists, a New Orleans jazz band playing on its upper deck. The warm notes floated on the chilly November air; a street away, a police siren suddenly wailed in counterpoint. Yasmin and Alice looked at one another and, in an access of glee, threw their arms round one another's shoulders and walked along, lightly in step with the band.

Leaving Diss, the train picked up speed but almost immediately seemed to slow down again. For a while it crawled through the darkness. Jamie got up from his seat, picked up his small rucksack and moved to the lobby near the outside doors. The light was dimmer there, and some night air blew in through a half-open window. He pulled on his padded anorak, shivering a little, then leaned on the closed door of the toilet compartment and looked out through the juddering window. A string of chilly distant lights showed, he supposed, some Norfolk village. Near Norwich, they must be. He had heard his parents talking – arguing – about moving here, about Norfolk schools. Didn't look very likely, now, with Mum and this Alan on the phone talking about new lives. Anyway, he didn't want a Norfolk school, or Fincham, or any school.

Didn't want anything. He was tired. Didn't want bright chat from Dad, or artfully organized treats, trips to flumes and air museums. Didn't want Camden, or school, or Battlezone even. Bugger, bugger, bugger the lot of them! A violent kind of depression seized him. The dim gloomy lights of a small station showed up alongside the train and with a brief jerk, which knocked Jamie's head against the toilet door, the train stopped. He peered out of the window, and saw a damp glistening black platform and an unreadable station sign. Knowing perfectly well it was not Norwich, in a confused anger he reached out of the window, wrenched the handle and felt it give.

The door swung open and Jamie McDonald and his rucksack alighted, against all regulations of Anglia InterCity, on the platform of an unscheduled halt. As he slammed the door and the train again began to move, the driver far away in his cab frowned and cocked his head to the left, listening. "Was that a door, Eric?" he asked the trainee sitting next to him. But neither of them could be sure, and nor could the guard when asked. Soon, the forward movement of the train through the drizzle took their attention from the matter. Jamie watched from the platform for a moment as the lights moved away from him, then turned and trudged towards a flaking, fading sign saying WAY OUT.

13

Daniel waited for five minutes, then five minutes more, pacing under the indicator and looking at his watch. Dave strolled out from the station bar between drinks.

"It's quite often late," he said. "But hardly ever very late." Indeed, a minute later the train pulled in, warm and steamy in the cold night air. Daniel stood by the barrier, peering into the crowd of Friday night travellers for his son.

There were several boys of the right height, one so dark-haired that Daniel almost darted forward to greet him. Five minutes later the platform was empty and Daniel filled with cold dismay.

"No Jamie?" said Dave, who had been buying a London evening paper from the newsstand.

"No," said Daniel. "I can't understand it. Alice definitely said this train. The five thirty from Liverpool Street, arriving seven thirty."

"Sure she didn't muddle up nineteen thirty and nine thirty on the timetable? Women do that," said Dave.

"No. We discussed the later trains because the time was so tight after school. But I thought it would make a late night for Jamie, by the time we'd eaten." Daniel was positive in his worry. He paced up and down. "Perhaps he got off too soon," he said suddenly. "I'm going to check."

Dave came too. In the area manager's office, an obliging youth rang up Diss, Stowmarket and Ipswich in turn to check whether anybody had found a twelve-year-old boy wandering around after getting off the train by mistake. They had not.

"Is he the sort of kid to make a mistake like that?" asked the young man.

Daniel admitted that he was not. "Were there any other stops?" he asked. "Unscheduled stops that might have muddled him? After Diss, perhaps? When he could have thought it was Norwich?"

The young man offered to ask the driver, but the driver had gone off shift, and so had the guard. Nobody remembered the trainee. After ten minutes the area manager himself came in, heard the story, and ventured; "Obviously, it's worrying, sir. But perhaps you should just check that the boy was on the train at all. He might have missed it. Just before you worry too much."

So Daniel went to the newsstand and bought a phonecard for two pounds and rang Alice and got the answering machine. For some reason he was unwilling to leave a message. He could not think what to say. Not a naturally anxious man, rather a solver of problems as they occurred, he hated the sensation of helpless vague concern. Irresolute, he stood outside the telephone box and chewed the end of his thumb.

Dave was not malicious. He would never deliberately have plotted to turn his new friend's worry into anger and make co-operation into hatred. But the fact was that if he had calculated, Iago-like, for weeks beforehand he could not have chosen a more effective moment to say, "Women do do that, you know. Bugger you about, over access. I once spent the whole weekend hanging about because she said Emma could come up, then on Sunday night I finally get her on the phone and she says oh, Emma had something on with a friend. Turned out she'd told Emma it was me who cancelled."

Daniel stared at him. Suddenly, he felt all the rage that he, as the guilty party, had conscientiously suppressed during the weeks of silent struggle. He burned at the thought of the lonely nights in the big bedroom, and the ludicrous half-term ones with Alice wrapped papoose-like in her duvet lest his touch contaminate her. He felt the rage of an orphaned child when he thought of the atmosphere of cold resentment which had sent him to this new place alone, unsupported by even the slightest goodwill. He even, in that moment, remembered the embarrassment about the M11 and the A12, at Adam and Sue's.

"Do you think that's what she's doing?" he asked Dave. Which was no tribute to his powers of logic, since Dave had never met

Alice and could not possibly know. But Dave was a little tipsy, and replied with bonhomous confidence.

"Sure to be. He obviously wasn't ever on that train. He's twelve, you said, nearly thirteen. Not a little kid. And you've checked everything."

Daniel, at that moment, really thought he had. But still a cautious inner core, the instinct of a father, made him protest. "All the same, I ought to speak to Alice."

"If you can, mate. If she's anything like the rest of them, she'll make herself scarce."

So when Daniel rang the Camden answering machine again and found Alice incommunicado; when his phonecard ran out of units just as he was about to speak his anger, he did not go and buy another one. He went back to Dave's local instead, right up until closing time. And, for once, he did not try to steer Dave off the subject of women's iniquity in the matter of divorce.

And so it was that when Alice, on the way from the wine bar to supper at Yasmin's flat, made the taxi take a detour to Camden to check that there was no message about a problem with Jamie, she found the light on the answering machine not even flashing. It was a new machine, which did not register silent calls. Assisted by Yasmin, she laughed at her misplaced maternal anxieties.

Jamie went through the little gate in the flaking white wooden railings and stood for a moment irresolute in the dark lane. He pulled up the hood of his anorak against the drizzle, and hesitated, shivering in the cold. Behind him lay the station. Bleak and dim-lit and empty as it was, it was a plain link with everything he knew. Those iron rails through it led on to Norwich and Dad; or to London and Mum, and Finchamgrove. The unmanned station in the middle of nowhere represented a kind of security.

He rejected it. He had got off the train, off the rails. He, Jamie McDonald, a boy not thought much of at his school, a warrior disgraced in Battlezone, a child ignored in his parents' mysterious battle and eclipsed by his brilliant, strong, agile sister, had done something which changed everything. He had seen a poster once, in Simon and Stevie's flat, a faded old poster of a woman in evening dress with a cigarette holder and black words saying, "Stop the world, I want to get off!"

He had stopped the world and got off. Now let them see if he cared.

He walked down the lane, thinking vaguely about the night ahead but still too dazed by his own action to be clear about it. The coloured lights of a pub led him forward, and as he got closer and saw round the corner he recognized the shape of a single-decker bus. He shrank into the hedge in his dark jeans and jacket, and watched it, unnoticed.

The bus's indicator said NORWICH, and a placard on the side NNDF FAMILY DARTS TOURNAMENT. A handful of people were aboard already, and others began to come out of the pub, laughing, and climb up its steps. The warm beery smell from the pub door made him suddenly long for human company and the indoor world. There were, he noticed, teenagers not much bigger than him getting on to the bus. A daring scheme came into his head.

It said Norwich, so it must go there. He would stow away. Turn up at his father's place – he had the address ("In case," Alice had said, tucking the paper into his pocket). He would say to his presumably distraught father, "Thought I'd come another way." That would show him he was not a child. Sauntering, swaggering a little like the bigger boys, he slipped into the line of customers leaving the pub for the bus, climbed the steps and, with his head down, moved swiftly to the only single seat, in the corner near the front where there was no room for a double. Resolutely, he stared out of the window, trying to look eighteen and moody so that nobody would speak to him.

Yasmin's smoked salmon, curled with cream cheese and caviar, was delicious. The two women drank some cold white wine and talked into the night about their first meeting, about Alice's old forgotten promise as a radio journalist, and Yasmin's adventures in the world of ambitious editors and media executives.

"Blokes in this business are all vain as monkeys. That's the weak spot. Always remember they're just big boys, frightened to put their cocks on the table in case you chop them off."

"Yazz, honestly. Don't you like any of them?"

"Oh, I *like* them. But I wouldn't live with one again. Waste of life, men are. No woman needs a husband, every man needs a wife. Look at the health and life expectancy statistics. Married women are less happy and live less long than spinsters; married men, the other way round. Men are leeches. Face it."

Alice did not think of Daniel, still less of Jamie. Instead, she thought of her life and how she had let it stand still during her long affair with the Opera House and her dreaming years of cosy family togetherness. Now she would, as they said, get a life. A career. Move ahead. She would be like Yasmin: strong, funny, invincible, independent, casually kind but unsentimental. Sexy but neat; smiling, but sharp enough to make big cats like Alan respect her. Into her mind, unbidden, swam a picture of herself setting out like some half-baked operatic heroine in her floating grubby scarves and Puss-in-Boots boots, to plead on Daniel's behalf with Lisha's cold angry parents. She flushed with embarrassment. Not that Alice, no, never again.

The bus blundered along the lanes, sometimes between deep banks where it brushed aside the rattling branches of trees, sometimes across wide black plains. Once it seemed to cross a glimmering river. It stopped once or twice at other pubs to pick up players but never did it seem to go within sight of the city. Jamie wondered uneasily whether NORWICH had perhaps just been its depot. Perhaps it was going somewhere quite different. The darts players laughed and shouted, and at one stage sang "why was he born so beautiful" when a large jovial man with a beard boarded the bus and whisked open his jacket to reveal an unevenly stuffed woman's black corset. Pretending to be asleep, at last Jamie slept in reality, hunched in his anorak; a fieldmouse again, a lost, insignificant speck moving northwards through cold Norfolk space.

14

He awoke with a jolt, aware that the bus had stopped and that people were trooping past him, on to the clanking step and out into the road. Snatching at his rucksack, Jamie got up and groggily, automatically, followed them. The driver, who was writing something on his pad, seemed to notice him in the mirror and turned, curious.

"Bit young for this, aren't ya, strawberry?"

"I'm just *small*," said Jamie. "I'm sixteen." The answer came automatically; he had been challenged, although never very rigorously, in numerous arcades and cinemas. It was accepted folklore in Form 8X that you could usually get away with saying sixteen if you acted tough enough and stared them down. This Norfolk driver seemed unconvinced. He shrugged.

The boy was moving away now towards that group from the Plough and Anchor at Wetheringham. Must be one of theirs, he thought. Although there was something that didn't quite fit. The driver frowned, and turned back to his form to note the arrival time: 2125. The League secretary came back on board to sign it.

"Thank you very much," said the driver, forgetting Jamie. "Have a good night, then."

"That should be a good one. Eleven teams, plus the home lot. That's why we had to book in here. None of the pubs is big enough. Eleven o'clock, then?"

"Won't be me. I'm off. Be Charlie, prob'ly."

"Fine."

The secretary moved off along the cinder path towards a long low concrete building marked LEISURE AND COMMUNITY

CENTRE. Jamie was still walking in the same direction, carefully halfway between groups so that each should think he belonged to the other. He was properly awake now, and panic churned in his stomach. This wasn't Norwich. The dark wide stillness of the sky behind the concrete building, the silence, the air, made him realize that he must be a long way from any city. He looked back. The empty bus was pulling away now, a fuggy moving island of warmth leaving him alone in the night.

Not really alone. All around were adults and big teenagers. Ahead of him lay a building which must obviously have a telephone. He was not, after all, as lost as all that. He moved between the swing doors of the leisure centre and stopped by a booth in the lobby. Yes. Telephone. The darts teams surged past him into another warm beery room and once more he was alone. He would ring home. Ring Mum.

But at the thought of ringing Alice a strange tightness came into his chest, a squeezing panic. Dad would come and get him, obviously, once they knew where he was. He would probably be a bit annoyed, but that would be all right. Only, after that the weekend would be over and he would be sent home on the train, and it would be the shrunken family again, just him and Mum. Mum doing this new life business, him at Finchamgrove. Mrs Davis. All the same, all of it waiting for him in the smelly little booth if he put money in that grey, battered telephone coinbox.

But he was the boy who had changed the world by getting off that train. He was a whatsit, that Russian thing Mrs Alcover was always going on about. A dissident. "Someone who does not agree with the laws and systems of the country they are in and is prepared to suffer disadvantages by saying so." She had tried to explain about people with long names like Sollynitsin and Rat – ratty something. A woman who wrote poems in the soap in a prison camp. Most of the class were only interested about the prison camps and the rats, but Jamie had remembered more. Mrs Alcover had talked about dissidents leading "heroically uncomfortable lives" even when they were not imprisoned. Their letters were opened, they were not allowed to do proper jobs, their children got banned from football teams, and if they were painters they couldn't show their work (Jamie felt a pang, there, thinking of Mrs Davis and her insistence that his pictures weren't proper). He liked the idea of the dissidents out there, proudly not caring about any of that stuff.

Well, his life was unbearable too and hopeless, and nobody would help. He would try being a dissident: heroically uncomfortable. Abruptly, hefting his rucksack on to his shoulders, the boy turned and walked back out through the doors.

The leisure centre, and the few houses around it, barely constituted a village. The black shape of a church was just visible through the treetops and for a moment Jamie wondered whether to go and sleep there. But it might be locked, and would certainly be cold, with that terrible bone-coldness of the church where Godgran made them go when they were camping in her orchard. And besides, there would be a churchyard to go through. He turned and walked in the other direction along the lane.

Soon he could sense farmland on either side, great bleak sweeps of fields with a chilly wind rising, smelling slightly of the sea. He walked on, his trainers noiseless on the road, grateful for their padded air-pumped heels. On the wind came fog; tendrils of it at first, then damp clouds which lay in lumps upon the lane so that he could walk right into the blinding whiteness and out again into clearer dark. This intrigued him for a while, and kept him walking, in and out of the clouds, without much thought or worry about his destination.

Then the fog grew thicker so that it was not always clear which was the lane and which the land. Once, he strayed on to a grass verge and fell sharply down a gully cut at right angles to the road to drain it. His ankle was slightly twisted; gasping with pain, he sat on the damp grass rubbing it. An idea had been forming in his mind about sleeping, as tramps were said to do, in a ditch. He had in his rucksack one of his treasures, a "Space Blanket" compacted to the size of a matchbox. He knew, from Scout camp, how you used it, rolling up in it with the shiny silver side inwards to throw heat back at your body. It had been far too hot when he put it round him at camp in summer. It must be good.

But intimate contact with the verge and the ditch made the idea of sleeping there a good deal less appealing. What else did you do, in the country? The Famous Five, long scorned in his reading but once his most vivid friends, were always sleeping in barns. A barn sounded good. Straw, hay, sacks; warm dry things. In the morning he could think what to do. Ring home, probably. At least he would have been a dissident for one night. It might make them see they had to help him. Meanwhile, he would find a barn.

A huddle of farm buildings and vehicles began to take shape in the fog ahead. There was a high open-sided Dutch barn and a confused jumble of other shapes: trucks and sheds and machines covered with canvas and two big lorries and a giant drum with a pointed lid. A little beyond them, a small farmhouse or cottage had one window lit, upstairs. The Famous Five used to knock on farmhouse doors and get fresh milk and permission to sleep in barns. The idea of asking such a thing made Jamie quail; besides, there were murders in the country as well as in London. Suppose it was a nutter's farm? Much better to sleep somewhere in a dry corner, get up early, and creep away. Back to the leisure centre place with the telephone. If – a curl of doubt disturbed him – he could find it. There had been some forks in the road, in the fog.

For the moment he would sleep. He turned into what must be the farmyard, and stumbling slightly on the uneven ground moved towards the tall Dutch barn where he could see gaps in the stacked bales of hay or straw or whatever it was. A dog barked. He froze. Then, moving very slowly, without a sound, he tiptoed away from the direction of the dog. It barked again, but a chain rattled. Obviously, it was on a chain.

Still, the barking would make the farmer come out and look, wouldn't it? Softly, Jamie moved away, and suddenly saw looming out of the fog at his side another building, a curved one. A sort of building, anyhow. It had no door but the front seemed to be a dark canvas flap, laced almost to the bottom. A little to his left there were wobbly wooden steps. Carefully, he crept up them and dropped on all fours to lift the flap and peer inside. Cautiously, he crawled through. It was very dark, and spiky things were lying around. But the floor was dry planking, warmer than the ground anyway; obviously whatever kind of roof was on the building must have kept the earlier rain out. Jamie, still on all fours, stopped and tried to sit up, but knocked his head on a sharp piece of something which was inexplicably pointing down from above. It did not seem to be very wide, so he shifted, cautiously sat up with his head in clear air, and groped in his rucksack for the small hard shape of the compacted foil blanket.

It was there. He had been almost sure, because he always carried it, like his knife with the little compass in the handle. But the confirmation of its presence cheered him. He was self-sufficient, like a soldier. He had warmth, and a weapon and compass, and – he groped again in the bag – food. One chocolate bar, one muesli bar, some very old sticky Murraymints left over from Scout camp, and a small waxed box of apple juice. Mum must have put that in. At the thought of her, he trembled for a moment and the tightness returned to his chest; but then, in the darkness, he set his face firmly and returned to his preparations like a soldier. Releasing the thin crackling material of the thermal blanket from its rubber bands, he spread it out, silver side up. He could just see the silver in a glimmer of light from the lace holes in the canvas flap. He lay down on it and rolled himself up into a neat sausage, keeping his arms in their anorak sleeves outside.

He laid his head on the stuffed rucksack, wriggled it a little to avoid the harder shapes of his book and his Walkman and, listening to the rising wind and a new patter of rain on the canvas, slept.

15

Alice woke on Saturday morning, dry-mouthed and stale, to find herself looking at an angular abstract painting hanging on a pale dove-grey wall. She sat up cautiously, to find that she had slept on a low, very comfortable sofabed. The sheet beneath her was linen, the duvet cover grey and apparently silk. The wall opposite was lined with books on matt black shelves, and a modernistic black steel desk stood beside the chimney breast.

Yasmin's study. Or spare bedroom. Alice remembered deciding not to go back to Camden, so here she was, having spent her first night ever at Yazz's flat off Portland Place. It made her oddly shy. She swung her legs out of bed, and padded across in her T-shirt and pants to look out of the window. The corner of Broadcasting House extension was just visible, and beyond it the pale-green futuristic building occupied by Euradio. She stretched, suddenly happy in this minimal bed-room, glad to be free of the energies and associations of her own house. Despite her hangover, Alice smiled into the black-rimmed round mirror over the mantelpiece and thought that she was, after all, still quite young. From the kitchen, Yasmin called.

"Coffee? Croissant?"

Alice wandered through. Yasmin, even in her Saturday jeans and faded denim-yarn sweater, had the air of a woman who had been up for hours working. She smiled crookedly at Alice's disarray.

"Do you want a dressing-gown?" She went through into the small sitting room, opened a cupboard to reveal neat ranks of clothes, and hooked out a red silk kimono. Alice put it on, gasping a little at the weight and the embroidery, while Yasmin poured coffee.

"Are you sure? This looks precious."

"It was Alan's. Now do you see what I mean about these chaps?"

Alice giggled. "This is not the way to begin a career as a humble underling in the Euradio newsroom. Wearing the boss's kimono."

"Exactly the way to begin," said Yasmin. "Besides, you won't be an underling for long."

"Yazz," began Alice, reaching for her coffee, "I don't want to be some sort of favourite."

Yasmin glared at her. "You are not a sort of favourite. You are a piece of long-dormant talent which I have very cleverly enabled the organization to pick up for a song. In a few months, when we go on air, we are going to need editors, senior producers, executives. People who speak French and Italian and know about news systems. You spent five years at the BBC."

"I don't speak French and Italian," said Alice. "Much."

"Yes, you do," said Yasmin flatly. "Heard you. You used to be over there all the time."

"Well, a bit," said Alice. "But if you're giving this bullshit to Alan, I had better start learning more."

"That's my girl!" said Yasmin, and pushed a basket of croissants towards her. "Breakfast. Real ones. Patisserie Jacques. I have a special deal with the guy who delivers them to the café on the corner."

"You have a lot of special deals," said Alice, breaking the corner off a croissant.

"Yup. And you don't have enough," said Yasmin. She was not eating, but watched Alice over the rim of her coffee. "We'll get you in the way of it, though. Just you wait."

Daniel, despite Dave's pressing invitation to "doss down", had got himself back to Mrs Hammond's after closing time. The car was still parked at the station. So on Saturday morning, with an angry hangover throbbing at the back of his head, he took another taxi down to retrieve it. Its windscreen was decorated with a £20 fixed penalty fine. Plus twelve quid for the two cab rides, plus what he spent in the pub. By the time the car was outside Mrs Hammond's cheerless domain, Daniel's dull hangover had turned to smouldering resentment. Mainly against Alice. Bloody hell, was she planning to send Jamie today, or what? He had a right to his son.

He told Mrs Hammond he had made a mistake about the arrangements but might still need the second room for Saturday night. She sniffed. He asked whether it was possible for a message to be left on her telephone, and again sniffing she said that she supposed so. Might he make a call now, if it went ADC through the operator and he paid for it? Mrs Hammond observed that if she made an exception for one guest, it could Cause Difficulties with others. Daniel gave in. Walking down first to the newsagent's for a new phonecard, then to the box on the corner, he rehearsed his lines. "*I suppose you think that's clever . . . You're the one who's always so censorious about people using children as weapons . . . this really won't do . . . do I have to see a lawyer about access? If you can't be civilised . . .*"

The answering machine, his own voice speaking from his own house, drove him into a worse paroxysm of irritation. After the bleep, he said, "Alice, it's Daniel. Are you going to send Jamie today? Or are you planning to keep up this campaign? Think about it. It isn't fair on him. Either way, I'd better know. You can ring in to Mrs Hammond's." He gave the number, walked back up the road, hating every neat sickly urban tree and clipped front garden, let himself into No. 23 and fell asleep on top of his candlewick bed.

Hours later, a tap on the door roused him. Rubbing his unshaven chin, he walked in his socks to the door and flung it open. Mrs Hammond looked up at his angry hawk face and dishevelled grey-streaked mane, and started back.

"Telephone message, Mr McDonald. Ring your wife *immediately*."

"Can I use the house telephone?"

"Mr McDonald, if I make exceptions . . ."

Daniel closed the door on her, kicked on his shoes and slammed out of the house. Reaching the box, he found he had forgotten his phonecard. Grimly, he dialled the operator and reversed the charge. Alice answered on the first ring, sounding oddly strained.

She snapped, "Yes, yes, yes," to the operator's question about accepting the charge, then, "Dan?"

"Yes."

"Dan, what do you mean about Jamie? He's with you."

"No, he isn't."

"What?"

"I said, he isn't. You said you'd put him on the five thirty, arriving seven thirty."

"You mean you never picked him up?" Alice's voice was shrill, accusing. Daniel swung between fury and terror.

"I was *there*, on the station."

"Norwich station?"

"Where bloody else? Alice, *did you put him on the five thirty?*"

"Yes!" She was shouting now. "And you didn't pick him up!"

"Alice." Daniel heard the hysteria in her voice and, with a great effort, suppressed his own crazed terror. "Listen." He spoke quietly, damping down all the emotion he felt. "Listen. At first I thought he must have got off early by mistake. But I checked all the stations, and there was nobody his age loose. It doesn't stop anywhere else. So Dave – so I thought maybe you never put him on the train. I did try to ring."

"There wasn't a message. I checked at nine o'clock or so. No messages."

"The card ran out. I thought . . ." He changed tack, looking at his watch. "Allie, I left a message at ten o'clock this morning. It's nearly six."

"I was out. I stayed at Yazz's. We went shopping. I had a haircut. I didn't do the machine till half an hour ago."

A silence fell between them, each crushed by the guilt of their dereliction of duty. Phonecards, friends, drinks, sleeping off drinks, shopping, haircut, unpacking of shopping: and all the time Jamie not anywhere. Twenty-four hours missing.

"Oh Christ," said Daniel at last. "What do we do first?"

"Police," said Alice, and a sob caught her halfway through the word. "Dan—"

"Just one thing," said Daniel suddenly. "Just let me ring Godgran. Just in case he went to her. She seemed to think . . ."

"What? You think she's been interfering?"

"No," said Daniel, not allowing himself to be angry. "But she rang me and said it would be best if I saw him soon. And she said," he frowned, trying to remember, "that she had something to tell me. After I'd seen him."

"You think he might have gone there?" Alice's voice was slack with relief. "Yes, he might. Ring now. Quick. I'll stand by. Quick."

A girl in a short leather skirt, waiting outside the telephone box with a green card in her hand, caught Daniel's eye and raised her eyebrows inquiringly. He shook his head, looked away, and rapidly began dialling Violet's number before looking at the blinking display and remembering that he had no card to pay with. Pushing the door open with his foot, he said to the girl, "Emergency. Any chance I could buy your card? Please. Please?"

Daniel, pale and shaking and unshaven, looked both handsome and desperate enough to make the girl immediately thrust it at him. "Don't worry," she said, and scuttled off down the road. He grimaced gratitude at her retreating back, jammed the card in the slot and dialled again. Five, six rings; then at last Violet answered, and sank his hopes in a second.

"Daniel. How nice. Did you see Jamie? Is he well?"

"You haven't got him, then," said Daniel stupidly.

A pause, and then, "No. Daniel, what has happened?"

Daniel told her, briefly. "I must ring Alice. If he isn't with you, it's a police matter."

"Oh dear. Oh yes. Oh, Daniel, good luck. I do feel guilty in this."

"Why?" Daniel was impatient to get back on the line to Alice but her words caught him, forcing him to stay.

"James wrote to me. He sounded more distressed than is normal, even in the circumstances. He said he had torn up his pictures, and that – well, he seemed upset about you and Alice. But I felt it was best that you saw him. Rather than the letter."

"Why not the letter?"

"Because things about it made me feel that he maybe did not know he had written it at all. I had a pupil like that once, who wrote letters of great distress and then forgot. It was a mental—" She had said too much. Abruptly, Violet ended, "Anyway, ring Alice."

In anguish, Daniel did so.

In Wetheringham, Violet walked across to the dresser, pulled a drawer and took out a candle and matches. She placed the sweet-smelling wax candle carefully in a pewter stick. When the Colonel arrived an hour later, he found her kneeling before the picture of the Virgin, the candle burning on the dresser, a rosary between her old hands and her lips moving steadily, silently. She looked up at him and said, "My godson's son has gone missing. Twelve years old."

"Jamie?" said the Colonel.

"Yes." Violet returned to her beads and after a moment's hesitation, creakingly, the old soldier knelt down beside her and lowered his head.

16

The wind and fog of the night passed early; if Jamie had woken
on his plank floor, he would have seen clearing skies through the
gaps in the canvas, and even a few stars before a pale calm dawn.
But he slept on in his strange shelter, comfortable on the hard
boards as only the young and light and weary can ever be.

It was full morning when he woke, and the sun was streaming
dustily in. The boy lay for a moment, looking at the green boards
he lay on and the canvas curtain around him. His small horizon
was, to all appearances, round; the edges of the boards swept
round like a miniature horizon. Sitting up, he saw that the
circle went further, presumably to completion on the other side
of the—

Of the engine! Jamie raised himself on his elbow, rubbed his
eyes on his fists, shook his head, and looked again. A few feet
away from him were gleaming brass pipes and pistons. He stared,
trying sleepily to make sense of it. Bolted things, riveted bits, arms
and belts and wheels resolved themselves into the unmistakable
shape of a neat little steam engine.

Incredulous, he looked up. Above the engine soared golden
organ pipes; beside the organ, a concertinaed stack of punched
paper zigzagged up to a slot in the machinery. As his eye
travelled wonderingly upwards, he saw a pattern of dark metal
rods overhead, a series of right angles; a top which looked like
a circus tent, red and white in triangular segments. Below it,
he saw that he and the engine and the pipes were all topped
by a decorative wooden frieze of roses and thistles, scrolls and
sunflowers, winged white horses and angels. And between them,
patterns: coloured curls and swirls and arabesques, crowns and

arches, a symmetrical riot of brightness even in the dim watery light through the red-and-white canvas roof.

Jamie sat up and wriggled round. He was facing a gilded, twisted pole like barley sugar, and looking up at a horse.

It was wooden, or so he supposed. Its mouth was open, its nostrils flared at him, lined with red, and its big eyes stared with a manic ring of white all round the black pupil. Its harness was red and gold, painted on with the same brightness that had made him gasp when he saw the canopy. Its dark-gold mane looked real enough to stroke. A red flower bloomed on the horse's breast, amid moulded green leaves; across its back were more scrolls and a smooth red-and-gold saddle, and over its bottom a pattern of medieval-looking square purple shapes, each turret or floret carefully lined with black and then again with white. Entranced, the boy reached up carefully and touched the horse; it was hard and smooth and cold. His eyes could not stop devouring it: the colour, the richness, the craziness of the creature was something he had never seen. Or never so close. For of course he knew what it was: a fairground horse, an old-fashioned one. Down the Portobello Road you saw them in antique shops. But this one was where it belonged, on a roundabout. With an engine. He had slept in a roundabout. There should be more horses, a whole parade of them.

He scrambled to his feet and began to walk round the circle, between the gilded twisted barley-sugar uprights. On the far side, there were eight or nine more horses in place on their poles, some black, some dappled, some as splendid as his first one but others chipped and faded. Several looked oddly smoky, dark along one side, their hooves charred. Each had a name: Spicey, Frank, Carrie, Minerva. More were off their poles and stacked or propped in groups. Two had been rubbed right down to the bare wood, and one had been propped up on a piece of canvas and painted a base colour – a sort of gingery bay. It was marked with faint, tentative lines to indicate where the saddle and its decorations should go. Jamie knelt to examine it. Beside him, an old sheet lay over a large metal tray with high sides. He pulled it off. There were paint tins and brushes and white spirit in a workmanlike jumble. He looked at them, hesitated, and walked back round to his rucksack.

Reaching it, he pulled out his carton of apple juice, poked in its straw, and took a long suck, leaning against the twisted pole. His mouth felt better for it and his head clearer. He ate the muesli bar and the chocolate, which was not much of a breakfast but better than nothing. Eventually, he would have to think of what to do next. He could hear the wind fluttering the canvas and whistling in the distant trees. It was winter. Dad would be wondering.

Jamie, who had felt interested and capable and even powerful for a few minutes while he considered the horse, shuddered suddenly and shrank into his padded jacket. Sitting down, closing his eyes, he deliberately blanked them out one by one: father, mother, Camden, school, the train, the darts bus, falling in the ditch, all of it. He opened his eyes again on the present. It was quiet inside the cave, peaceful. It was a good place. Someone, some lucky person, came to this quiet colourful haven, pinned aside a flap – they would have to, for the light – and worked with those paints to make the horses beautiful. They had not come yet. Perhaps they would.

Jamie huddled for a moment, his head on his knees. Around him, clamouring to get into his head and disturb his bright horse thoughts, were flurries and batterings of other ones: nervous thoughts of discovery, of home, of anger and bustle and worry and school and police. Something had to blot it all out. Raising his head, he saw the finished horse above him on its golden pole. "Champion" said the scroll on its neck, white on dark gold. Its eyes stared forward, fixed. It would look wonderful when it moved, up and down and round and round, forelegs lunging, hind legs out behind, galloping. The pattern across its rump and hind legs intrigued Jamie; it used the carved relief scrollwork but echoed the same shapes on the flat sections.

Jamie pulled himself up and ran his hand over the patterns, tracing them. Eventually, as if he had made a decision, he patted it abruptly and walked back round to the side with the painting things. Looking at the ginger horse, he hesitated, then stooped to pick up a flat piece of wood which lay near the paint tins. A few flakes of old red paint clung to it, and there were worm holes dotted across it. It looked like part of an old step, one of those he had stumbled up in the night. It would do. Jamie brushed the dust off it with his sleeve, laid it down, and carefully chose two brushes from the bundle wrapped in rags on the paint tray. Not too fine, not too broad. He flipped the lid off two paint tins, red and black, and carefully, slowly at first but with increasing confidence and pleasure, began to paint on the old plank, beginning with an orangey-red rose and spreading his lines out from it, faithfully copying the pattern on the horse's chest.

Two hundred yards away, inside the farm cottage, Susan Bailey pushed back her lank black hair with a movement of irritation and called up the narrow stairs.

"Ed! Breakfast!"

"Dad's gone out," said a surly adolescent voice. "Went to catch Robert, about getting some space covered over for Rowley to do the gallopers."

"He's not had his breakfast!" The woman returned to the kitchen and picked up a plateful of bacon and eggs and fried bread, shoving it into the warming oven of the old coke range and shutting the door with her scuffed shoe. She laid the bare wooden table, avoiding the corner on which lay a grubby pile of bills and letters and a folder inscribed, in rococo style, "Edwd. Bailey's Great Norfolk Steam Fair. ACCOUNTS."

Sighing, she straightened the papers and sat down with her own breakfast, a slice of buttered toast and a mug of tea. After a moment, she pulled one particular letter out of the heap, a much handled and creased letter. She was still looking at it, the mug in her other hand, when the door swung open and Ed Bailey came in. Susan gave him a half-smile of welcome.

"Breakfast in the bottom oven."

"Thanks." He bent and opened the black door. "I had to go out and catch Robert before he took off for the day on that tractor."

"Yes," said Susan. "For the gallopers, Tim said. Did you get the space?"

"Not in the barn. He's got all that hay. What we'll do is, we'll put tilts across between the lorries, with the end of the barn to keep the wind out. Rowley can work like that. That's one thing about Rowley. He don't fuss. We'll do it Tuesday, and if he turns up in time he can start on the gallopers. Tim can check out the cranks."

"Good." Susan spoke absently, still staring down at the letter. "Eddie, can we really do this?"

"The Cold Fair? We have to. It's a chance."

"We've never done it before. Never travelled after October."

"We have to," said Ed again, sitting down and attacking his breakfast. "The money's good, the publicity's good, there's all the stalls and big advertising, it'll be full of Norwich people for five days, right up in the Christmas holidays. They could have asked any number of fairs, and they chose us. Said they wanted it all traditional, like an old-time Cold Fair. Steam and frost, the woman said."

"If they'd only written earlier!" mourned Susan. "We'd not have done Garboldisham, or Henham. We'd have got everything back here laid up earlier, got the work done, specially on the gallopers."

"Well, they didn't and we didn't," said the big man, spearing his fried bread. "Be all right, girl. The engine's fine, Tim's happy with it. He's just got some to do on the cranks. And Rowley won't take long to sort out the horses."

"Rowley! That's another thing," grumbled Susan, although by now it was obvious that her husband's sanguine mood had lifted her own. "Rowley said he'd be here Friday, latest."

"He'll get it done, girl. He's bringing his sister's lad too. Prob'ly stopped off to pick him up."

"Does the lad know the trade?"

"Rowley says he's a good little painter. Weak in the head, Rowley says, dun't talk much, but a good steady hand if you tell him what to do. Used to work with Rowley when he was a nipper. Fifteen now. Rowley says he doesn't bother too much with school and that." He sucked at his tea. "Shouldn't be surprised if they got here today. Once they're here, it'll be a horse finished every two days, with you doing the base coat. There's only ten need work, and the four cockerels touching up. That's four weeks, top. Don't you worry."

"I would do more," said Susan, "myself. Only you know it's never right. I can do the base, even the dapples and the mane. But I can't do the decoration. Not the freehand. Besides, if I keep on doing the Flats while Joyce is off—"

"Yes, you got enough to do," said Ed hurriedly.

The topic of Susan's winter job cleaning the old people's Flats was a grievous one to him. But a travelling fair could not employ a whole family any more, not properly. Carters did it in Berkshire, but Berkshire was pig rich compared to Norfolk, and they had all that talent in the family. A small travelling steam fair, its equipment venerable and vulnerable, was not economic. Not really. Not even with free winter quarters on a son's wife's family farm. Not even with other sons and nephews who obligingly worked winters elsewhere and only drew pay in the travelling season. Baileys stuck together, and stuck to the fair; but the whole thing, thought Ed as he often had before, was the same as they said about a bumblebee: technically, it couldn't fly.

But ah, when it did! When the crowds came and the horses flew and the organs played! The gallopers whirled, the swingboats with their angel roof echoed to the cries of children – 1990s children, thought Ed with satisfaction, lost space-age children won back for one evening into his world of gentle benevolent enchantment. Children lured away from the crude and garish images of violence and warfare and the pounding rock beat of the modern funfairs. Yes, thought Ed, when it flew, it damn well flew. That was something hard to give up.

"Maybe we should have taken the contract with the HoliPark people," he said suddenly, polishing up the last drop of egg yolk with his bread. "Gone fixed. Got regular money, permanent site, we'd know where we are."

His wife looked at him, tired and fond. "You don't mean that, Ed Bailey, you do not."

"Well, I'm not one of the real old Baileys. My dad was new to it, never was a showman till he ran off with my ma. Just because he travelled the fair, that doesn't mean *we* have to." He sighed, cradling his tea. "Maybe we ought to be on concrete. It makes sense. Steady money. We could get some trust to give us a hand with the rides, then. Conservation. Like a museum, only working. You could have a proper house."

Susan pressed her lips together, smiling, shaking her head. The conversation was a well-worn one; she knew that if she showed any sign of enthusiasm for this idea, an idea he in fact deeply hated, Ed would take it as his duty to give up travelling for good and become a HoliPark exhibit, as miserable as a beached whale.

She considered for a moment, pretending to think it over. Then, theatrically, she shook her head. "We'd never get Rowley to do the painting! Not at HoliPark!"

This was a familiar joke, and Ed laughed. Together they embarked on a well-worn imitation:

"A true fair, my dears – " croaked Susan.

"– should come up like a magical mushroom on the clean grass," continued Ed, in a quavering voice.

"And light up the night, and be gone in the dawn like a dream," finished Susan. "Leaving only flat grass and a memory for next year. There wouldn't be a beer, my dear, I suppose?" She rolled her eyes, wheedlingly.

"Ah well," said Ed, recovering himself. "Gypsy or not, he's one of the best fairground painters I know."

"*When* he turns up," said Susan. She cleared the plates off the table and clattered them into the sink. "I tell you, if he keeps us waiting one more day, he's not getting any beer till Saturday week."

Inside the roundabout, oblivious to everything, Jamie painted on through the morning. The sun streamed in through the canvas where he had unlaced it and hooked it back. The old waste board was now covered in patterns and flowers, swirling and interlocking, and he had raised his sights and begun work on the leg of the ginger horse. On to the black base coat on its hoof he carefully drew a yellow V, and a red line following the shape of the foot. He glanced across constantly at a nearby finished horse, catching the style but improvising the detail. He loved the way that they were all different, yet held a family likeness. The first hoof finished, he sat back and frowned appraisingly. Good. Another hoof. He shuffled sideways a little and dipped his fine brush into the red enamel, just the tip.

He was moving the brush along in a smooth, careful curve of red when first the light intensified, and then a shadow fell over his work. He clucked with annoyance, thinking it was a cloud; but when he looked up, the canvas flap was thrown right back and above him in the opening loomed one of the biggest men he had ever seen, with one of the biggest black beards.

"What the hell?" began the man, angrily. Jamie shrank away. But the man's eye fell on the decorated plank, and then on the brush in the boy's hand and the neatly decorated forehoof of the horse. Miraculously, the beard split into a big smile. Jamie, uncertain, smiled back. It seemed safest.

"You're Rowley's sister's boy?" said the man.

Jamie nodded. It was plain that Rowley's sister's boy was a safe thing to be.

"Where's Rowley? I don't see his wagon. Where'd you sleep?"

Jamie pointed to the crumpled space blanket and his rucksack, beyond the engine. Ed looked at them and laughed. "So he's gone off somewhere? Old bastard. Never even came up to tell us. Left you to make a start?"

Jamie nodded again, uncomfortably. Now that the canvas was thrown aside, beyond the big man he could see more closed-up fairground vans and rides, each with lettering in an expansive, bulgy, festive style: BRITISH AND BEST . . . FARE £1 ALL CLASSES . . . JUBILEE CHAIR-O-PLANE FLYERS . . . EXCELSIOR SUPREME STEAM YACHTS . . . JUMBO FLOSS, FISH & CHIPS, DONUTS . . . His stomach let out an audible rumble, and he clutched it in embarrassed dismay, leaving a streak of red enamel on his anorak.

"Didn't Rowley give you breakfast?" asked the man. Jamie shook his head. "Come on then." Jamie bent to wipe his brush with the spirituous rag, rewrapped it carefully in the damp cloth, and climbed down after Ed to trot behind him to the cottage. Saying, nothing, nodding and obeying, was obviously the safest thing to do. It led to food, anyway.

17

They rang the police. Once Daniel had used the last of the strange girl's phonecard on telling his wife that Godgran knew nothing, it was agreed between them that she, from the family home, should be the one to report Jamie's disappearance.

"I'll ring you, obviously," said Alice to Daniel, almost choking. She wanted to say, "Come, come home, quick, now, help me!" but could not.

"I'll ring in. To check. Meanwhile I'm going back to the station to see if the train did stop anywhere." He wanted to say, "Alice, let me come home, now, quickly, we need to do this together." But he could not. So all the company Alice got was a young WPC who took every kind of particular and stood by while Alice rang Gavin's home, and Tim's, and even George's, although Jamie and George had fallen out two terms ago. The policewoman glanced around the house with a look Alice somehow did not trust, and left her with an admonition to "Ring a friend, to sit with you, I would".

So Alice rang Stevie. Something stopped her from calling Yasmin or Jenny. Guilt, probably, she admitted to herself. She could not bear even the faintest bat's squeak of blame to add to the private guilt which encumbered her so heavily that she could hardly breathe. And although neither of them would have expressed it openly, there would have been blame in the air. From Yasmin a continuing criticism of Alice for lumbering herself with children in the first place. From Jenny the much more onerous criticism of a fellow mother, needing in sheer panic to convince herself that such a thing could never happen to her.

But Stevie would not criticize. She dialled his number, her hand trembling.

"Stevie? Oh, Steve, are you doing anything?"

"Not." He was oddly terse, but softened immediately, as if he had heard her shallow, panicky breathing. "I mean, sorry. You caught me at a bad time, sweetie. Simon's gone off."

"Oh, Stevie, I am sorry. Look, I won't—"

"No, no. Drown our sorrows together. Daniel, is it?"

"Jamie. Oh, Steve, he's gone. I put him on the train to Norfolk and he never turned up. We've only just found out. It was *last night*." She began to cry, holding the telephone tightly, dashing her other sleeve across her eyes and nose.

Tinny, distant, Steve spoke. "I'm coming. Hang on, Allie. He'll be all right. He's a boy. We boys, we do these things to our mums."

When he had rung off, Alice stood holding the telephone as if for comfort, and steadied herself. Boys do these things. Boys run away. Always have. Think of *Brandon Chase* and Hornblower and Dick Whittington, the Famous Five and *Moonfleet*.

Don't, don't for a minute think about pederasts and sadists and murderers, about the newspapers and the television appeals, the terrible procession of well-brushed smiling school photographs of boys, *twelve years old, last seen wearing a blue anorak* . . .

Not that. Murder is a rarity, child murder even more of an aberration. Yet children live on the streets of London, in cardboard boxes, earning their living in God knows what squalor—

No, not that either. Alice shook her head fiercely. Daniel! Daniel should be here. In spite of everything, the thought of him steadied her. He had been there when Clemmie was born, singing "Clementine" to the newborn wrinkled thing, making Alice laugh; he had been there all through that other night when slowly, awkwardly, Jamie was born. He had sung softly then to Alice alone, cradling her through the endless pains. Afterwards, he held the newborn Jamie and said gentle things to him while she sobbed and retched and deliriously fought the midwife who delivered the afterbirth. She had seen them there communing, father and son, and felt angry and excluded; but before the feeling could take hold, Daniel had handed Jamie to the nurse and bent down to hold her instead, murmuring, "Well done, you did it, it's over, it's all right."

Why was she thinking of these things? Because, she suddenly realized, she could smell them. Not only did her womb ache, a deep long-forgotten hurt inside her, but the scent of new maternity was all around; there were even, she incredulously felt, damp milky patches in her brassiere.

Alice put the telephone down and walked upstairs to the bathroom. She threw off her clothes, neat black Yasmin clothes, and stood under the shower for several minutes, trying to wash away the terror. When she opened the door to Stevie twenty minutes later she was wearing a long, cosy, red-and-gold velvet kaftan with moth holes in it and was almost calm.

In the Saturday night bleakness of Norwich station, under the cold lights, Daniel stood beside the driver's cab of a London train, the same service that twenty-four hours earlier Jamie should have arrived on. He was talking to the driver.

"I know you don't officially stop anywhere else, but does it happen?"

"Certainly does. Signals, bridges knocked up by lorries, all that."

"Do you know who was driving the seven thirty arrival last night?"

"As it happens, I do."

"Who, then? It's important."

"Charlie, I'd say. He's off now. Only thing is . . ." The man turned away into the depth of his cab, to speak to another figure in the gloom.

Daniel tried to climb up, persisting, "I really need to know. It's my son—"

"Hold your horses. I'm trying to find out for you. What say, Eric?"

The other figure in the cab mumbled something. The driver turned back.

"Eric's a trainee. He was in the cab with Charlie."

Daniel leaned forward. "Please, tell me. Did you stop after Diss?"

And Eric told him everything, up to the curious sound at the unscheduled stop which could have been a door slamming, but might not be. There were funny echoes, said Eric, that bounced along the train in some of these old brick stations.

"Tell you something else, too." He paused, as if for dramatic effect. Daniel waited, holding the notebook in which he had just written down a place name. "The door locking wasn't on."

"What do you mean?"

"It was the train they haven't done the mod on."

"What mod?"

"The modification. Central door locking. Stop people falling out on to the track. After all the accidents."

"You mean you normally can't get out without the central lock being undone?"

"S'right. Only that train, that don't have the mod. Last one."

"So he could have got out?"

"That's what I'm saying."

Daniel barely thanked the two men before turning to run back across the concourse to his waiting car.

"Tell me about Simon," said Alice to Stevie. "No, I mean it, tell me. I need my mind on something else. We can't do anything until the police ring."

"Nothing to tell," said Stevie. "The usual little note on the bed. Having the weekend with a friend."

"Well, it might be just that," began Alice, but fell silent at Stevie's glare. "Oh, all right. It is rotten. Why don't you, I dunno, show him what it feels like?"

"Throw him out? Get revenge? Go cruising myself?" said Stevie. "Alice, you are a grown-up lady, which is why I love you. Don't start sounding like your friend Yas-meanie."

"She's not—" Alice began, then stopped and laughed. "Well, all right. I know what you mean."

Silence fell. The gas fire, which Alice rarely lit, hissed and gave off a cosy smell reminiscent of student digs. Stevie, who was kneeling on the floor, moved closer to its sharp, over-focused heat.

"The real problem," he said, staring into the redness, "is not how to treat the little bitch when he comes back, but how to believe that he will come back."

"Yes," said Alice, and suddenly burst into tears again. Stevie moved closer and threw his arm across her knees.

"Jamie will be back. You wait. It'll be an adventure he's having. He's a *boy*."

"You keep saying that," said Alice. "You're so macho."

"There's a lot of Baden-Powell in me," said Stevie with a smug campness. And she laughed, as he had meant her to. And at that moment the doorbell rang and they both started and scrambled to their feet. Alice made for the door. Two police officers stood there, and she screamed.

Violet Lancing and her Colonel had by now risen from prayer and taken to drinking tea. "I feel confident," said Violet, consideringly. "I have never quite believed in direct consolation during prayer, but somehow I feel confident about the little boy. That he is in the hand of God."

"Wish I did," said the Colonel. "Wish we knew more."

"We shall," said Violet. "Soon. I only wish," she added, "that I felt as confident about his benighted parents. They are the type to *squirm*, perversely, right out of the hand of God."

Daniel stopped outside the little station and his heart sank. If ever a place was nowhere, the back of nowhere, this was it. In the thickening darkness, dull lanes led away from it in two directions past leafless trees which stood sparse against the cold sky. There was no shop, no house, nothing that might have drawn a lonely small boy to its shelter. He climbed back in the car and went further down the lane. Half a mile on there was a pub, a small one with coloured lights round its door. He parked and went in. A group of men sat playing dominoes in one corner, and a large barmaid looked across at him inquiringly. Something in her look implied that foreigners were not wholly welcome.

"Half a pint of shandy, please," said Daniel. When the woman brought it, he fumbled a moment for change and then casually said, "I don't suppose you saw a boy in here last night? Quite a young boy?"

"We don't serve underage," said the barmaid coldly. "Plain clothes, are you? Give it a rest."

"No, no. I'm not police. It's just that my son – well, I thought he might have come in."

"I'd a' seen," she said. "Darts tour last night. We only had half a dozen, all evening. The other regulars were all on the tour."

So Daniel left, cold and sad, his shandy hardly touched. When he had gone, and the comfortable local silence had fallen once again, one of the men in the corner raised his head and said, "Funny, that. There was a kid on the bus that we thought came with the Woolsack team, only they said not. They thought he was ours. He warn't there, later."

"D'you think we oughter run after him and tell him?" said the barmaid who was not naturally unkind.

But Daniel's car could clearly be heard accelerating off down the lane.

"Did the feller leave his name?" asked another card player.

"No. Can't a'been important."

"Divorced, p'raps," said the youngest player. "There's always rows about what the kids do while they're with the other one. Prob'ly trying to catch her out bringing his boy to a pub under age."

Heads were shaken, briefly, over the awkwardness of modern family life. The game of dominoes resumed.

For Jamie the day had grown magical. He ate, silently and voraciously, in Susan's kitchen where nobody intruded on his supposed feeble-mindedness with questions. Then, glancing at Ed for permission, he received a jerk of the big man's head and trotted back out to the roundabout. Climbing the steps more confidently now, an accepted worker, he folded the canvas flap right back, crouched by his tray of paints and rapidly began work.

The light from the watery westering sun was good. He finished the forehoofs, shuffled round to the hind legs and did them; then, cleaning off his old brushes, he chose a slightly wider one and began on the red flowers and saddle. The brushes were good quality and slid easily round the carved petals on the animal's chest and flanks. On its hind legs there were no guiding lines for the decoration; after a moment's scrutiny of the finished horses, Jamie decisively began some arabesques of his own, like curled snakes at the top, only headless, with pointed forks to follow the line of the leg. They didn't have to be anything. They were just shapes. He loved them. He took some darker red, wiped his brush quickly, and began lining and shadowing the work he had done.

At four o'clock, Susan brought him a mug of tea and a slab of cake. The tea was well-sugared, which he disliked normally, but he drank it hungrily for the sake of the heat and munched his cake. Susan sat on the step and admired his work.

"That would've taken me two days, that lot. I'm better sticking to base coat. I'd say you'll be as good as Rowley when you've been at it a bit longer. Fifteen, did he say you were?"

Jamie grunted, "Mmmm." Grunting, he had found, was oddly acceptable to these people. Perhaps they thought he was foreign, or dumb.

"You ain't very big for fifteen, boy." Susan privately thought that he must have a problem with numbers. Thirteen, more like. It did not particularly surprise her that Rowley's sister did not have him in school; that was Rowley's family for you. Jamie stuffed some cake into his mouth and said nothing. Susan continued her train of thought. "Thing I'm thinking is, where you going to sleep if blasted Rowley doesn't turn up tonight? Do you know if he's coming back? Be dark in an hour, and he don't have lights that work, or never has had."

Jamie shook his head. The arrival of this problematical Rowley would, he realized in the small part of his head which he allowed to think of the past and the future, change things irrevocably. The longer it took the better. That Rowley might not come that night was a blessing.

"Well, our living caravan's all stripped out," said Susan. "I think we'll put you in the small 'van. Tim's old one. That'll be warm enough if I light you the stove. I'd better get that ready."

She got up, smiled at him, and went away. Jamie painted on until it was too dark to see and too cold to hold the brush, then packed up the brushes again, put the lid on the paints, and straightened up.

Real uncertainty hit him now, for the first time since he had set eyes on the horses. His parents would be wondering about him. The thought of them sent a wave of panic all the way up his body, and he grasped a twisted brass pole for support. He could not go back home.

Home! A warmth came to him, compounded of kitchen suppers and Dad cooking and Mum's trailing clothes brushing past his head as he read at the kitchen table; but it was rapidly overlaid by another sense of home, and another wave of panic. Suddenly he could see the torn-up paintings in the corner of his bedroom, the computer with its grimy keyboard, the scuffled homework papers. Nothing ever finished, nothing ever right, everything to be done over again. He could smell the air of that room, saturated with panic and anger.

Jamie pressed his head against the pole, closed his eyes and then opened them again to see the bright beautiful heads of the finished horses on their poles, for ever leaping, galloping through their vivid landscape to the music of their golden pipes. He must stay and finish this job. The Rowley man would see that he could do it, and accept his help. Perhaps one day he would see the lights on and the horses moving, plunging and rising in their perfect livery, their livery that he had painted.

A hard knot of resolution formed in him. Later, that resolve made it easier to slip down the road after his silent supper with the Baileys and enter a telephone box which stood on the corner beyond the farm and near what he now saw to be a crossroads. Ed, coming in for his tea, had mentioned "nipping out to ring the Norwich woman about hard-standing". Jamie had watched in which direction Ed nipped, and a couple of hours later in the eight o'clock darkness he crept from the paraffin glow of his little caravan and followed the same road. Ten minutes along, sure enough there it was, a lonely lighted kiosk where two lanes met.

Inside the telephone box, well fed and with the certainty of his bunk and blankets ahead of him, Jamie steadily dialled the Camden number. He knew what to do: treat whoever answered like an answerphone. Say his piece and hang up. No arguing. He pushed in his 10p piece.

"Mum, it's Jamie," he said. He held the earpiece away from his head and, with a great effort, blocked out the hysterical response. "I'm all right. I'm fine. Food and a place to sleep and everything. Please leave me alone. I'll ring when I want to come back." Suddenly, the preposterous unlikelihood of his mother leaving him alone hit him, and he added more unsteadily, "You *have* to leave me alone, or I can't bear it." And, before the sound of frightened mother could begin again, he put the phone down and went back to the little caravan, to sleep.

18

The WPC and her colleague, Detective-Sergeant Clough, could not have been more solicitous when faced with Alice's doorstep scream. "No cause for alarm – " began the policewoman hurriedly as Stevie, running up behind Alice, took her shoulders and led her back to the sitting-room. The police followed, and when Alice had been placed sitting, like a rag doll, in one of the chairs Detective-Sergeant Clough introduced himself (the WPC did not, and Alice had forgotten her name from the earlier visit, and felt a brief surge of anger at being wrong-footed at such a time). The senior officer took up the theme.

"There's no cause for alarm. I'm sorry, madam, we should have made that clear immediately."

"I didn't," said Alice, shakily, "exactly give you time, did I?"

"You'd be surprised how many people think a police officer on the doorstep always means the worst," said Clough sagely. "I sometimes feel we should have a set of different coloured hats. To indicate the type of news." With which unexpected piece of frivolity he calmed Alice to a surprising degree. Breathing deeply, she said:

"So you don't have any news?"

"No. I'm afraid not. But we need to eliminate certain possibilities. We have made enquiries. It transpires that the five thirty train stopped shortly after Liverpool Street Station, an unscheduled stop at" – he looked at his notebook – "Maryland. In East London. It would have been possible for the boy to alight there."

"Why would he?" Alice felt suddenly defensive.

"We need to ask some questions about the background," said

the policeman steadily. "The boy's state of mind, family situation, friends, that sort of thing."

"You think he might have run away?"

"Young boys do run away." The policeman stated it flatly, as if giving a lecture to pupils in some Formica classroom at Hendon. "Unfortunately. But in a case like this – " he glanced around the house, not disapprovingly – "it may be more easily possible to find out why, and therefore where. And who with. If your husband and yourself could answer some questions . . ."

Alice quickly interposed.

"This isn't my husband. My husband is working in Norwich. This is – a friend. Mr Dent."

The police officers, man and woman, looked carefully at the woman and man in front of them. Sergeant Clough, in particular, seemed to revise his earlier opinion of the household as a stable, desirable middle-class family setting.

"I see," he said heavily. Alice was distractedly alive to nuances, and a phrase darted through her head – *"more in sorrow than in anger"*. She could not let the policeman's sorrowful imputation lie there between them. Stevie had flushed slightly, but sat quiet, not interfering.

"Officer, I should make it clear," said Alice. "I may as well be frank and admit that Daniel – my husband – and I are temporarily living apart. For various reasons. But Mr Dent is merely a friend." She was going to say "family friend", but a desperate dogged honesty prevented her. Stevie was her friend, her personal friend. "He is visiting me. On the suggestion of your colleague here. She suggested I ring a friend for support."

The WPC's eyebrows rose, only a little but enough to make it perfectly clear that a female friend would have been more the thing. More suitable for a Mother in a Crisis. Alice bit her lip and flushed. Stevie spoke suddenly.

"And besides," he said, "I have a partner of my own –"

The two police officers looked at him. Throwing his head back, tossing it even, Stevie continued,

"– whose name is Simon Quinlan."

There was a silence, the gas fire hissing, the policeman breathing heavily, Alice stock-still. She spoke first.

"I can't see that any of this matters. I can answer any questions about Jamie."

"Of course," said Clough smoothly. And the questions began, far more searching than the WPC's earlier interrogation. There were questions about school, about Jamie's friends, about what in his parents' situation might have upset him. Alice answered truthfully, including Clementine's revelation about the truancy.

Then came questions about adult friends, male adult friends, confidants. Alice wavered, realizing with a shock how little she knew of his life, compared to the total knowledge she would have had two or three years earlier. She had not realized how Jamie's occupations had broadened, moved away from her with his move into secondary school at Finchamgrove. She had not seen how much of his time was his own. Until she went to the kitchen drawer to check, she could not remember the name of the Scout leader who had taken him to camp, and was nonplussed when asked for that of Gavin's uncle, with whom both boys had been to the cinema a couple of times. She could not remember whether it was LaserQuest or Battlezone that he favoured. She became aware of sounding like a woman who knew little about her child and cared less, at least until a crisis broke. She felt herself identified by these questioners with some feckless draggled mother in a news story, swearing that her boy never done nothing like mug an old lady.

But it was wrong, she told herself desperately. It must be wrong. She did know about Jamie, she cared, he was her baby. She never left him alone – well, only with Clemmie there or next-door on call – she did not let him out at night alone. But children these days, she wanted to cry out, their lives are their own, this is London . . .

Her answers were taken down by her unwaveringly polite, noncommittal listeners. Stevie weighed in, supporting her: said Jamie was a very capable boy, went around on his own on the Underground, was nearly thirteen, very intelligent, very artistic. He told them about Simon's supplying Jamie with pattern-pieces, and of how often Jamie would rework the pattern and, in his and Simon's view, improve it. Still the pencils moved, the unanswerable questions went on. At last the two of them rose, and with both promises and demands of frequent contact, left.

When they had gone, Stevie crossed over to Alice and put his arms around her. She wriggled away, glancing at the window; but the police were not there, and she sank back gratefully into his embrace.

"Oh God. They think I'm a complete slag, don't they?"

"Probably," said Stevie. That was the comforting thing about him, thought Alice. Her woman friends would have said, "Oh, no, of course not." Stevie faced the facts.

He left her to move across and close the curtains, then turned and said:

"When I was letting them out, when you were still in here, they took my address."

"Why?"

"God knows. Perhaps they want some really good fresh linguini." His sad clown's face drooped, making her laugh. Then:

"Oh God," said Alice. The momentary diversion had faded. "Where *is* Jamie?" And she would have begun crying again, only the telephone rang and sent her haring into the hall.

Stevie watched her stand there, trembling, inarticulately stammering, "Where – darling – tell me – no, don't go – " He went over to stand beside her, neither too close nor too far away, so that he was there when she turned towards him with the dead line purring in her hand. Her face was white, a gleam in the unlit hallway.

"It was Jamie," she said shakily. "He said he was fine, and had food and a place to sleep and – "

Stevie waited while she fought for composure. "– and to please leave him alone."

As she wept, standing there in the dark hall, he took the telephone from her hand and replaced it gently on its rest. He stood frowning for a moment, one hand absently placed on her shoulder, then picked up the receiver and began to dial.

"Not the police yet," said Alice, through her sobs. "Not yet. I have to tell Daniel. And he wanted to be left alone, suppose they come after him, suppose he panics, he said he couldn't bear it, Stevie, he might do something – "

"Not the police," said Stevie. "Ssh!" He had only dialled four digits and now was listening. Alice could just hear a tinny voice saying "Service Activated". Stevie began scrabbling in the cracked mug which held the pens and pencils by the telephone. Pencils were broken, pens dry. At last, his lips moving silently, he found a child's crayon and wrote a number in grainy orange wax across the front of the Business Directory. Then he put the receiver down and turned to Alice.

"Fourteen seventy one," he said smugly.

"What?" Alice thought it was a date, cast wildly back through a long-forgotten history degree for what might have happened. Caxton and the printing press? Ferdinand and Isabella? 1471?

"It's a new thing. You dial it, and it tells you the number that last called your telephone. One uses it," said Stevie coolly, "when one lives with Simon. One uses it a lot. Surprised you never got round to it."

Alice could hardly take in the import of what he was saying.

"You mean – that number you wrote down – that's where Jamie is?"

"Was, a couple of minutes ago," qualified Stevie. "It's a start, flower. Things are looking up. Stop crying. Five minutes ago you didn't know anything. Now you know he's got a bed and some food and an attitude problem. And you've got a way of finding where."

Alice grabbed the telephone book, and scanned the number as greedily as if it was her lost child's face.

"We must go there. Now. Tonight."

Daniel, wretched, returned to Norwich and Mrs Hammond's. She had, he noticed, recovered the pot-pourri from its hiding place, undone the Sellotaped bundle, and hung it back in the cupboard. He kicked off his shoes, then stood up and padded out into the corridor to knock on the door marked PRIVATE in sloping stick-on capital letters, gold foil on grey. It opened, just a crack. Looking down he could see a bare shiny leg and the hem of a towelling gown.

"Mrs Hammond? Might I ask, are there any messages for me?"

"Messages are left, when appropriate," replied a voice, "on guests' doors." The door closed and he padded back. Nine o'clock. Alice might still ring with news. Or maybe he should go home? But suppose Jamie turned up? He had been given the Hammond address; Alice would have given him emergency taxi money. He must stay. The rule in such situations, surely, was that any parent in a known place must stay put. Mrs Hammond was quite capable of turning Jamie away, under some rule she had invented. Sighing, he stretched fully dressed on the bed. It was quite impossible to undress and put himself to bed until this crisis should be resolved. Any potential port of refuge for a lost child must be permanently, reliably, wakefully manned.

The same reasoning, powerfully advanced by Stevie, kept Alice from her proposed rush into the night in search of a telephone number. He might ring again. What kept her from feeding the news directly to Detective-Sergeant Clough, whose number had been pinned above the telephone by his own hand, was something she never afterwards could explain to anyone's satisfaction but her own.

"I think," she sometimes mused to an uncomprehending, disapproving Jenny or a bored Yazz, "I think it was because he said to leave him alone. He sounded as if it might be dangerous for outsiders to find him. And the thing was I never thought, once I heard his voice so determined, I never believed he had been harmed . . ."

The awful presumption of this, the accusing eyes of the dead children in the news reports, would sometimes take her by the throat even years later, and choke her off telling any more. "Maybe I wasn't in an altogether normal state of mind myself," she would conclude lamely. And even Jenny accepted that. She had read articles about Traumatic Stress Syndrome.

Stevie, after an hour, went home. Alice would have liked him to stay in the house to alleviate its awful emptiness but gently and firmly, mindful of the expression on the policeman's face, Stevie left.

"I'll be at home, petal. Not going anywhere. In the shop tomorrow. Just ring. Keep me posted."

So Alice eventually slept, the ripped cover of the telephone book under her pillow, the telephone itself plugged in beside the bed. A photograph of Jamie, torn from the kitchen table lay in an envelope next to it.

Long winter miles to the north-east of her, Daniel slept too, still dressed and lying on top of the candlewick bedspread, uncomfortable and cold and haunted by pot-pourri.

Violet Lancing, flat on her back, arms folded on her breast as the nuns had taught her to sleep seventy years ago, passed her usual five or six hours of serene unconsciousness before waking to lie listening to the World Service and watching for the dawn.

Jamie slept the best: a long dreamless oblivion amid the fusty blankets, with a great mustard-coloured moon streaming through the dirty end window of the little caravan. It lit the tumbled bedding turned out by Susan Bailey, the smouldering woodstove, the cheap, tattered plastic mattress and the last, almost vanished, baby curves of the sleeping boy's cheek.

Alice woke at five, in darkness, and lay rigid for a moment, remembering and reorganizing the events of the night before. After a while she rolled over, lifted herself on her elbows and scrabbled under the pillow for the telephone book cover. For one heart-stopping moment she thought the pillow had rubbed off the crayoned number, but turned the ragged paper over and found it there, as clear as when Stevie had written it: 01328 890909. She stared at it for a moment, then laid the paper carefully on the floor beside the low bed and rolled over on her back again, her hands behind her head, thinking.

Despite Yazz's loyal praise, back in her radio days Alice had never, in fact, been a very competent news journalist. Not only did her priorities differ sharply from those of all normal editors, but she suffered a prevailing vagueness when it came to finding out hard facts such as addresses and figures. Certain memories and instincts, however, remained. One of the reporters whose tapes she edited had left to work as a public relations man, first for Telecom, later for one of the new independent companies in the same field. Barnaby had beautiful long eyelashes and a collection of Venetian glass, and had been something of a flirting partner for Alice in the office. His number, long undialled, must be somewhere in her old leather book. Barnaby would know a way of finding out where 01328 890909 was. Without involving the police.

Without the police. As she spelt out this aim to herself, Alice was shocked. It was irresponsible, it was crazy not to call Sergeant Clough. She should have called him last night, while Jamie was still near that telephone. Suddenly, she visualized a motorway service area with hundreds of cars and lorries coming and going, and Jamie stepping out of one to telephone briefly before roaring on down the highway to anywhere. Or, being forced out, someone standing over him as he spoke. Bile rose in her throat, but steadily, firmly, she put the thought aside. He had not sounded like that. Nor, she remembered, had there been any traffic noise in the background. So it was not a motorway. She closed her eyes, trying to remember his words, to hear what kind of place they were spoken in: "*I'm all right. I'm fine. Food and a place to sleep and everything.*" A telephone box, she thought, but could get no further.

As she lay there, staring at the ceiling, the words he had spoken replayed themselves in her mind. "*Please leave me alone. I'll ring when I want to come back. You have to leave me alone, or I can't bear it.*"

Alice came to a decision. Rolling out of bed, she went to the messy top drawer of her dressing table and rooted about for her old address books. Coming back to the bed, she hooked the telephone up on to the mattress beside her, riffled briefly through the Cs and found Barnaby Conway's number.

A sleepy male voice replied, American in intonation, its tone a protesting wail. "What? What the hell? It's haff-past five in the morning."

"Barnaby?"

"No. He moved a year ago, for Chrissake. Same exchange, but three two seven nine. How many dumb friends does that asshole *have*?"

Alice thanked the voice then grimaced at her watch, but still remorselessly dialled the new number. This time a woman answered.

"Who's that? . . . Barney – Barney, I don't believe this, but it's some woman for you. Alice. Ummph." She sounded as if she would go back to sleep, and Alice held her breath, but at the end of a brief scuffling moment a sharp male voice came on.

"Hello? Hello?"

"Barnaby, it's Alice McDonald. Remember? From the Beeb. Barney, I need a small bit of help, but it's very urgent. Very urgent. Please."

Barnaby's voice, more recognizable now, came back. "Allie, do you think it could wait until eight or so? No? OK. Don't hang up. I'll take it in the kitchen. Susie is glaring."

Alice waited impatiently. At last Barnaby, sounding vertical this time, came back.

"Right. Anatomize this emergency."

"I have a telephone number. I got it from the thing you dial, the fourteen thing."

"One four seven one. Don't tell me. I know what you want. Daniel has had mystery phone calls from a female breather who puts the phone down. You want me to trace her so you can do a napalm attack."

"Do a lot of people ask you that sort of thing?" said Alice, briefly diverted.

"Yes. Hundreds. And I say no, no, no. One, because I no longer work for Telecom. Two, because even if I do happen to know people who do, I am not keen to see them sacked for breach of confidentiality just so a lot of furious women can rip each other's hair out."

"Well, it's not a bimbo," said Alice. "It's a child. My son. A boy of twelve. He's lost. Run away. And I have the number of where he rang from last night, and I have to find him. Barnaby, I do. Please."

"The police could trace the number in two minutes. Legally," said Barnaby's voice. "Are you on to them?"

"Yes," said Alice. "Only there are reasons. I'm scared that he'll—" She had to stop. "I'm scared he'll kill himself or something if they go clodhopping in. But if I knew where he was it'd be safe for me to find him, I know it would. Please, Barn."

There was a long pause.

"Look," said Barnaby at last. "Will you promise me something? Promise to bring the police back into the picture as soon as you possibly can bear to? Don't faff about on your own, Allie. You're not fit to be out alone."

"You mean you'll do it?"

"I mean, give me the number."

Alice read it out, slowly. She heard a pen scratch on a notepad.

"I'll ring you at half past nine, when I've spoken to somebody."

"Oh Barn, oh Barnaby, thanks!" She was overcome. A thin baby wail came down the telephone line. "Is that – Barnaby, I didn't know—"

"Yup," said Barnaby. "I too have a son. As of six weeks ago, which is why Susie is not grateful for your call. His name is Donald."

"Tell Susie I'm sorry. And thanks for helping. Really, thanks. It could make all the difference, I just know it could."

"Don't thank me," said Barnaby. "I am a law-abiding man. Thank Donald for corrupting me into sentimentality."

Alice replaced the phone and lay back. She slept.

In Norwich, Daniel dreamed of Lisha. She was sitting on the grass at his feet, beside some sort of river, and twisting her head to laugh up at him through her curtain of dark hair. Her arm was on his knee, her weight warm against him. He rested his hand on her hair and felt its silky softness. Looking down, he saw with a start that his hand was young, a little boy's hand, soft and chubby. It dwindled before his eyes until a baby's fat hand lay against the dark hair, then a kind of claw, and his arm was shrivelling up against his side, the thumb crashing towards his big head which curled over on his chest, a foetus—

He opened his eyes, coming sharply out of the nightmare. It was dark and cold in the room, and his hand lay on the stalky roughness of the candlewick bedspread. He moved stiffly, grabbing the material to roll round him as he turned on his side. Lisha. Why should he dream of Lisha, especially beginning in such a romantic, pastoral way? They had never had such moments. They never sat together in a landscape in silent, timeless companionship.

Their talk and arguments had been – he knew now, to his shame – brief and irrelevant, the important thing between them the hum and growl of sexual tension. On those afternoons at her friend's empty bedsit up Gray's Inn Road they had wasted no time talking, or sitting, or leaning. They had fallen on each other voraciously, dragging off clothes, grabbing and crushing and scratching and thrusting their bodies together. Then, with him achingly guilty and her proudly indifferent (or, as he had found far too late, simulating indifference) they would part with a few brittle words. Until the next time.

Rolled in the harsh candlewick, Daniel shuddered. How did other men, other husbands, recover their self-respect after such affairs? Did they have some way of not caring, of dismissing it as a man's fun? Or did they build it up into romance, into a part of the search for true, blinding, archetypal love? Was it his training, his academic discipline, which stopped him from inventing a bearable moral framework for his own history? Why did he feel so permanently dishonoured over something which other men did and forgave themselves easily for?

The sex, he saw, was part of the problem. He could not, would not, dismiss it as a sporting activity, a bit of fun. What he had done with Lisha was a mistake but it also partook of eternity; it stood for ever, unchangeable and on the record as all human couplings must. If he held sex as a sacred part of his marriage, a gift of his identity and his utter trust to Alice, it followed that the sacredness attached also to the same act within the affair. All human couplings could produce human life, could result in a living soul. And indeed, oh Christ, this one had done so.

Daniel curled up tighter, miserable at the act and the aftermath. He clung to the thought that if he were not miserable, he would be a lesser man.

Would the burden ever lift? He was not a Catholic, not any more; could not confess or properly repent, and so could not be forgiven. He must be condemned for ever to look back at this animal interlude, this error, this ugly betrayal, and to see it as part of himself. It was a permanent disablement.

These thoughts had troubled him much over the months. Telling Alice had, for a while, dispersed them. Her apparent forgiveness, her anxiety to help him with the material consequences, had been a balm. For those few days he had walked more lightly, sensed a vista of blessed forgiveness, begun even to forgive himself. Alice's relapse into fury had taken all that away and returned him to his disablement. Now, far from home, with Jamie vanished into some invisible danger, he seemed to stand on the edge of a precipice.

Even that would be bearable, he thought, if he stood there with Alice beside him. But she was on the far side of the chasm. Last night she could have asked him to drop everything and come home, to face the terror with her, and she had not done so. And it was not his place to suggest it, not now, because of Lisha.

On his bed while the weak dawn rose outside the fussy lace curtains of the window, Daniel lay and suffered alone.

Jamie woke early and sat bolt upright on his tousled bunk. He felt alert, expectant, as if it was the first day of the holidays. The caravan in daylight was a pitiful enough sight. Decaying vinyl and stained plastic were everywhere and the odd little woodstove in the corner, protected with a roughly bent sheet of tin, was haloed with a sticky, tarry bloom on walls and ceiling. Jamie saw none of this but knelt up on the bunk to peer through the dripping, misty window.

The roundabout was still there, a drum-like shape in its green canvas. The horses were hidden, but he could see the roundingboards above the canvas, painted with jungle scenes: flamingoes and leopards, storks and hippos and crocodiles, all mixed up with golden curls and wreaths and pineapples and giraffes and arabesques and paisley shapes in red and gold. Swiftly, Jamie began to dress, pulling on his tracksuit trousers, T-shirt, socks, sweater and anorak. When he had finished he glanced down and noticed that his underpants still lay on the cold floor of the caravan, and after a moment's hesitation kicked them into the corner. His watch said seven fifteen. Susan had said she would call him for breakfast; obviously it wasn't yet. He pushed his feet into his trainers, hopped down from the little caravan, and walked across the frost to his day's work.

It was an hour later, with the sun fairly up, that Susan Bailey came out to look for "Rowley's boy" and found his bed empty. He was up on the roundabout, immersed in lining the horse's saddle. The dark-red line on the paler red turned itself, at each end, into a primitive rose. She watched for a moment in silence, then; "Mornin'," she said. "Up working early!"

He jumped slightly, and turned towards her, but did not speak.

"Rowley oughter be pleased," she said conversationally. "Anyway, your breakfast's done. I'm now going to put it on the plate. Come on."

Obediently, he stowed his brush and followed her to the

cottage. The taciturn Tim was there, and Ed, nursing a mug of tea and talking about something called a Gavioli. Jamie had seen the word on the roundabout. Gavioli must be the organ. He slipped into his place at table and, when his tea and a plateful of sausages and eggs was put in front of him, gave Susan a sudden radiant smile of thanks.

Charmed, she looked down at him. "Don't you ever talk?" she asked. "Go on. We all know each other now."

Jamie only smiled again, and began to eat.

"He dun't have to talk," said Ed jovially. "He just has to paint."

But when the boy had gone back to the roundabout, Ed remarked to Susan; "D'you really think he's fifteen? Fourteen, even?"

"Could be," said Susan cautiously. "Rowley said about that. But he does have his gypsy attitoods to all that."

"But Rowley reckoned it was all right, about school and the council and all?"

"Well, what he said to me," said Susan, "was that the boy was feeble-minded, didn't take to school one bit, and Rowley's sister didn't know what to do with him all day but that he was a handy painter enough if he wasn't fussed. So he was doing everyone a favour, bringing him."

"Better not fuss him, then. What I want to know is, when's Rowley coming?"

"A lot of people want to know that, a lot of the time, moi dear." Susan had fallen back into the imitation, and both laughed. Tim, silently eating bread at the end of the table, looked up and spoke for the first time.

"So long as it *is* Rowley's sister's boy," he said.

They stared, uncomprehending. Tim shrugged, and went back to his gnawing.

When the phone rang at half past nine Alice snatched up the receiver. It was not Barnaby.

"Mum?" said Clementine's glad voice. "Mum, 'smee. Just rang to say, I'm in the event team. And the sprint. For the winter series. And we had our Academic Assessment, and I got eight pluses and no minuses."

Alice could not take much in but listened numbly to her daughter's news with small "Ahs" and the occasional "Good for you". When Clementine said, "And home? Everything OK? Dad back this weekend?" she merely said, "No, it's very busy in Norwich. With the new job. Jamie went up there," and prayed for her voice to betray nothing. Clementine rang off sounding as blithe as ever, so Alice, sinking on to the hall chair, assumed she had succeeded. It was another half-hour before Barnaby rang.

"I haven't got anywhere yet. Or not anywhere much. It is Sunday, remember. I'll be on to you as soon as I get it."

"When—?" began Alice

"Look, I am not the police. They'd get it straightaway. You could just ring them, you know. Explain about being worried, and how they've got to be tactful. Allie, you ought to."

"I know," said Alice, desperately. "But oh, Barn, do try. Please."

"I am," said Barnaby, and rang off.

She roamed the house, desolate and jumpy, too nervous to tidy up and too preoccupied to read. She rang Stevie, but he sounded equally preoccupied and a little sharp. Alice had to remind herself that it was the sharpness, the lack of soft emollient platitude, that she normally appreciated about Stevie. She could not expect him to turn into an agony aunt just because she wanted comfort and had deliberately rejected softer sources of it. She stopped herself from ringing Yazz or Jenny. Both would thunderously disapprove of what she was doing over the telephone number. Her heart failed her when she thought of it.

Once, she began dialling Mrs Hammond's number in Norwich to leave a message for Daniel but realized that there was no message she dared give. "He rang, and I know the number, but I haven't told the police yet." No, impossible. Besides, she must not block up the phone. Barnaby, on a fraught family Sunday with his new baby, must be given every chance to get through. And besides, another feeling held her. It was like the time she had her first positive pregnancy test, from a chemist's kit; for two days she had walked around hugging the secret baby to herself, neither seeing her GP nor even telling Daniel. Even this dangerous secret made her feel strangely close, privately close, to her son for the first time in years.

"Please leave me alone. You have to leave me alone, or I can't bear it." He had said it to her, and she would keep the faith. He would not have chosen those words under duress, on that motorway forecourt of her nightmares. He did not sound deranged, or even very strained. Just determined. She would not, of course, leave him alone; but she would make sure that others, more heavy-footed and alarming, did.

Even the knowledge that she was wrong and irresponsible gave strength to her resolve. She was Milton's Eve, vainglorious, scorning simple sensible obedience and taking the path of free will. A small voice told her, every few minutes, that her silence might be the instrument of harm to her child, but she deafened herself to it. For the first time since the day she lost the Opera House job, she put on music all over the house, great swelling, heaving, passionate overtures. *Leave me alone, you have to, or I can't bear it*. OK, Jamie, she said silently to the kitchen wall. OK, leave it with me, I'll come on my own, gently.

It was a long, terrible morning. The loneliness and the suspense and the music together wrought her to a high pitch of emotion. Her breathing grew swift; she walked endlessly around the house, from the ground floor to the basement, up to the bedrooms, along the landing, to and fro, measuring her cage like a lioness confined.

When the doorbell rang, Alice was listening so hard for the telephone that it took her a moment to recognize the sound. Descending from the landing barefoot and wild-haired in her long velvet dress, she opened the door, half expecting another terror of police uniforms. But a slight, dark girl with severely cropped hair stood there instead. Alice stared at her without recognition. The girl looked chilly and pinched in a T-shirt and cotton jacket over black jeans.

"Mrs McDonald?" said the visitor, hesitantly.

"Yes?" said Alice.

The girl looked at her with – Alice recognized with surprise – something not far from fear.

"Could I – do you think – could I come in? And have a word?"

Alice was a Londoner, a streetwise Camden resident. Newspapers and television for ever flickered stories of doorstep attacks, of girls like these with knife-bearing boyfriends waiting round the corner. There was a moment of assessment and hesitation. Finally Alice stood aside and said, "All right. But I've only got a couple of minutes. Is it a charity thing?" For she had noticed that beneath the fashionably threadbare cotton jacket the girl's T-shirt said JESUS SAVES. It said it, moreover, without any flippant additions along the lines of "With the Woolwich". Also, the jacket's lapel bore, in cheap metallic gold, the Chi-Ro silhouette of a fish. Muggers in Camden were not, Alice decided, yet sophisticated enough to disguise themselves as Young Christians.

The girl walked in and followed Alice into the kitchen where the two of them stood on either side of the table with its damaged family collage. The girl looked down at that, and seemed to have some trouble speaking.

"Well?" said Alice, impatient. "Look—" But the girl spoke then, with a rush, in rehearsed words.

"I'm Lisha Danforth. I know you know about me. I came because I heard someone at college saying that since Dan – Mr McDonald – had gone to UEA, you hadn't gone with him. And they thought you were splitting up."

Alice stared in horror at this pale and flimsy teenager, babbling across her kitchen table. She recognized nothing at all of the smiling face amid abundant hair which she had seen on the photograph in the Danforths' house. Nothing at all of her own young self. This girl was almost gaunt. Suddenly, a wave of hostility made her gasp, and when Lisha drew breath, she broke in, "You heard we're splitting up? Oh yes, so you thought you'd come along and stick the knife in? Check out the terrain? Maybe see if you can get him back?"

"No, no, no!" There was real agony in the girl's tone, and she brushed her arm violently across her eyes. There was a desperate, jerky quality about her movements generally, and seeing this made Alice quieten a little. She listened to the next part of the rehearsed speech.

"No, I couldn't, I wouldn't. You see, I'm not like I was, the devil's driven out. I've become a Christian. I truly want to atone. Chris – that's my priest, at the group I go to – he said we must step backwards and undo the work of our old devils. Like the drug dealers, they go and give back money and stuff, and help people they used to sell to. And when I heard them say Dan had split from his wife, I told Chris about me and what I did. And he said I had to bear witness to Christ by coming back and confessing to you. I had to do anything I could to make whole again the family I damaged."

Alice sat down suddenly and looked up at the creature who stood, thin and blazing-eyed, before her.

"I do not need this," she said. "I really, really do not need this at all. How dare you barge in—"

"Chris said," continued the girl, "that my own sins could be washed away by Christ's forgiveness, but that it was my responsibility to deal with the effects, the shadows cast by my sins. Like, a burglar can't just say 'I repent'. He has to give back the stuff, or as near as he can."

Alice motioned Lisha to the chair opposite her, only because this towering evangelism was too overwhelming to tolerate when it came from above.

"That's the point," she said coldly. "As near as you can. Do you want to know what shadows exactly you have cast? And then perhaps you can tell me what the hell you propose to do about them, to make yourself feel goody-good?"

"Yes," said Lisha simply, her pale face glowing. "Tell me. Only if you want to. Chris says the point is not to intrude—"

"Indeed," said Alice. "Don't think of intruding. Just bloody listen. Shadow number one is that Daniel has lost his job and gone a hundred miles from home to a strange place and a probably worse one. Shadow number two is that, as your friends in college rightly report, we seem to have split up as a family. A split which dates from my birthday, in case you're interested. Shadow number three – the really big one, Alicia, so concentrate – is that our twelve-year-old son, who is upset by all this, has apparently run away from home and can't be found." Her voice was beginning to break treacherously. This could not be allowed to happen, this girl must not offer her sympathy or see her cry.

At that moment, the telephone rang, and Alice leapt up, saying harshly, "Wait. I haven't finished."

But again, the call was not from Barnaby. Lisha, sitting at the collage table, watched through the kitchen door, her elbows on a ripped picture of Daniel on a waterslide with small Jamie in his arms, about to land in St Mark's Square. Alice stood cradling the telephone to her ear, uttering small, distressed sounds. "Oh . . . oh no . . . oh Stevie . . . Christ, what can we . . . no, don't be – how could they think . . ."

At last she stopped speaking and stood with the telephone for another moment, as if the other speaker had cut off abruptly before she was ready. Finally, Alice put back the receiver, came in and over to the kitchen table, sat down exactly where she had been before, replacing her elbows on the table. She noticed, to her irritation, that the cat had jumped on to Lisha's lap.

"Shadow number four," she said, "is another big one. My best, kindest friend, Stevie, just rang to inform me that the police have arrested his boyfriend Simon on suspicion of abducting my son. Stevie is upset. He also informs me that he wishes he and Simon had never set eyes on any of us, and that he never wants to see me again."

And this time, she did cry. Alicia Danforth stood up, pulled a piece of paper out of her pocket and silently put it in front of Alice before letting herself out of the front door, which she closed with care. When Alice raised her damp eyes from her arms and found herself alone, she saw the paper. Under the neatly printed name and address were written, in tiny, careful script, the words, "IOU. Only ask, day or night, and I shall pay. God's love be with you. A. Danforth."

Simon's arrest had followed his return to the flat by only half an hour. Detective Sergeant Clough had moved fast and, it should be understood, in perfectly good faith, after a series of coincidences. A conversation with social services concerning the presence of homosexual men in the "close circle" of the missing boy had set alarm bells ringing in his mind. Frequent police lectures on relations with the gay community had, it is true, emphasized that predatory paedophilia was far from being an inseparable part of homosexual orientation; but the fact remained that there had been two sex murders of young boys in London – East London, as it happened, not so far from that unscheduled stop at Maryland – within the last twelve months. The horror of these, and their unsolved state, set every detective's teeth on edge and his or her antennae twitching.

Simon's lost weekend had not escaped police notice either. Alice and Stevie's portrayal of the boy's life had included his keenness on art, and Simon's generous provision of wallpaper and fabric print samples for him to make collages and copies of. The next question, "Did he get on with adults? Was he confident with them?" had elicited an eager positive, and Stevie had volunteered, "Certainly with Simon. Same mental age." He had given a fond, affected, slightly bitter laugh. But the policemen had not laughed. They had called on Stevie on Sunday morning at nine thirty, asked for Mr Quinlan, and been told that he had "blinded off into the blue" on Friday afternoon, and that such blindings-off were far from unusual.

So a PC had stayed discreetly outside the flat door alongside the shop; and when Simon came home, as he always did in the end, he had only twenty minutes' affectionate vituperation from Stevie and no time at all for news of the McDonalds before the policeman's radio had summoned up two colleagues and a warrant. Sergeant Clough, to do him credit, had thought that a quiet voluntary questioning would initially be enough. The bloke might after all be eliminated by alibis within ten minutes, and harassing gays for being gay was not at all his line. But from higher up the chain of command came the order for speedy dispatch, for handcuffs and a van and a bit of drama.

There was, in Covent Garden, sufficient of a community atmosphere for the handcuffs, the van, the angry pallid prisoner and the distraught screaming of Stevie Dent in the street to be widely noticed and discussed. Even if it was Monday morning before the newspapers drew their attention to it with the banners: GAY KILLINGS – THIRD BOY SOUGHT – LONDON MAN HELD.

After half an hour of sitting numbly at the kitchen table, Alice had almost decided to telephone Sergeant Clough about Jamie's call and allow police proceedir.gs to take their course. She owed it to Stevie. Not that he had asked, during that brief angry telephone call. In his terror and humiliation he had clearly forgotten about the number she still held. The number which would let Simon free: for wherever 01328 890909 was, Simon, she was confident, had not been. It would give him a clear alibi.

That he might have other alibis she acknowledged to herself. But she flinched away from imagining what damage the police might do to them, given the kind of people they would come from. Like many liberal-minded but conventionally married women, Alice drew private boundaries round her tolerance of the "gay scene". To love a man as Stevie did, live with him, comfort and support him in almost matrimonial fidelity seemed to her an entirely acceptable way of life. As good as marriage; which is to say, as good as the behaviour of the people in it. She happily went further: to amuse oneself in drag clubs and gatherings, to dress up in suspenders and padded bras as an ironic commentary on the culture and the gay condition was, again, something Alice could appreciate and enjoy. She and Daniel had watched *The Adventures of Priscilla Queen of the Desert* with both children, and laughed with it, and discussed it in the family without unease.

But the wilder shores of gay life were different. The desperate frivolous promiscuities, the cruising and cottaging, the bizarre equipment, explicit magazines and stimulant drugs were as repellent to her – she hoped, no more repellent – than the heterosexual equivalent. Simon, she knew from recent increasingly confidential talks with Stevie, occasionally adventured to those further shores of sexuality and Alice did not like to know it. She had challenged Stevie.

"How can you bear it? Most husbands and wives would be out of their minds if the other one went out brothel-creeping."

He had mocked her a little and said, "It's delayed adolescence. Remember, most gay men don't come out and admit it until they're over twenty. We hang around brooding and wondering why girls look so revolting with their kit off. So we miss out on the wild oats, the teenage bit. Remember? When you snog someone for a dare, or get so pissed you don't know who had you at the party or whether you just passed out on a bag of clothes pegs? Remember dressing up to go out on the pull on a Saturday night?"

"Well . . ." said Alice. "I was never . . . but yes, I know what you mean."

"So tell me, Cinders," said Stevie relentlessly, "that you never in your born life had a man's tongue in your mouth until you had weighed up the serious spiritual implications of your relationship with him and his likely advantages as a life partner."

Alice had laughed, thrown up her hands and conceded the point.

"So," Stevie said, "Simon, being a teeny weeny bit of a retard, is just not quite over all that yet. He feels entitled to do silly things."

But not evil things, not with children. Picking listlessly at the dead pictures on her kitchen table Alice thought, sadly, that of all people she was probably the last in the world to believe that Simon would have hurt or corrupted Jamie. Once, in Stevie and Simon's flat, there had been an *Evening Standard* lying on the table with the latest East London murder on the front: the picture of a fourteen-year-old boy, and GAY MONSTER'S NEW VICTIM as a headline.

"Do you, when you see that, do you feel angry?" she blurted, without thinking.

And Stevie had said steadily, "Yes. While you're about it, ask Daniel sometime how he feels about rape reports. I bet he feels angry and embarrassed too. You know: 'all men are rapists!' QED, all gays are child molesters."

It was at this point that Simon had surprised them both – for he did not join in serious conversations if he could help it – by turning from the flyblown French café mirror in which he was frowningly adjusting his bow tie for a night serving in the bar. Abruptly, he said, "Very pretty boys of seventeen, yes. Lead me to them. As long as they know the score and make the running." He turned back, tossing his head sideways to improve the fall of his carefully bleached forelock. "Even then, duckie, to be shamingly honest, I'd rather look and yearn. But kids? Forget it. I might go out and kill that bastard myself. Believe it or not, Allie, years ago before I was a screaming queen I used to be a little boy."

"Why did you tell me that?" Alice had demanded almost angrily. "I didn't ask if you fancied boys, I wouldn't be so insulting. I asked if you felt angry about gay monster headlines."

"I told you because you're a mother tigress, dear. And *you* know that *I* know that you sometimes wonder about gays. And that you maybe wouldn't hire one as a babysitter, not if there was a podgy moon-faced thing with a bust that you could hire instead." He preened for a moment, while Stevie sat silently watching him, then continued, "And do you know, tiger-mummy? I'm glad you have these *murky* suspicions. Murkier the better. Protect your children, Allie. Keep them safe. It's a bad, bad, bad, bad world."

And Simon, flippant happy sexy Simon, had blown her a kiss and gone out whistling "Donna é mobile". Alice had believed what he said and knew she always would. She also knew that she would never repeat the conversation even to Daniel, in case a more suspicious listener take it for a smokescreen or an example of protesting too much. She believed Simon. His boundaries might be a lot further back than hers, but they existed. And he was as repelled by what lay beyond them as she could be.

Perhaps Simon, then, understood his arrest. Perhaps he could even sympathise with the police conclusion. Or at least accept it with better grace than his lover. Alone now at the kitchen table, Stevie's hysterical "I wish we'd never set eyes on your sodding family!" ringing in her ears, Alice shed tears for them all. For Simon, across a table from some impassive questioner, trying to stop himself making cheeky jokes in his nervousness; for Stevie, who hated her. For Jamie, out there somewhere. She was moving to the telephone to ring Sergeant Clough when it rang and at last it was Barnaby.

"Alice? I have the address. The bad news for you might be that it isn't a private address. But if it had been, I don't think even my source would have given it to me. It's a phone box."

"Oh, Barney! I thought it might be. Where?"

Barnaby read out two B road numbers. "It's on a crossroads, apparently. Near Walsingham. Norfolk."

Alice let out a great sigh. "So he did go to Norwich. He did go. He must have given Daniel the slip. Or Dan was late. Oh Christ, if I could get my hands on Daniel . . ."

"Can I go now?" said Barnaby's voice. "Only, I do have a wife and child, and it is Sunday."

"Yes, sorry. Oh, I am so grateful. Let me read the road numbers out again." She did. Barnaby confirmed them and Alice was alone again, looking down at the co-ordinates of the place where her son, eighteen hours earlier, had stood and told her to leave him alone.

Jamie worked on in the watery sunshine, and by Sunday lunchtime had finished another horse. The silent Tim came and unscrewed something from the engine and took it indoors; Susan came out after lunch and worked alongside Jamie through the early afternoon, putting undercoat and base coats on several of the naked rubbed-down horses, and tentatively marking in some dappling and shading around their heads.

"I can do this bit," she said, tongue between her teeth, concentrating. "Just about. But I can't do real fairground, I can't do the scrolls and patterns, they always look wrong. You've really got the touch. Did Rowley teach you?"

"Um," said Jamie. Relaxed now, he really wished he could talk to the Baileys, ask them questions, find out about the Gavioli organ in the middle, and the engine, and why there was a tiger snarling on each of the four corners of the pay booth, and who Mr Isambard Kingdom Brunel was, painted in his top hat on the screen round the engine base. It was lonely just saying "Uh" and "Um".

But if he started talking, they would soon find out that he was not Rowley's boy at all, and he closed his mind to the consequences of that discovery. Already he was looking foward to supper, and having the stove lit in his little caravan, and sleeping there again with the moon outside the misted window. He would wake the next day and start on the black horse which was drying out in the sunshine. He loved the black base, so deep and glossy, and had an idea about the eyes: they would stare, he decided, with the thinnest of red rims to make their whiteness more startling. They would be dangerous wild eyes, rolled a little backwards. The small children might not want to ride that galloper, but he would. One day, he would.

He knew, now, that they were called gallopers. Not just horses. Gallopers. On the rounding board, on sections between the jungle paintings, it said EDWD. BAILEY'S SENSATIONAL NORFOLK GALLOPERS BRITISH AND BEST. He had learned quite a lot about this little fair from careful listening and piecing together of conversations; also from Susan's absent-minded chat while she painted. Bailey's would normally have been laid up weeks ago, for winter, with the work being done slowly at leisure in the barns or under canvas tilts between the lorries, to smarten up the rides for April. But money was tight, and an offer to do a revived winter fair, the Cold Fair just outside Norwich, had been too good to miss. Only the gallopers and chair-o-planes and steam yachts were going, plus the food stands. There would be three weeks up to Christmas, with flocks of people coming to craft stalls and the steam fair right at the heart of it. "They din't want modern rides, Sue," Ed had said triumphantly, reading his letter again at breakfast. "Just the hooplas and the food and their charity stalls, and us in the middle of it. We might take the juvenile roundabout, if Joe can bring his boy."

Jamie had not quite sorted out in his mind how many Baileys there were. He knew Tim, who was in charge of the steam engines, and that Ed did the carpentry and travelling, and that Susan looked after them all, ran the accounts, and kept up the simpler paintwork. Other brothers were mentioned from time to time. Or maybe they were cousins. And in the winter, of course, they had the mysterious Rowley.

"And we wouldn't have relied on him, wouldn't be so stupid," said Ed, half to the silent boy and half to his wife, "if it warn't for the fire, and the new hosses we had to put on. The old paint would've done, if it wasn't for all that smoke."

"We could do it without the gallopers," Susan had said doubtfully. "Take the other kiddy roundabout."

"No, we couldn't," said Tim fiercely, looking up from his roast beef. And:

"Gallopers are what people expect," added Ed. "They're the heart of the fair. You'll be wanting us," he said with scorn, "to hire a waltzer next."

Jamie had wanted to ask why a waltzer was so terrible, but now, out in the afternoon sun, he began to see. He had been tidying up the paintwork on a fire-damaged horse, and Susan had decided he looked cold and sent him off to "run up and down for ten minutes, or your fingers'll seize up". He peered around the other rides, lifted some canvases, and admired Rowley's other paintwork. Scrolls and angels, arabesques and checks and rococo curls, like the ones on the top of the gallopers which, Susan had teasingly told him, were "real gold leaf". He read the lettering in the dim green light under the tilts: DE LUXE TOYTOWN PURE DELIGHT . . . FARE £1 ALL CLASSES . . . BRITISH AND BEST . . . BAILEY'S FUNFAIR HERE TODAY GONE TOMORROW COME NOW . . . SAMSON STRENGTH STRIKER RING THE BELL.

It was, he suddenly thought, kind. The letters were loud and colourful and rowdy, but nothing about them suggested an intention to hurt. The funfairs he had been to, at the seaside, were all about skidding and shrieking and clinging on with white knuckles and dicing with fear. The lights were strobe, the music hard rock, the pictures showed Terminators and guns and bombs and monsters. They had the same feel as Battlezone, only brighter.

But this fair, as he began to explore it, was different. It existed to thrill, not to frighten. There were birds and biplanes, angels and animals, gold and silver curves instead of neon zigzags. It was a thing of swinging and flying and galloping, not jerking and screaming and banging. A waltzer would not fit in. Anyway, Ed went on about steam as well, and you could hardly have a steam waltzer. Suddenly, before him rose up a vision of the coming Christmas fair, and how the steam would rise amid the glittering gold leaf and hang on the freezing air with the music all around, and how the coloured lights would blur in the fog as night came down. A Cold Fair. The idea charmed him. And his horses at the heart of it. He ran back to the gallopers and picked up his brush again. It was cramped, working on the roundabout platform; he also knew by now that this was not considered at all satisfactory, and that a proper shelter would be ready by Tuesday for Rowley and his boy to start painting in earnest.

"Only, since we had to build up for Tim to test the cranks, after that stoopid safety inspector," Susan had said, painting in a dapple, "I thought I might as well make a start, like. Just as well, boy, else where'd you have crept in like an old rat to sleep the other night?"

Jamie laughed, but said nothing.

At about the same time, Violet Lancing stood at her back door, summoning her cat. "Kittykittykittypest!" she called, banging a tin of cat food with a fork. "Kittykittymurderer!" The shaggy black animal slunk towards her, tail in the air. "Here," said Violet, abruptly forking out half the tin into a stone bowl which stood on a rickety wooden table. "Dins. Eat it. It's already dead. I know that takes the fun out of it, but it might stop you bringing in more fieldmice. Kittykiller."

The cat began eating, with greedy jerks of its head, and Violet was about to turn back into the kitchen when through the hedge at the bottom of the garden came a tall figure in a long, greasy black coat tied at the waist with string. His face was weathered, wrinkled beyond his years, yet beneath it all rather pale, with a suspiciously red nose. His hair was dark, heavily streaked with grey and curled over his collar; his beard was not long, but on the other hand gave no impression of having ever been trimmed. It was more as if the hairs grew to a certain length, and then simply lost heart, or could draw no more nourishment from the unpromising soil of his chin. At his heels trotted a yellow brindled lurcher, its tongue hanging out.

Unperturbed, Violet raised the hand which held the cat food

fork in grave salutation, and stepped back indoors to dispose of the half-empty tin. She put it in the fridge, slammed the door, threw the fork into the stone sink, and came back outside.

"Why don't you ever come to the front?" she inquired. "I only ask, out of curiosity."

"Oi left the van off the road," said the man. "Ain't no lights. Not all of 'em. Walked up from the Pea Field."

"Goodness, only you still call it that," said Violet. "There haven't been peas there for years. You used to do the picking, didn't you, with your sister?"

"I did. Before the big machines." He was standing outside the back door now, and Violet stood aside to let him in.

"Come in, do. Geoffrey and I will be having supper early. You're very welcome. No, let Nadia come in."

She motioned towards the silent yellow dog.

"Naow!" said the big man. "Dirty gorgio habit, dogs inside. Nadia – tscha!" The dog lay down, resignedly, on the step, and he came indoors, rubbing his hands. Violet moved towards the kettle.

"So tell me, what are you up to?" she said conversationally. "It must be a year since we saw you."

"This an' that. I've a painting job to do down at Little Hincham. Ed Bailey's place."

"Oh, I am glad!" said Violet. "You were always so good at painting, you did such wonderful things for me when you were little. You've no idea what it is for a teacher to have a child who doesn't paint like a child. A real thrill, every time I came over from all the rainbows and stickmen to look at your work."

The Colonel appeared in the doorway from the sitting room. "Ha! Rowley back again, I see," he said, in more of a bark than was usual to him these days. His clipped straight-backed tidiness was in marked contrast to Rowley's appearance, which fact might well have made both of them uneasy. As it was, however, only the Colonel ever seemed to feel it. But he fought it. This was, after all, one of Violet's protégés.

"What sort of thrill was this, Violet?"

"Rowley was one of my Infants when I first came up here after the war to teach at the old Wetheringham School. At least, he was whenever his family stopped by for a month or two for some farm work," said Violet, pouring three mugs of tea and emptying a packet of digestive biscuits on to a very old and chipped, but rather pretty, pink-flowered plate. "He was wonderful at painting, especially circus and fairground patterns and gypsy caravans, but I never got him too enthusiastic about reading."

"'Rithmetic was good, though," said Rowley, slyly.

"Only for working out Newmarket odds," said Violet, primly. "Goodness, how you shocked that inspector!" And they laughed together, the old woman and the gypsy, and once again for a moment Geoffrey felt excluded. Where had he been, in the dry years after 1945? Married to Celia, down at Aldershot, no children coming, nothing happening year after year, time standing still. He used to wonder at night, lying sleepless apart from Celia in the married quarters, where Violet had gone and whether she was all right. And she had been up here, teaching these ragamuffin children, pinning up their paintings, making small friends who would grow up into great hopeless cases like Rowley. Suddenly, he looked at Rowley with a spurt of affection. The man saw the good in Violet, anyway. Treated her with proper respect, as his old teacher. Mustn't judge by appearances.

They talked for a while, then ate spaghetti together with a bolognaise sauce which Violet expertly expanded for the three of them by throwing in a can of tomatoes and some late field mushrooms which Rowley produced, rather to the Colonel's dismay, from the pocket of his horrible coat. The talk fell on Little Hincham and the fair.

"You're a bit early, aren't you?" said Violet. "I thought Ed and Susan never started with the fine work, the painting, till after Christmas. Ed's father used to say, engineering before Christmas, painting after."

"I'm late, more like," said Rowley complacently, wiping his mouth. "They've got a Christmas booking. Cold Fair, at Norwich. Got to get straight. And they got their gallopers half smoked up in that fire."

"Oh, that's wonderful!" said Violet. "I read about the Cold Fair idea, and I hoped they'd have steam rides. But I never thought Bailey's would go."

"I told 'em," said Rowley, "I'd bring my sister's boy to help out. S'why I'm late."

"Where is he?" cried Violet in sudden dismay. "Rowley, you have *not* left your nephew down there in that cold van in the Pea Field while you—"

"He warn't *there*," said Rowley crossly. "She gone and sent him to a training scheme." He spoke the last two words with intense contempt. "As a house decorator." He looked as if he would have spat, but recollected himself in time, perhaps helped by the Colonel's steady gaze. "So a' go all the way to Walsingham, and she says cool as a cucumber, posh as a fruit, 'Eaow neaow, Joby's gone off training for his NVQ.' Bloody old cow."

Violet laughed. "So you're turning up late and understaffed. I see."

"I'll git it done," said Rowley sullenly.

"You'd better. I shall come to this Cold Fair, to check. I might bring my godson's children—"

Suddenly, the memory of Jamie fell on her and silenced the table for a moment. Rowley rose.

"Thank ye for the food. You've three tiles missing on the wood house. I'll do 'em in the morning."

He left, trailing down the garden with the silent yellow dog at his heels, blending quickly into the darkness before he slipped through the gap in the hedge. Geoffrey stacked the three spaghetti plates and said, "He'll be off down there to get drunk, you know."

"I know," said Violet imperturbably. "That's why I take such care to line his stomach first."

22

On the wrecked patterns of the kitchen tabletop lay Lisha's note and the paper with the Norfolk road numbers on it. Alice stared at both. Five minutes earlier she had spoken to Detective Sergeant Clough, said she knew that the boy was alive and well and in Norfolk and that Mr Quinlan could not possibly be involved. Something, perhaps Clough's polite, wary, mistrustful refusal to discuss the matter of Simon at all with this mother who was also a close friend of Simon's lover, had made her dissemble. She mentioned the telephone call but not the 1471 recall or the tracing of the number. Instead, she had asked, "If I get a real clue to where he is, can I come with you – with whoever goes to trace him? I'd have to be there when he was found."

The answer was a polite, still wary, negative. The Norfolk force would be alerted. Alice would be notified. If she stayed quietly at home it would be much better. South or North Norfolk, did she know?

Alice, wildly, had said she was not sure. In front of her, the road numbers burned up from the paper. She closed her eyes. Sergeant Clough had signed off with something else about "dealing with it" and "no reason to think the worst". Now, turning the two papers over and over in her hands, she came to a decision. She was going straight there, straight to the heart of the problem, straight to where Jamie was. She had reconstructed the rest of the conversation, the part before that terrible "Leave me alone". *I'm fine. Food and a place to sleep and everything.* He would not have said it quite that way if he was travelling on. More like "I'm going somewhere I'll get food and a place to sleep". No. He was close to that phone box. She would find him.

Alice had a car, although these days she very rarely used it. Once, she had rather enjoyed the bad-tempered sport of London driving, priding herself on her sharp hand on the hooter and her ability to find secret, cunning rat-runs away from the peak-hour traffic. But since her parking space at the Royal Opera House had been taken away two years earlier the car had barely stirred, and she had hardly missed it. Every December, the cost of its MOT, third party insurance and tax made her pause and exclaim ruefully that it really must go. But she had owned the rusty, pale-blue Citroën 2CV since 1977. Once, early on, she had painted orange flowers with psychedelic leaves on its front doors; Jamie had been allowed to decorate the back doors and boot with his own patterns when he was five, and he had been immoderately thrilled to be allowed so to deface a real motorcar.

"Oh, keep it," Daniel always said. "Come in handy when mine's in dock." And gratefully Alice had agreed and paid up. Besides, remarkably for London, this raffish vehicle had a free parking space. An unattractive and occasionally flooded patch of cracked concrete near the canal had been rented cheaply from the council by the street for twenty years in some complicated deal over rear access to the properties, and the McDonalds found themselves allocated two spaces by brisk Mrs Geary from No. 42. "It keeps local property prices up," she explained, "if there are parking spaces. But it is best if the householder uses them."

"There you are," Daniel had said, at the Christmas when this happened. "It's a positive community service to keep your car. Mrs Geary will be grateful. Besides, suppose mine breaks down?" So she kept it, and Dan used it occasionally while his was in for service, and came back marvelling that it still went. "Nothing to go wrong, I suppose. It's a sewing-machine engine, basically. But I wouldn't trust it much beyond Wembley." The car stood there, month in month out, and never seemed to get broken into or vandalized. "Not worth their while," Daniel said. "That's the kind of car they make young ram-raiders drive as a *punishment*. A ritual humiliation."

Now, Alice took the keys of her car on their ancient Sergeant Pepper keyring – older even than the car itself – and left the house, taking only a long dark coat with Jamie's photograph thrust deep into its pocket. It was two minutes' walk down to the canal, but when she got into the car park she saw a difficulty. It had been invaded by Sunday market shoppers at Camden Lock; cars were parked in file right along the middle. This presented no problem for most of the cars in the residents' bays, but her blue 2CV and one other were blocked in by a battered old Mini, parked carelessly on a slant in the time-honoured style of Mini drivers who like to believe that their vehicle takes up no space at all.

"Sod!" Alice stamped, so suddenly intense was her fury. The one time she needed the car, really needed it, urgently! There was nobody around she could ask for help. She turned back and ran round the corner and along the road to her house, fumbled the keys impatiently, and slammed back into the hall. Picking up the telephone, she dialled Jenny's number. Rod would help, he was only five minutes away, he played squash. Together they could bounce the Mini round a foot or two.

The phone rang twice, and then, "Yes?" It was Jenny's voice.

"Jenny, is Rod home?"

"No," said the tinny Jenny voice. "He's away with some clients this weekend. Anything I can do?"

It was not an inquiry intended to be answered in the affirmative. Alice rang off, and thought of neighbours. No. They would want to know where she was going, and why. They knew she never drove the car. She was too tired to make up lies. Wandering through into the kitchen, thinking, she saw the paper on the table: "IOU. Only ask, day or night, and I shall pay. God's love be with you. A.Danforth."

The telephone number at the top was Kentish Town. Alice paused only for a moment, then carried the paper back to the telephone and dialled the number. A boyish voice answered.

"Christian Reunion Group, North Hostel, God is Love, can I help you?"

"Is Lisha Danforth there?"

"She is. One moment, please." Footsteps retreated along bare flags with the hollow sound of an institutional corridor, and in a few moments the breathy voice came on the line. Alice spoke rapidly.

"Look, your IOU. There is something you can do. Now."

"Yes. Willingly. I meant it."

"Are there a lot of you there? Boys, as well as girls?"

"It is a mixed hostel, yeah, and Father Chris—"

Alice did not want to hear any more about Father Chris. These eager, tambourine-bashing young Christians could do a practical work of charity, quick, then make themselves scarce.

"OK. You know where I live. Can you get five or six strong people down here as quickly as possible? I have to move a car."

"We could get Chris to drop us in the minibus," said the voice eagerly. "He's just off to Leicester Square to pick up the evangelism group. I really am grateful to you for allowing—"

"Yes, yes," said Alice. "Just bloody get here." While she waited, she fed the cat and took a key out of the teapot on the dresser, tucking it into her purse with short, impatient movements.

Lisha brought ten comrades, in the event; eight of them splendidly fresh-faced, clear-eyed young men in the same Jesus Saves T-shirt that Lisha wore, and one muscular blonde girl in a baseball cap saying HALLELUJAH! They stood on the doorstep shining with goodwill, and Alice led them to the car park and pointed to the Mini.

"I need to get out. Mine is the blue 2CV. All it needs is that Mini bouncing round a few inches."

But the leading young man thought that bouncing might harm its suspension, so they picked it right up, the ten of them, and shuffled carefully backwards, putting it down next to another car's rear bumper. Alice backed out, in the usual cloud of black 2CV smoke, and saw them preparing to lift the Mini back into its old position. The wild thought crossed her mind that she now had a permanent personal army of muscular young Christians to do any heavy work she wanted. Perhaps they could be a bodyguard, like the Praetorian Guard around the Emperors of Rome. Or carry her about in a sedan chair. That would impress Yazz. Until, of course, they started singing "Gimme oil in my lamp, keep me burning".

She flapped up the window of the·2CV, clipped it insecurely in place, and leaned out.

"Alicia!" she called, and saw Lisha turn from her place at the Mini's rear and move obediently across to her. "One more job!"

"I really am grateful," said the dark girl earnestly, but Alice cut her off.

"This," she said, dangling it through the window, "is my spare key. The cat will need feeding and the plants watering, and the milk and papers taking in. Because of burglars. Be sure to double-lock it after you."

Lisha nodded, apparently not too bemused. Alice suddenly wondered whether she was actually going mad under the strain. *Fatal Attraction* came to mind. Would this girl, this girl who had slept with Daniel, cook the cat in a pie for revenge?

Looking at the mild, Christian faces now gathered around the car, meekly waiting to help in Lisha's atonement, she pushed the thought aside and continued, "Ring this number," she scribbled Yazz's number on a piece of scrap paper which lay on the front shelf of the car, "and tell that name there, Ms Yasmin Hunter, to tell Alan that Mrs McDonald won't be in for work tomorrow. A family crisis."

"Oh, I am sorry, is the little boy . . ." began Lisha, but Alice just grimaced fiercely, said "Do it!" and eased out the clutch. In another choking cloud of illegal exhaust fumes, the little car rolled forward, and was gone.

23

Somewhere north of Colchester, watching her vibrating hands on the wheel, Alice remembered Daniel. The train of thought that led to him was triggered off by the rueful reflection that Daniel would never, ever have let her set out on such a journey in this particular car. Although it had trundled only around London for years, at the slow speed of London traffic, Alice always had a secret feeling that it was a car perfectly capable of going anywhere. This was perhaps because she had driven it to Venice in 1979, not long after she bought it fresh from the showroom with her father's legacy. Indeed, it still had a string of Venetian glass beads wound round the metal frame of the rear passenger seat, as a trophy, by Sam and Erica who had come with her.

But even that, she now reluctantly admitted, had been a slow business. The car could do 65 mph then, but the wind used to shake it so much at its highest speeds that she feared the wheels would leave the road. Now, it climbed to a sedate 45 and stuck there, straining and vibrating. It had taken her two hours to get this far, and already the light was visibly fading. Daniel would have stopped her trying it, in mid-November anyway. The heater was not quite working; at least, it would blast scalding smelly air on to her feet for a few minutes, then cut out and deliver ice-cold wind instead. She had stopped in a layby near Chelmsford and put on her long black coat.

Now, she stopped again for petrol and a bar of chocolate, and rang Mrs Hammond's from the comfortingly bright neon lights of the filling-station call box.

"Could you tell Mr McDonald," she said, "that it's Mrs

McDonald, and not to worry, because I'm on the trail. No, just that. On the trail. Say it's a good trail."

Mrs Hammond could have told her that Daniel was there, not ten feet from where she was standing. She could have described the way he was lying in the dark on his candlewick bedspread with his clothes and sweaty socks on. But she didn't. Her glimpse of Daniel through his uncurtained window (from the flower bed, where she stood in her galoshes) had filled her with righteous distaste. Uncouth lodgers who lay on bedspreads and made free with her potpourri did not deserve to be called to her personal telephone. She wrote in her neat, crabbed hand on a scalloped message pad, "Mrs McDonald rang to say not to worry she is on the trail," tore off the sheet and went to put it on his door, tucked behind the screwed-on number. She did not knock. He had, she noticed, failed even to shave today. One had certain standards.

Colder now, Alice went slowly back out into the gloom, and over to the little old car which stood patiently, its orange flowers flaring oddly white in the sodium lights of the forecourt. She would have really liked to speak to Daniel. If only to ask him whether it was the A14 she changed on to at Ipswich, or the A45, or whether perhaps they were the same road now. Sighing, she started up again, northwards and eastwards.

Lisha rang Yasmin, who was dismayed and a little angry at the bald message. Saturday's trip around the shops and the hairdresser with Alice, as if they were single girlfriends again, had been wonderful. All their old comradeship was reborn as if Alice had been suddenly brushed clean of the soft fusty accretions of marriage and domesticity. She shone, thought Yasmin; shone for the first time in years. The two of them, bright and sharp and energetic, reflected one another's glitter again as they had not done for a long time. Hell! What "family crisis"?

Yazz kicked the leg of her black steel telephone table with a petulance and lack of cool that would have surprised her colleagues. She would not tell Alan until morning. Allie might think better of it. Family crisis!

The little car coughed and vibrated across Suffolk in that Sunday dusk while Rowley ate his spaghetti in Wetheringham, Yasmin waxed her legs, angrily and painfully, alone in London, Daniel lay staring unseeingly at Mrs Hammond's nubbly Artex ceiling, and Jamie in Little Hincham wrapped up his brushes in turps and tiredly, happily, helped Susan light the stove in his caravan.

Alice followed signs for Norwich, and gradually the miles counted down. For a moment, she thought that she would go into Norwich, find Mrs Hammond's and collect Daniel before venturing further north in the winter darkness to the telephone box. But on the ring road, the thought of searching in the dark for some obscure street made her carry on. He would probably be out, anyway. Her arms ached, her leg over the accelerator shook with fatigue as, foot on the floor, she drove the car at a steady 40 mph away from the lights of Norwich City and northward and westward, towards Fakenham. It was up there somewhere. Once, she stopped under one of the last streetlamps of Norwich to check her route. She had trouble reading the map, but with a shock of surprise realized that the spot itself was not very far from Wetheringham, from Godgran's. Could Jamie . . .? Could that explain why he sounded happy about eating and sleeping? But why a telephone box?

No. Alice had never been entirely comfortable with Daniel's godmother. It was not only the dry wit and quizzical, school-mistress's eye that made her uneasy, but the Catholicism too. She suspected that Violet Lancing prayed for her conversion. But Godgran would not conceivably have lied to Daniel, or kept Jamie secretly. Alice tried for a moment to believe that she would, that she was senile enough for anything; but they had seen her in the late summer, spoken to her since, and the very idea of Violet in anything less than total control of her mores and her morals was laughable.

Still, it was close. There might be some local network Violet knew, some way of finding out who would shelter a runaway boy . . . Alice, on a particularly dark and threatening patch of road, wondered whether to ring Godgran Lancing straightaway and enlist her help and, even better, the help of that splendid old boyfriend of hers. But again her heart failed her. Violet would be horrified that she had not told the police everything. Just as Daniel would be. Just as, actually, she was herself. Tears began to roll down Alice's face as she drove on through the darkness.

A few miles past Fakenham, something under the thin tinny bonnet of the car exploded. Alice, almost asleep, heard a loud bang and found herself struggling to control the lurching, slowing motion of the 2CV. When it drew to a halt, she had pulled it on to the verge with one wheel jolted uncomfortably into a drainage gully. She opened the door and got out, to stand beside it helplessly for a moment. That had been what Daniel called an Expensive Noise. Something had gone. Even if she had been more competent, there would have been no point in looking. The car was dead, as surely as a model aeroplane whose elastic band had snapped.

She sat down again in the driver's seat and turned the ignition key, but nothing happened except a curious and ominous smell. Hastily she jumped out, remembering stories of cars bursting into flames with less warning. She had her coat on already, and reached inside quickly for the road map, her purse and the rest of the chocolate.

The car did not burst into flames. She stood there, while nothing happened. It was seven o'clock. Alice looked up and down the road, but no car had passed her since Norwich. She tried to look at the map, but it was too dark even if she held it close to her face and took off her glasses. Kneeling on the damp grass verge she pulled an old cigarette lighter out of her pocket – a sentimental souvenir of the days when Daniel smoked – and let it flare over the map. It could hardly be more than three miles or so, round a couple of corners, to the crossroads. The crossroads where, she knew, stood a telephone box which had been working twenty-four hours ago and presumably still was.

There really was no alternative. Locking the car, Alice began to walk rapidly on along the road, her map in one hand, the other thrust deep into her pocket.

After a while this hunched and inhibited walk began to give her backache. Making a conscious effort, she shrugged and relaxed her shoulders, stuffed the map in her pocket and began to walk more freely, her arms swinging. She was not at ease. Lines ran through her head:

> *Like one who on a lonesome road*
> *Doth walk in fear and dread*

> *Because he fears a frightful fiend*
> *Doth close behind him tread . . .*

Was that right? Odd, how the absurd old lines could take on meaning in a dark, strange landscape like this. She tried to raise her spirits by remembering the *New Statesman* competition to imagine misprints in well-known poems:

> Because he fears a frightful *friend*
> Doth close behind him tread.

She smiled, not out of inclination but on principle, forcing the corners of her mouth upward and outward. She kept on walking, and after a mile saw opening to the left a smaller road which she remembered from the map. It had high banks and trees either side, and looked even more ominous than the main road. "I am a townie", said Alice fiercely to herself. "I am a tremulous pathetic townie. There is nothing wrong with a country lane." All the same, she would have felt happier among the addicts and the cardboard box beggars in Camden High Street.

Not five miles away, Violet and the Colonel finished the washing-up and discussed Rowley.

"Why does he travel on his own?" asked Geoffrey. "You always said he was from a big gypsy family."

"Even gypsies," said Violet serenely, "get irritated by thoroughly unreliable people. It's quite hard work being one, you know. Rowleys are a liability, just as they would be in a school, or a regiment. Anyway, he doesn't want to. Even gypsies can want to get away from their families."

"D'you think he makes a living? Enough to eat, warm clothes and all that?"

"Yes and no. He gets a fair rate from people like the Baileys but he doesn't spend it on food and clothes. Just drink and a bit of petrol. He's actually better off not being given much money at all. Just food and clothes and the odd bottle of dandelion wine. That's what I do." She slid the last plate into the rack and threw a sly, sidelong glance at the old man. "Except that my clothes aren't much good to him. He needs a nice widow woman to call on. Or, you know, 'off she went to her grandfather's chest, and brought him a coat of the very very best . . .'"

The Colonel sighed. "Hint taken. Shall I give him the loden coat with the half-belt at the back?"

"Dear Geoffrey," said Violet, moving into the sitting room and lowering herself into a chair. "A double blessing. To have you not looking like an Austrian psychiatrist, and Rowley kept warm this winter."

"So *he* won't look like an Austrian psychiatrist, I suppose? That hair's right for it," said the Colonel.

"Mm. But not the beard. That's more Australian than Austrian. Geoffrey, since I've mentioned it, would you like some dandelion wine right now? I would. Since you're on your feet, corner cupboard."

Daniel woke sharply from the sleep which had succeeded his long miserable reverie. Eight o'clock! Had Alice rung, was there news? He stumbled out of his room on to the fluffy synthetic pile of the corridor carpet and stared wildly up and down past the oak-effect candelabra lights on the wall. Turning, he saw the scalloped note fixed to his door.

Mrs McDonald rang to say not to worry she is on the trail

He snatched it, stared at it, looked around again helplessly, then kicked on his shoes and set off again for the telephone box and a fruitless encounter with his own answerphone voice, recorded in very much happier days. Afterwards, he stood poised with his green phonecard, wondering who else to ring. But then, quite suddenly, the heart went out of him and he walked back to the only shelter, bar his car, to which he still had any rights. The potpourri was waiting for him.

24

Walking rapidly with her head down, Alice turned off the first lane into the second one, which seemed to run across more open country. After a mile or so of silent, thoughtful trudging she saw yet another lane leading off it, and knelt on the grass again to flare the cigarette lighter at the spread map. The flame guttered, and her eyes took time to accustom themselves; but it fitted, all right. Standing up, her knees unpleasantly damp even through the long coat, she knew herself to be on the way to the crossroads she needed. As she walked on, it began to snow. Not crisp flakes, but wet hateful sleet which blew into her face in sharp cold prickles and found its way inside the collar of her coat. She blessed its unfashionable length and weight and walked faster, her head down.

At last the shapes of distant farm buildings formed against the night and a pale glimmer of light appeared. A telephone box. It was an old-fashioned red one with bars, obviously saved by some strict preservation society, and it stood on an unmistakable crossroads. Alice supposed that when it was first put there the telephone must have served several scattered dwellings, and that the Post Office of those days avoided conflict by cannily putting it nowhere near any one of them. But it was, it must be, Jamie's box.

She pulled open the heavy door and thankfully stepped inside out of the cold wind and the sleet. Nine o'clock. Not too late to ring Violet Lancing but, she thought with sudden dismay, Violet had no car. She used some local taxi all the time. Nor did she have Violet's number. Or any small change. And there was no book in the kiosk. Stupidly, she picked up the receiver anyway and heard only a thin dispirited wail. The box might have worked last night, but didn't now.

Alice began to feel panic rising. The question of Jamie, she now saw, would have to wait until morning. She could not stumble around in the darkness knocking at strange, threatening farmsteads, being barked at by collie dogs, getting into God knows what difficulties and maybe even risking Jamie. The delay was pain enough. A shudder went through her at the thought of another night, a third night, with her son under no known protection. The foul breath of all the old fears rose around her, whispering of Jamie dying in a ditch, Jamie captive, Jamie tortured, Jamie waiting for her in vain. Then Stevie's voice came back, light and affected and wise: "He's having an adventure. We boys, we have adventures." Yes. Hold on to that.

Meanwhile, it was snowing wetly outside, and inside the kiosk it was dry and light, if not particularly warm. Alice hesitated, then bent her knees and slithered down until she sat on the concrete floor – mercifully not smelly as a London one would have been, but only coldly fusty – and wriggled her back against the panes, trying to avoid the sharp edges of the red bars. As she slid with surprising rapidity into sleep, the thought briefly tormented her that Jamie's feet in their grubby trainers had stood here only a day earlier, while he said *I couldn't bear it*. If – when! – she found him, she must make it a gentle encounter and not a hysterical maternal grab. It was her last thought before oblivion took her.

Rowley, remarkably, did not drink that night. He sat in his small caravan whittling idly at a piece of softwood by the light of a paraffin lantern. What he made was the small sharp-featured head and torso of a man. When he had finished he laid it aside, picked up some smaller pieces and began, with a few absent-minded strokes, to shape them into arms and hands, legs and feet, each in two sections. At last he laid the puppet out on the red-and-yellow painted dresser, narrowed his eyes to judge the proportions, and decided that the legs were too short. Never mind. He would adjust that in the painting. Paint it right, and anybody would believe it was right. He would give the puppet to Miss Lancing for her godchildren, with a rod in its back and a springy plank to make it dance. Finish it down at Bailey's.

He yawned, kicked off his boots and stretched on the bunk. Full of food, tired from the long day's towing of his 'van along the winding winter lanes, he closed his eyes. He would not sleep well without a drink but was too tired to get up and pull the bottle from under the bunk. Beneath the wagon, he could hear the yellow lurcher stirring and scratching in her sleep. "Night, Nadia," said Rowley.

At four o'clock he woke, his eyes snapping open. He knew that he would not sleep again. An evening without drink always affected him like this. Sometimes, he thought that the reason he drank so much was merely to woo sleep, which had eluded him all his life. Maybe if he had been able to sleep better he would have stayed with the family, travelled in company. Or maybe not. It suited him this way, though he would have liked his sister's boy Joby to travel with him, and paint alongside him. But she had left the family too. She had left off travelling, married the man with the house – a man whose name Rowley could never be bothered to remember. She was having Joby trained as a house painter. Make him as dull as she was.

He rolled off the bunk, pulled the clothes to one end, and stepped down from the wooden caravan on to the cold grass. "Tcha!" he said to the dog. It woke abruptly and trotted after him to the hedge, where they both urinated companionably. Rowley yawned, ambling back on his big knotted bare feet to the caravan and the old car that pulled it. He pulled on his boots and outer clothes, and set off again up the field towards Miss Lancing's hedge. Might as well do those tiles.

Violet Lancing lay awake, the World Service chuntering gently from the portable radio at her side. She heard Rowley at work, hammering back the tiles on the woodshed, but did not move. Life, she thought, was far more interesting when you were old than people thought. Passionate girlhood had been tiring, full of titanic struggles with conscience. Middle life, with its long hours of work and responsibility, passed too quickly to be savoured or reflected upon. Nor had she enjoyed the single woman's enforced stance of respectful humility towards the married, the status of spinster aunt or godmother. She had worn it gracefully enough, and enjoyed the children, but to be free of that visible stigma was nothing but a blessing. Only now, as an old woman, could she rest and act according to her own rhythms and desires, and speak her mind as she fancied. The difference between her and the married women had all but gone; even when they were not widowed, their children seemed to have scattered and lost interest in them, leaving them oddly more forlorn than she was. Violet had vigour, she had intelligence, she had the godchildren and their children coming to her out of choice not duty. She was used to solitude, but had Geoffrey, the best friend there could be and the only true sharer of her private history. She had passing friends, relics of her teaching days when she knew all the village secrets – friends like Rowley. The social worker, she reflected, would not be very pleased at the idea of an unkempt gypsy erratically mending her woodshed roof at five in the morning in the pitch dark. She would write it down as an Indicator of Increased Risk. Violet smiled to herself in the darkness.

When Rowley had finished, he loped back to the Pea Field and his caravan, and decided that it was almost light enough to drive. He could get breakfast at Ed Bailey's. Surprise them by being early.

That he was actually five days late, it did not occur to him to acknowledge.

Alice woke at three, then four, then five, each time changing the angle of her knees and aching pelvis and shoulders. At six she knew that she must stretch out fully or die of misery and cramp. She pushed the door open and crawled out of the telephone box, to find the morning milder than the night before, and mercifully dry. Standing up, shaking out her black coat, she raised her arms over her head and let the groaning muscles contract and relax in their proper way. Never, never, never again. She should have rung the police. She lay flat for a while in a crucified position, then rolled upright and, kneeling, rubbed cold dew from the grass over her forehead and eyes. Then she pulled out an old scarf from the coat's voluminous pocket to dry her face on. There was a mirror in the kiosk, which showed her that she did not look as bad as she might have done. That, no doubt, was thanks to Yasmin's hairdresser with his promise of "zero maintenance for a busy lady, OK?"

She ran and skipped up and down to restore life to her limbs, then pulled out the picture of Jamie she had torn from the kitchen table collage. The hunt would begin. Seven o'clock was not too early. Not in the country. They got up early for cows and things. Briskly, Alice set out down the wrong arm of the crossroads, towards the chimney of a distant farmhouse.

Jamie slept late. It was eight o'clock before he opened his eyes, and curious sounds were coming from the direction of the gallopers. Kneeling on the bed, rubbing the mist off the caravan window, he saw that the canvas tilts were off the roundabout. For the first time he could see the whole of it, from gilded and jungled rounding boards to the red platform from which rose the twisted brass rods. The loose horses and paints had been cleared off it, presumably into the new shelter Ed had made with canvas stretched between the lorries and the barn. In the centre, amid the dazzling muddle of mirrors and medallions and top-hatted heroes, Tim was grappling with something in the engine. A puff of steam rose from the chimney pipe.

Jamie snatched his tracksuit and jacket, pulled them on, found his grimy socks under the pillow where he had kept them for dryness and pushed his feet into his still-laced trainers. Tim had got steam up and he had missed it! Tim had said that he might do it early, but this early! Jamie tumbled out and ran towards the gallopers, almost forgetting not to speak.

Tim looked down at him. "You slep' well, nipper," he said. "Go and have breakfast. Got an hour yet before she's ready to run."

"Hah," said Jamie in a relieved tone, and ran towards the cottage. There was a new vehicle outside, he saw; a square, not particularly ornate but cheerfully red-and-yellow wooden caravan that looked as if it ought to be pulled by a fat piebald horse. Instead, the shafts had been replaced by an old agricultural towing bracket which was fastened to the rear end of a very old Hillman Minx with one green door and three brown, on a blue body. The caravan was, Jamie noticed, quite newly painted and adorned with a few discreet curls and brackets, red on yellow.

The car in contrast was utterly uncared for, and had one headlight glass missing. It was as if someone acknowledged and respected the caravan but preferred not to admit ownership of the car. Maybe they didn't belong together. None of his business, anyway. Without knocking, a favoured son of the house, he pushed the kitchen door open and savoured the smell of bacon.

25

Half an hour earlier, as Susan was clattering the breakfast together, the sound of an unsilenced exhaust outside the window had caused her to stop, cock her head, and say to Ed, who sat reading *The World's Fair* magazine at the head of the table, "That's Rowley. Know that car anywhere, Ed."

"You could be right, girl." Ed stood up, stretched, and moved towards the door. Outside he could see Rowley's caravan and Minx.

"Travelling early, I see," he said in greeting. "Before the police get up, by the look o' that car."

"Too right, me dear," said Rowley, slamming its door so that flakes of rusty blue and brown fell in a little shower on the weed-cracked concrete of the farm drive. The yellow dog had come out with him and now slunk into its habitual place under the wagon. "Any breakfast?"

"Sure," said Ed. "Susan's frying for all of us. 'Cept Tim who don't eat anything but Cornflakes and he's out on the centre engine anyway."

"Good news, good news," said Rowley, coming in. "You git the engine going, I'll do the horses."

"Better late than never," said Susan tartly. "Wednesday, you said."

"Leave off, girl. He left the boy, and that's been dang useful."

"That's true," said Susan. "That's a grand boy for painting, Row. Bit o'luck, with the Cold Fair so soon."

Rowley stared at them. "I don't see," he said, "how that's to be called a bit of luck that my sister's Joby is a bloody old NVQ housepainter, and I'm left on my own with half a set to do up by December. I call that bloody *bad* luck."

"But you're not on your own," protested Ed, staring back. "The boy's here. Been here since Friday night when you left him sleeping in the gallopers. Done nearly two hosses, bloody well, too."

Rowley scratched his chin. Perhaps, after all, his blessed sister had seen sense. Or perhaps Joby had run off. Nah, wouldn't have the wit to find the Baileys, not out here in the middle of nowhere. Anyway, Joby wouldn't have done two horses. Rowley was fond of his slow-witted nephew but had no illusions about his ability to work without strict direction. Strict, as in "Now with the red paint, follow that line exactly like on the side I just did. Now clean your brush, boy, and take the yeller . . ." Running Joby was hard work. Joby was not the kind of boy you left sleeping in gallopers to get on with it.

At last he said, "That ain't my boy, whoever it is. You got a friendly ghost, or what? Gimme a cup o' tea, for God's sake."

"Oh Ed," said Susan suddenly. "I knew it wasn't right. I knew he was never fifteen. Whose *is* the boy? He must've run away."

"My dad ran away to join the fair," said Ed, dreamily. "Thirteen, he was. Ended up owning it."

"It was different then," said Susan, agonized. Ed seemed not to realize that one could not simply take possession of a stray boy because he happened to be useful. Not these days. There were school inspectors, social workers, police. Rowley, however, looked suitably thunderous.

"Whoever he is, meddling around pretending to be my sister's boy Joby, he'd better have a damn good reason."

"I don't think he ever pretended anything," said Susan slowly. "He just let us think . . ."

"Well, we had to think it," said Ed. "Nothing else to think. He did the job. Early Saturday morning, he practised on a bit of old step for a bit, then just started in. Bloody well. Nearly as good as you, Rowley. And drinks less."

"Whose *is* he?" said Susan again. At which moment, Jamie pushed open the door and, still exhilarated from the sight of

Tim's wisps of steam, walked in grinning broadly and trustingly at the whole company.

"Boy," said Ed, taking control. "This here is Rowley. We thought you was Rowley's boy."

Jamie's face paled, and he took a step towards the ragged bearded figure. Rowley jumped back like a scalded cat.

"Not a step, boy! Not a step!" he cackled. "I don't know you, I've not seen you. And don't you go telling your Gorgio parents that the gippos stole you, because we didn't and we never did and we wun't want to."

"Oh, calm down, Rowley," said Susan wearily. "Nobody's saying you stole him. Don't be so *paranoid*. It's out o' date." And to the boy: "What is your name? You can talk, I bet you can."

"Jack," said Jamie promptly. It was what he wished school-friends would call him, less babyish than Jamie. But they always called him Jamie because Clemmie always had at school. "I'm Jack."

"What you doing here?" said Ed.

And Rowley simultaneously, "Who taught you to do my job?"

Susan quelled them both with a look and asked more gently, "Who do you belong to? Where do you live?"

"Nowhere," said Jamie, or Jack, stoutly. "I live on my own. I do painting for people and they give me food. I'm nearly sixteen. Actually."

The adults exchanged glances. His piping, well-spoken middle-class tones told them much of what they needed but feared to know. But Susan intervened before Ed could carry on.

"Come on, Jack boy," she said gently. "Have your breakfast, then tell us."

Grateful for an opportunity to invent a more satisfactory background for himself, Jamie sat down and began to eat his breakfast.

The Colonel arrived just after Violet's breakfast, carrying a dark-green loden cloth coat over his arm.

"What ho on the Rialto," he said as usual. "Rowley not up yet? Drunk, I suppose."

"Wrong," said Violet. "He was up at five, mended the roof, left one of his bits of woven grass on the knocker – I think it means blessings, or thanks or adieu or something – and he's gone. To work, I should think, down at Bailey's."

"It's a bit bloody hard," said the Colonel, "when you can't even rely on Rowley to be drunk and unreliable. I'd better take it down there, since you say the deed must be done."

"I'll come with you," said Violet. "We'll book Charlie for ten o'clock. I like Susan Bailey. Sensible girl. Very efficient blackboard monitor, I remember."

When Jamie and Rowley had both finished eating, Jamie maintaining a cautious silence, Susan said, "Tell you what, anyway, Rowley. You go out there with the boy, have a look at the work he's done."

"All right," said Rowley, a little sulkily. "C'mon, boy."

"I'm Jack," said Jamie, suddenly a little defiant.

"C'mon, Jack," said Rowley, and stumped out of the cottage. "Is my 'van all right out there?"

"No," said Susan. "That's right in my way." She was smiling.

"Oh, well, then," said Rowley, also with a lurking smile. Jamie looked from one to the other, detecting some old joke between them. He felt suddenly comfortable among these strange adults. He also knew, with strong unwonted confidence, that Rowley would change towards him when he saw his work. It was good work.

Tim was still fiddling with the engine and organ in the centre of the steaming roundabout when they arrived. Jamie addressed Rowley directly.

"The horses that still need painting are under the big tilt now, by the barn, behind the lorry. But the one I did first is the ginger one, and Tim's put it back on its pole."

"Not ginger," said Rowley irritably. "Bay."

"Here," said Jamie, who was up on the platform, standing beside his horse. "Here it is. *Nancy.* Susan told me what name to put on the neck scroll. It was her mother's name."

Rowley stood, silent, looking at the horse. He dropped to his knees and looked underneath its chest, closely, at the breastplate and the leaves around it. He laid his hand on the flowing carved gold mane.

"Susan showed me," said Jamie, "how you have to put the silver layer on first, before it takes the gold. But I wouldn't have messed about with the gold without asking."

"Thass not real gold," said Rowley. "Real gold leaf I only use up there," he pointed to the crowns on the rounding board, "where bloody old public can't get at it."

A silence fell. Rowley looked at the horse again and Jamie, relaxed, looked with him. At last Rowley turned back to the boy and said, "Who taught you that?"

"Nobody," said Jamie. "I copied. And I put a few bits in of my own. Like the tassels."

The horse's painted numnah, beneath the painted saddle, had yellow tassels at its four corners, and they were not painted hanging flat and stylized but alive, as if tossed by the horse's motion, flying back.

"Where'd you get the idea of the tassels?"

"Off a fabric sample, called Arabian Nights, that my friend Simon gave me. I used to practise them at . . ." a shadow crossed his face, "at school. In art. I did a whole page of red and gold tassels. Mrs Davis said I was wasting time."

"Mrs Davis," said Rowley, "sounds a right old cow."

"Yes," said Jamie. The two of them looked again, then Jamie pointed to another horse, dark brown with sumptuous trappings, rolled-back eyes on bright blueish whites, and a coat of arms on its breast.

"That's my favourite of the other horses. Figaro."

"That's the best of them," agreed Rowley complacently.

"Did it matter that I borrowed the tassels from the Arabian thing?" said Jamie. "Only, Susan said the decorations were all traditional. Victorian, she said."

"The tradition, Jack," said Rowley, "the tradition is to borrow anything you like, from anywhere you like. Look there, the ropework on the top of the pillars. That's borrowed off the Navy."

He moved round, pointing high and low. "That there's Roman, with the square edges. That's Romany – old circus, old fairground, caravan painting. That over there, that's French, off a foot of an old chair my grandad saw when he was working for John Anderson in Bristol. That there, that's sailor knots again. That's Boy-zantine, we used to call it, that's what they call rock-ocko. Up there, that's medieval. This here is Scottish tartan."

"I did a tartan rug on my other horse, the one that's not quite finished," said Jamie. "I did red, orange, yellow. Because it has those colours in the flower on its chest."

"Quite right," said Rowley. "You don't put too many colours on one hoss."

There was a silence. Jamie hesitated, then said, "Did I do it all right?"

Rowley looked at him. "Better 'n all right. Better 'n Joby by a million miles."

A few minutes later Tim, who had finished whatever he was doing to the engine, gave one of its brass faces a quick triumphant polish with the duster and shouted across to the pair deep in conversation over a horse; "Hold on, then. I'm goin' to test the cranks."

Rowley put his hand on a post, and Jamie climbed on the Figaro horse. Tim eased a lever down and, slowly at first, the roundabout began to move. Tim was looking up, watching the overhead cranks moving up and down with the horse poles under them. Figaro began slowly to buck and gallop, and Jamie sat on its back, laughing. The roundabout gathered speed, with Tim still fixing his eyes on the cranks, his smile gradually widening.

"I guess that's got it," he said over the hissing of the engine. "Come on, boy. Music to celebrate. Test the Gavioli."

Jamie dismounted and came over to Tim's side, on the still centre of the platform. The horses, the empty poles, and Rowley continued to revolve round him. There was a wooden box beside the organ, with several stacked zigzags of punched paper in it.

"Choose," said Tim. Jamie looked at the cover sheets of the music. Each one listed its tune in small, crabbed print. "Me and My Gal," "You Are My Sunshine," "Daisy Daisy". He laid it aside. "Favourite Hymns for Fairground Service: Abide with Me . . ." He turned another. "Great Tunes from Grand Opera." He thought for a moment of his mother, that distant insubstantial figure from the past, and handed the opera sheets to Tim. Tim fiddled for a moment, feeding it carefully over a brass drum with raised brass pimples. Jamie, close to the warmth of the engine, watched carefully how he did it.

26

Daniel left Mrs Hammond's early, just after seven, and drove down to the university. He had showered, washed his hair with savage thoroughness, put on clean clothes and, while shaving, given the reflected Daniel in the mirror a stern talking-to. He was no longer going to lie supine on a candlewick bedspread off the Norwich ring road, indulging in lachrymose remorse and shirking his responsibilities as a man and the head of a family. He was going to London, to support – or perhaps confront – Alice. He was going to talk personally to the police officers investigating his son's disappearance. He was ready to take control.

Going into his cubbyhole of an office, he pulled out his pad and wrote a brief note to the head of his department, posting it under her door as he left. Then he drove back to the ring road and made for the Newmarket and M11 route south. A motorway, this morning, would suit his mood.

Until that morning's walk through narrow, pointlessly winding lanes, Alice would never have believed that houses could be placed so far apart. What were they thinking of, these old rural people who lived in such places before the motorcar? From the first farm cottage (where they stared at her in perplexity and shook their heads over her photograph) to the next one along that lane (where much the same thing happened) it was fully three-quarters of a mile. Then she had to walk back, footsore and hungry, past the first one again (where the curtains twitched) in order to take the second arm of the crossroads towards two more dwellings. One was empty, a holiday house by the look of its untidy garden and expensively cottagey furnishings. She crept around, peering through the windows, but there was no sign of recent occupation amid the pastel pine and rustic rocking chairs. A sense of the futility of her mission began to crush her spirit. At the next house, half a mile on, they had seen no strange boy at all. But if they had, would they tell her? The inhabitants were old and fearful and genteelly aggressive, and the door was liberally plastered with police warning stickers and kept on the chain while she spoke. Probably, thought Alice gloomily, they thought she was an antique dealer come to con their valuables out of them.

At last, she was back at the telephone box. With diminishing hope and a sob rising in her breast, Alice set out to walk the third arm of the crossroads. The huddle of farm buildings she had noticed the night before did, presumably, include some kind of dwelling. She had no knowledge of farming and its machinery, and was afflicted as she drew closer by a townie's sense of affront at the apparent muddle and asymmetry of the buildings, the wide muddy alleyways between them, the haphazard way that tin, wood or tarred canvas patches were roughly hammered on here and there.

As she drew closer to the chaotic jumble of red brick and weatherboarding, pantiles and rusty corrugated iron and vehicles with big tyres, she could certainly see smoke rising. Very white smoke, and a good deal of it, which was odd. There was a smell on the air too, one she could not quite catch but associated with long-distant holidays.

Still, the smoke meant that somebody was there. Alice walked on, more eagerly, using her scarf again to scrub the tears out of her eyes and polish her glasses. Abruptly, unbidden, an old prayer rose in her mind and its music rose with it: she had been brought up in a limp apathetic agnosticism, and religion only ever touched her through art. *Ave Maria, gratia plena, dominus tecum*, her mind murmured. It was Desdemona's last prayer from *Othello*. The words ran out on her after *tecum*, but she let the tune continue in her mind, steadying her as she walked. Again and again, *Ave Maria, gratia plena* . . .

It changed. The tune changed. The rising tone that ended the Ave suddenly speeded up, bounced into a rhythm, and the tune began to change as she hummed it into another, brighter Verdi aria. It blasphemously became *Libiamo! Libiamo!* the opening of Alfredo's drinking song from *La Traviata*. Nor was she only humming it. She was hearing it. Alice stopped, stood stock-still, incredulous. Music was rising from beyond the nearest farm shack, wheezy and joyful, Verdi on a showman's organ. They used to play his airs on a barrel organ, she thought wildly, in the streets of Milan during his lifetime, when he was as popular as Lloyd-Webber today. She listened, then walked on rapidly towards the sound.

Not a barrel organ. Fuller, prouder than that: a fairground organ. Almost running, like a child who follows a brass band down the street, she rounded the shack and saw a Victorian roundabout, strangely short of horses, whirling round. Its few gallopers plunged and reared, their ever-open mouths baring white teeth, their colours shocking against the grey tones of a November farmstead. Steam – of course it was too white to be ordinary smoke – rose from a chimney at its centre, where a tall, dark youth with long coal-black sideburns stood by the engine. Whirling round the outer ring, one arm on a golden twisted pole and the other spread outward, his black coat flapping, was a ragged, trampish figure of a man. And on a dark-brown and resplendent horse labelled *Figaro* rode a boy whose tracksuit trousers, whose trodden-down trainers, whose puffy anorak and dark flopping hair she recognized.

Her cry was not heard over the puffing, tuneful, joyful racket as she stumbled towards it, terrified of hallucination, convinced in her thudding heart that it would vanish. She tripped, fell to her hands and knees, and knew she could not get up again and face the unreality of this joy. She threw off her glasses, and buried her face in her hands.

Tim pulled the lever, stopped and slowed the roundabout. Rowley embraced his pole and yelled at him.

"What you doin', boy? Git to the end of the tune!"

Jamie sat on his horse, grinning at the old man's indignation.

Tim stolidly watched the roundabout stop, blew off some steam, and said, "I reckon we got a visitor."

Looking down, Jamie saw a woman kneeling on the ground,

her head in her hands. Scrambling down, he ran to her, and picked up the discarded glasses.

"Mum?"

Alice raised her head. The child before her could not be a hallucination. He was too dirty for that: dust in his hair, streaks of paint on his clothes, oil from the engine still coating his hands (although Susan had, to do her justice, made him wash them in the stone sink before every meal).

"Jamie?"

"Mum, are you all right?"

"Jamie," she said again, kneeling up, taking the glasses with an unsteady hand. "You are absolutely filthy." And she burst into a passion of tears, clutching her oily child to her, her head on his chest.

Rowley looked at Tim but only said, "I thought his name weren't Jack."

And Tim, whom nobody had yet bothered to tell about the morning's revelation in the cottage kitchen, just said, "That your sister, then? Sure you remembered to tell her you were taking the boy? She looks upset, to me."

"I – did – not – take – him!" shouted Rowley. And Alice looked up, bewildered and suspicious, at the raffish red-eyed figure on the roundabout step. Up on the engine behind him, Tim was looking at something over near the lane.

"Reckon we got more company," he drawled. This was one of the most enjoyable mornings he had had all autumn. The cranks were working fine, the engine ready, the organ was tested, Rowley and his boy assistant were here and ready to get the horses done. The Cold Fair project, which had filled his cautious engineer's mind with dismay, began to look both likely and lucrative. And now here was his mum's old teacher and her army boyfriend come to join the fun.

"Ahoy, Rowley!" said the Colonel, striding towards him with as much bonhomie as he could muster, to please Violet. "You missed your breakfast! I meant to say, I've got a coat that might fit you, since you've – er – kept your figure better than I have."

It was a bold attempt at tact, but Rowley was too well accustomed to accepting other people's clothes to need such niceties. He glanced at the green coat on the Colonel's arm.

"Let's try," he said, and slipped off his black coat, hanging it on a horse. He whisked the dark-green cloth round him and shrugged experimentally. "Well, I thank you. That fits perfect." He thrust his arms into the pockets, which were satisfyingly deep, bottle-deep, as he privately put it. "Tim," he said, picking up the black coat and tossing it towards the centre. "You can stuff this in that boiler o' yours."

"I wouldn't risk my boiler," said Tim repressively. "Nasty old fluff."

Alice had by now let go of Jamie, stood up, and put her glasses back on. Despite this, nothing around her seemed to make sense except for the blessed, dirty presence of her son.

"Good morning, Alice," said Violet, formally. "What a lovely surprise. So this is where Jamie was all the time? Or are you just visiting Ed and Susan?"

"I don't know," said Alice. "Jamie, how did you . . . how did you . . ."

"I said," shouted Jamie suddenly, "to leave me alone!" And he turned and ran stumbling towards the little caravan, tears carving through the dust and soot on his face. Alice made as if to follow him, but Violet caught her arm in a surprisingly strong grip.

"I wouldn't, yet," she said.

"But he might run away again!" said Alice, pulling desperately.

"Geoffrey," said Violet. "Go and guard that caravan." And to Alice she comfortably observed, "He'll be safe enough. Geoffrey used to guard all sorts of things. Explosives, top secret formulae. He can guard a boy of twelve. I think we need to talk to Tim and Rowley."

"Nothing to do with me," said Rowley, whose ragged beard above the collar of the smart Germanic overcoat did, uncannily, give him the air of an Viennese psychiatrist in a pre-war film. The Colonel, walking obediently to the caravan, reflected that Violet had always been right about the character of that coat. It really was not a British sort of cut. Too reminiscent of some assembly of Freudians in a Continental grand hotel in the late 'thirties.

Rowley, unaware of the associations that hung around his newly wrapped form, spoiled the effect slightly by spitting. He repeated, looking at Violet rather than Alice, "The boy's nothing at all to do with me. I only just come. Ask Ed and Susan. They've had him working here all weekend. I got work to do right now."

"Very well," said Violet. "Come on, Alice."

With a last look at the caravan, Alice unwillingly let Violet draw her towards the cottage. The old woman kept talking.

"I think, you see, that we ought to find out where we are exactly, before we go in any new direction. Olivia always says that's the rule in the bush, when they get lost on the way back from one of the villages. Do all you can to find out where you are, and you're less likely to stumble off into a crocodile pool."

Alice walked alongside her, head whirling, hardly listening.

"You mustn't worry too much," said Violet. "Susan Bailey was in my Juniors years ago, and she married Ed Bailey, and they took over this very small steam fair, and really, they've made a tremendous thing of it considering they started from nothing but the machinery. Ed's father died of drink, and Susan's ran off somewhere with another fair, but this generation really are hard-working, very respectable, excellent people. You never hear a thing wrong about them and believe me, that's rare enough in this part of the world, especially in winter when we've not much else to do but moral evaluations of our neighbours. And there's no harm in Rowley, I can vouch for that. He acts as a sort of roving handyman and painter. His family were gypsies, but he split off on his own. I've known him for forty-nine years, since he was six, so he isn't nearly as old or eccentric as he pretends."

"Jamie," began Alice. But Violet, for some reason of her own, was determined not to let her spill out her terrors before she was in the farm kitchen and could see the Baileys.

"I'm not a silly old woman, you know, I know about the harm that comes to children. But I don't believe it will have come to Jamie. Not here. Not if he's been here since the beginning, and it sounds as if he has."

Alice was aware that Violet was trying to soothe her, and despite a spurt of irritation, she did feel soothed. Talk of junior schools and respectability and handymen and gossipy winters round cottage fires was just what she needed. It took her into a Miss Marple world, and she felt happy to spend at least a while amid such archaic rural certainties. Her dreams had been too much haunted by the idea of a terrified child in some bleak motorway lorrypark, his small face colourless under the sodium lights.

Also, she trusted the Colonel to ensure that Jamie did not run for it. She followed Violet into the cottage, noticing that there seemed to be no convention at all about knocking.

The interior was bare and, to Alice's eye, comfortless. A smoky coke range in the corner held a blackened frying pan, and the stone sink was full of dirty breakfast dishes.

"Susan!" the old lady was saying warmly. "Ed! We have a mystery here, and we think you can solve it. That boy—"

"Oh, Miss Lancing!" cried Susan, as relieved as Alice to be drawn into Miss Marple country. "Oh, Miss Lancing, we only found out this morning that he warn't what we all thought he were! Is he a runaway, or what?"

"Y-yes," said Violet. "Or yes, maybe. This lady is my godson's wife, Alice McDonald. She is Jamie's mother."

"He said he was called Jack," said Ed, stroking his black beard nervously. "But to tell you the truth, till this morning he didn't say one word. We thought he was Rowley's sister's boy, who's a bit weak in the head, like."

"Not that he acts like a weak-in-the-head type," said Susan quickly. "It was just, I think, he didn't want us to guess he warn't Rowley's. And he talks that nicely," she added placatingly, "that we'd of guessed he weren't related to Rowley, no chance."

"When did he come?" asked Alice in a small, strained voice. "Who brought him? It's miles from Norwich, he was going to Norwich, he didn't even get that far—"

"We found him Sat'dy morning, he'd been asleep in the gallopers," said Ed. "By the time I got to him, he'd started work on the hosses. So I thought—"

"You thought he was Rowley's sister's boy, dumped on you. Quite understandable to think that," said Violet, and to Alice, "you see, Rowley might do something like that and not see anything odd about it. He's often slept rough himself since he was a boy. Once he wanted to stay on at school for an outing when his family moved on, and I found him hard asleep on the floor of the games hut. I don't think you can blame Ed and Susan. It's a very mobile world."

"Do you mean", asked Alice slowly, "that he's been painting – those horses?"

"Yeah," said Ed, eagerly. "Done two, really well. We were knocked out, thought he must a' done it all his life, come off some gypsy family, maybe," said Ed. "That's why we didn't suspect a thing. He's that good. We'll miss him a good deal, even now Rowley's here."

Alice was sitting at the table by now, her aching muscles relaxed, her elbows on the bare wood. Susan, through the conversation, had been making tea and now put a cup in front of her. Briefly, lightly, she laid a hand on Alice's shoulder, and leaning down while Ed and Violet continued talking, murmured, "He's taken no harm. He's eaten like a hoss, and slept warm, I saw to that, with the stove lit. And I've worked alongside him doing the base coats, and nobody laid a finger on him." Alice looked up, grateful for the words and the touch, and found herself putting her own hand on top of Susan's on her shoulder.

"Thank you. I've been so afraid."

"So would I have been. He's not fifteen, is he, nor anything like?"

"Twelve." Alice's eyes misted.

"I should ha' said something earlier, only Ed was so sure he was Rowley's, and he was doing so well, getting on with it, so keen . . ."

Alice drank her tea, thoughtfully. Then she stood up and said to Violet, "Could we have a word? A private word? Outside?"

"No need for that," said Susan. "C'mon, Ed." The two of them vanished, with alacrity, out of the back door.

27

Inside the cottage kitchen, Violet sat down opposite Alice, warming her hands on her mug of tea, and said, "Well?"

"When I came," said Alice slowly, "and I saw the roundabout, it was moving, and the organ was playing. Jamie was on a horse. I think it must have been one of the horses he painted."

She paused. Violet sat silent, listening.

"It might be just that I've walked a long way this morning, and last night," said Alice, "and I'm tired and I've been terrified for days. But when I saw him there, all filthy and happy, I saw his face for a moment before – before I couldn't see anything for a bit. And his face looked, he looked—" She broke off, uncertain, and sipped her cooling tea. "Well, I thought, when I saw him . . ."

Violet sat, waiting, as if for a small pupil to work out the answer to a schoolroom question.

"I thought," said Alice, "for a minute, that he's better off here than he has been for a long time. His face was – unclenched."

"Yes," said Violet, and sipped her tea. "Indeed."

"I know it's mad," said Alice, "but you saw how he ran off just now. It wasn't that he doesn't want me, that he isn't happy to see me, because he hugged and hugged me at first." She paused again. Violet went on waiting for the answer. "It's that he thinks I'll take him away from here, straightaway. Before he's done enough of this painting."

"Yes," said Violet again.

"I know it's mad," said Alice again. "And school would have to be dealt with, and all that. But you're not far off, are you? From here, I mean."

"No," said Violet.

"So could we stay with you for a few days? Even a week or two? Me and Jamie? So he could go on helping Mr Rowley?"

"Clementine is away at school, of course," observed Violet, noncommittally.

"Yes – that's it. I could stay."

"And your post at the Royal Opera House?"

"I was made redundant," said Alice. She did not think it the moment to face the matter of Euradio, of Yasmin, of Alan's expectations. "So you see . . ."

"Well," said Violet. "It all falls out well, does it not? As for schooling, might it not mollify the truant officer to know that I am a teacher?"

Alice stared for a moment. Old people were – old people. That Violet, seventeen years retired, might still consider herself a teacher in the present tense was extraordinary to Alice. But she saw the advantage of the situation.

"Yes! How silly of me! Oh, Violet, that would be perfect!"

"I think your solution to the immediate problem is a good one, Alice," said Violet. "Presumably Daniel—"

"Oh, never mind Daniel!" said Alice rather too quickly. "He'll have to put up with what I decide. I have the cust— I mean, I look after Jamie."

Violet looked at her, long and steadily, until Alice dropped her eyes. Then, briskly, the old woman got up and went to the door. "Ed! Susan!" she called. The two, who had been laughing together at the state of Rowley's bald rubber trailer tyres, trooped back into the kitchen.

"We have decided," said Violet, "that Jamie would be better off staying with me, and having the occasional *bath*, than he is living in the caravan. What time will you need him to start work in the mornings?"

Ed gaped. "You mean . . ."

"I do not suggest you pay him," said Violet. "There are legal difficulties about paying children who ought to be in school. You can feed him his dinner. Probably, knowing him, his breakfast too. And I am sure that a guarantee of unlimited rides would be an acceptable *quid pro quo* . . ."

It was agreed that Alice should go out to the caravan and tell him. She found Colonel Gordon not on guard and the door ajar, and briefly breathed too hard. But the Colonel was inside the caravan, seated on the bunk, in earnest conversation with Jamie.

". . . leg of an old French chair, Rowley said," Jamie was explaining. "If it looks right, it is right. He says it's like advertising, you have to make people want to ride. So you make the horse like a horse you'd dream of riding, really splendid, royal but wild, he said. You dream, and the punters will want the same dream. He said not to mind about Mrs Davis or any busybody old cow. He said that if you see something in your head and paint it as right as you can, all the people that matter will see that it *is* right."

Alice paused on the step. She had not heard such a long speech from Jamie in months. Certainly not since the beginning of the school year in September.

He could not see her, and continued: "And he said that if any people like Mrs Davis don't see that, they can go and stick their heads up a dead cow's bum!"

A gruff bark of laughter from the Colonel enabled Alice to break in, saying as gently as she could, "Jamie. Godgran and I have worked out something."

He turned towards her, his face closed again, impassive, stubborn. But he listened.

"We're going up to her house. It's only three or four miles. We'll stay there and you can come down every morning at eight thirty to start work on the horses, then come back at half past three when it's dark and do some lessons with her."

"Until it's finished? Until we've done all the horses?" said Jamie. "And touched up the rounding boards and shields?"

"Y–yes," said Alice. "It has to be finished by—"

"In time for the Cold Fair, December tenth," said Jamie. "Travel and build up on the ninth. Load up the day before."

"Right," said Alice, feeling suddenly excluded from some purposeful team. "Anyway, at least if we go to Godgran's you can have a bath. Charlie's coming back at eleven thirty, which is in ten minutes, so we can all go—"

Jamie looked at her in horror. "I can't leave while there's still enough light to work!" he said. "Rowley and I have got twenty more horses to do. I'll be starting on the black one after lunch!"

Alice was opening her mouth to protest, but the Colonel cleared his throat diffidently.

"Very willing to stay," he said. "Keep an eye on things, while you ladies sort out beds and whatever. Charlie can come back for us at four, maybe?"

"You could do some undercoating," said Jamie. He appeared to have struck up some kind of understanding with Colonel Gordon. "You'd manage that, wouldn't you?"

"Suppose so," said the Colonel. "A fairground horse can't be all that different from an armoured car, can it?"

"Did you used to paint armoured cars?"

"No," said Colonel Gordon. "But I used to tell other chaps to go and do it."

Violet and Alice got into Charlie's taxi together, Violet still having the air of somebody very carefully, soothingly, leading a nervous horse. As it moved off, she asked with studied casualness, "How did you get here? This morning, I mean?"

"Well, it was last night," said Alice. Then, "Oh my God, the car!"

Charlie braked sharply and looked round.

"No, sorry, my car," said Alice. "It's broken down, on the verge, not far from Fakenham or somewhere. I could show you on the map." For the map, crumpled and tear-stained, was still at the bottom of her deep coat pocket. She took it out, but it spoke so eloquently of the night's long miserable walk that she could hardly bear to look at it.

"Should Charlie collect your luggage, perhaps, and report it to a garage?" asked Violet.

"Um, there isn't any luggage. I left in a rush."

"Perhaps that's simpler. James might need some clothes, might he?"

Alice felt that Violet was perhaps trying too hard to pretend that she, Alice, was and always had been in full and thoughtful control of this situation.

"Yes, of course he will. I haven't thought of anything, or made any plans, I just so wanted to know he was safe—"

Violet held up a hand. "I know. Very understandable. Suppose Charlie takes him and Geoffrey into town this afternoon, to

Hobblers. They'll sell him some jeans and a sweater and some underwear." Alice nodded assent, and groped in her bag for some notes.

"And until your car is mended," continued Violet, "Charlie will have to bring him down each morning at eight thirty and fetch him at four. Charlie?"

The big man in front nodded.

"Good, you've got all that. Well, I think we're all arranged. You, Alice, while your clothes are washed will have to wear some of my old gardening trousers and perhaps a jersey of Geoffrey's. But I doubt we shall be going out much. For a week or so."

Charlie drove on, wonderingly. That was the best thing about the taxi business in a place like Wetheringham. You got a ringside seat. The show, however, appeared to be over. The two women rode the last miles to Moss Cottage in silence, Alice looking out of the window in a sleepy daze, and Violet with a superhuman effort holding herself back, in front of Charlie, from again raising the subject of Daniel.

The M11 motorway did suit Daniel's mood. It was quiet, and fast, and purposeful, and as he sliced past the M25 interchange he felt almost cheerful. He convinced himself, overtaking a row of slow lorries, that with resolution and efficiency the solution to the past weeks' problems and the past days' fright would soon be found.

As the motorway ended, however, and he crawled in a queue of choking traffic through the rundown north-east London suburbs, a darker consciousness descended. Suppose Alice was not home? Suppose her "trail" had led her elsewhere? Suppose she was there but still as bleakly cold towards him as before? Depression gripped him, mirrored by the helpless slowness of his crawl through grubby fluorescent cones and hopeless-looking roadworks and urban dereliction. It was no good. None of it was any good. The family was over, finished, fragmented, and he had done it.

In her bare and airy office high above Portland Place, Yasmin tried and failed to concentrate on the first quarterly financial predictions for the Euradio consortium. Where the hell was Alice? Who was this soft-spoken young woman who had telephoned her the preceding afternoon, against a background of what sounded like somebody singing "Kum-ba-ya" to a guitar, and softly announced that "a family crisis" precluded Alice's coming in to work on her very first vital day?

She and Alan were both, although now from separate directions, in the habit of coming to work early. At seven forty-five she had arrived, hung up her jacket, and gone to his office to tell him. Alan had not been pleased.

"Look, Yazza, 'family crisis' is not quite enough," he drawled. "You told me she was reliable, kids grown up, past all that stuff about getting home for bathtime and missing work because the nursery nurse got mumps. You said," he pointed accusingly at Yazz, "that she was red-hot, raring to go, on the case."

"She is. She will be. It must be a bad crisis to keep her away today. She was really keen. I don't understand it." Yazz detested being forced on to the defensive with Alan.

"Well, I don't *want* to waste time understanding it. I want her here, tomorrow, at eight thirty. Otherwise what does it look like to the others on her level? It's a small team, you know that. We're supposed to be running pilots from the end of this week, and she's not even properly trained on the new equipment."

"She'll pick it up bloody fast. I tell you, Alan, she's going to be good."

Alan began fiddling with the picture frame on his desk. "Caroline," he said dreamily, "has made a career plan to work part-time from home once the baby comes. Fairer on everyone. Working mothers . . ." Yazz stifled her fury at the way he liked to mention his new wife to her as often as possible. He clacked the plastic picture frame down on the desk with an air of finality, and resumed his harsher tone. "Family-fucking-crisis. Dear oh dear, Yazz, you'll be putting Personnel online to the local Brownie pack next."

Yasmin retreated angrily to her own office and rang Alice's number. The answering machine bleeped politely and Yazz just said, "It's Yazz. Ring work, Allie. Or there soon won't be any."

Daniel heard the telephone ring and stop as he fumbled with his key. There were no newspapers stuck in the door and no milk on the step, so he took it that Alice was, at least, home. He pushed the door open, and the smell of home met him with a rush of memory which stopped him like a physical blow. Oh Clemmie, Jamie! Oh, the family jokes, the suppers, the amiable bickering, the kitchen muddle and the drifts of Alice's mouse-nibbled velvet clothes across the bedroom! Oh, the plans, the giggling resolutions to do silly things, to spend the poll-tax money on a sleeper to Venice! Oh, the memories! Reeling a little, he stepped inside and closed his front door, tenderly, behind him.

In the kitchen someone moved. Daniel whirled round and his mouth opened in shock. Standing by the kitchen table was a clergyman, young and mild-faced in a black top and white dog collar. For a flicker he panicked, thinking of Jamie and someone come to break terrible news.

But it could not be that, he illogically thought, because the woman beside the vicar was not Alice but someone else dark, with shorter hair. A thin, pale, crop-haired girl in a baggy oversized Jesus Saves T-shirt. And she was not crying or even sitting down, but prosaically holding a tin of cat food and a fork. The tortoiseshell cat mewed and rubbed at her leg in a passion of impatience. There did not seem to be bad news in the air. But:

"Daniel!" said the girl in a shocked voice, and he realized who she was.

28

It was, Daniel later privately told Dave in the Goat and Boots, the most excruciating few minutes of his life. Unforgivable of Alice to put him through it. He was thrown by everything, he confided, even the damn clothes. Here was this new, scrubbed, crop-haired Lisha, unrecognizable as her old slinky Lycra-clad self; no longer the flasher of navel and tosser of hair who had so tormented his last academic year in London. This Lisha, standing before him in his own messy kitchen beside the wrecked tabletop collage of his family life, preparing to feed his cat, was another creature. She smiled at him, an eerily holy smile, forgiving yet apologetic. Next to her, the dog-collared parson smiled too, placatingly.

He stood there feeling foolish, saying, "Lisha? What the hell?" while she bent and forked the foul-smelling meat and jelly into the cat's dish. He went on standing there while she took the fork to the sink and washed it with earnest thoroughness. She then put the empty tin into a carrier bag she pulled from her jeans pocket.

"I didn't want to leave it in the bin to smell," she explained. And these were the first words she had spoken to him since before the abortion.

Daniel had never been the one who spoke first in awkward emotional situations. Coupled with Alice, he had never had much need to, for she would weigh in with a rush of exclamatory goodwill and defuse most problems that way. So he just shook his head a little, as if to clear it, and continued staring at the pair of them. Lisha glanced at the vicar and said, "Chris? Should I explain a bit?"

"This is Mr McDonald?" said the parson. He was, Daniel saw,

not as young as all that: a pasty-faced, amiable-looking man in his thirties. "If so, I think you should. This is his home."

"Well, how kind," said Daniel sarcastically, recovering his self-possession now that the man had spoken. An unknown male interloper, somehow, was easier to deal with than a transfigured ex-mistress. He addressed his remarks to the vicar. "Yes, do tell me what the hell you are doing in my house."

"Feeding the cat," said Lisha, and beneath the veneer of evangelical blandness she, too, seemed to be recovering something of her old dangerous spirit. But she glanced sideways at the clergyman, and almost imperceptibly he shook his head. Her face wiped to meekness, she turned and smiled gently again at Daniel, speaking the soft word that turneth away wrath.

"Mrs McDonald asked me to feed the cat, as a favour. And to do the milk and papers, in case of burglars. While she's away. I was glad to help. I owe it to her."

"You mean you came here to see Alice?" began Daniel, and this time the clergyman spoke, with firm authority.

"Yes," he said. "I had better explain. In our Mission, which Alicia has joined as a hostel member, we believe that the Jesus Movement involves taking personal responsibility for the outcome of our transgressions. We believe that sin must be not only repented and put aside, but atoned for. We have several young people who were formerly involved with drugs and now work with the victims of those drugs. Similarly with theft. In cases of adultery or fornication, it is obviously harder – "

Daniel was speechless again, but opened and shut his mouth a few times.

"– but," the man continued, "in this case Alicia very courageously offered a personal atonement to Mrs McDonald, who as it happens has a number of difficult crises to deal with at the moment, as you may know. And Mrs McDonald has been given the grace to accept this penance in our Lord's name. So Alicia will be coming here as long as it is needed, to feed the cat. Strange and wonderful," he added piously, "are His ways."

"What about me?" said Daniel. "Do I get any say?"

"If you're home now," said Lisha meekly, "obviously, there isn't any need to feed the cat. Are you home?"

"Yes – no, of course not – for God's sake, I work in Norwich!"

said Daniel. "But I am home right now, so if you wouldn't mind, Father, I really . . ."

He still could not bring himself to speak directly to this new Lisha. Shame, rage and embarrassment rendered him incompetent to deal with any of it. Silently, he opened the front door for them, and they went out into the early dusk, Lisha carrying the bag with the cat food tin.

"I'll come and feed him tomorrow, shall I?" she said.

Daniel muttered, "Yes," and shut the door before they could bless him.

He walked numbly back into the kitchen, and sat for a while watching the cat finish the last of its food and then sit, licking its fluffy white paws and attending to its ears as if nothing was wrong with the world at all. He remembered Jamie as a toddler, sitting next to the cat, earnestly copying its movements, licking his hands and pretending to wash behind his ears.

Eventually, he went to the hall, listened to the messages – a cryptic snappish one from Yasmin and something ineffably dull from Jenny about borrowing hamster cages. Then he rang the police station. It took some time before he could make his request understood, but eventually somebody came to the phone and said he was Detective Sergeant Clough. He seemed surprised that Daniel did not know his son had been found.

"We're delighted, obviously, that the boy is all right," he said heartily. "Just a bit of a crossed wire, it would seem. Staying with his granny all the time, up in Norfolk. A local officer will be calling on Mrs McDonald and the grandmother, and there should be some contact from Social Services up there. Nothing to worry about. Perhaps if you contacted your wife, sir . . ."

"I will," said Daniel grimly. He dialled his godmother's number and his temper was not improved when it was picked up and he heard a burst of laughter in the background. The voice that spoke was unsteady, as if the speaker found it difficult not to yield herself to the general mirth.

"Three four two eight – haha – sorry. Three four two eight. Miss Lancing speaking."

"Godma, what the hell is going on?" snapped Daniel. "I have just had a policeman on the phone saying that Jamie was staying with you all along. A crossed wire, he said. When I rang you on

Saturday you said you didn't know anything. Do you know what kind of weekend we've had?"

"Yes," said Violet. "And it was quite true, he wasn't here and I knew nothing. But given where he *has* been, and wanting to spare the Baileys any trouble, it seemed politic to Alice and myself that we should tell a small white lie."

"Who are the Baileys? No, forget that. Is Alice there?"

"Yes, and Jamie's just home, with Geoffrey, both of them covered in paint. Geoffrey has red ochre on his moustache, which explains our levity just now."

"Can you put Alice on, please, Godma?"

He waited. He could hear Jamie's voice high and blithe, the Colonel's deeper tones laughing, and Alice – taking her time – moving across the cottage living room still talking to them, something about white spirit and being careful not to set fire to it with a cigar. Someone said something, and there was another burst of laughter. Daniel, miles away and alone in a dank unoccupied house, waited. On the tail end of the laugh Alice finally picked up the telephone and said happily, "He's fine. In fact, better than fine. It's been a tremendous adventure, and it's not over yet." She was, Daniel could hear, immensely happy; so happy that she had forgotten to be distant with him. For some reason this made him angrier.

"What's all this about the police being told some lie about him staying with Godma? Where's he been?"

"Working for a funfair. Painting. He slept in a caravan."

Daniel leaned against the wall, his heart pounding. All the suppressed nightmares of the last forty-eight hours came back to him with full force. Funfairs were sinister, dangerous, lawless places. Boys Jamie's age vanished into the noise and confusion, lured by free dodgem rides, and were found decomposed in ditches months later. And Alice was laughing about it.

"For Christ's sake! Who found him?"

"I did," said Alice, and giggled. He began to suspect, correctly, that she had been drinking Violet's dandelion wine. He could not know the kind of night she had spent. His fury and terror rose.

"Do you mean you went off on some chase, some *trail*, you called it, without telling the police? To some fairground? Alice, even if you were lucky, that is the most irresponsible—"

"Oh, shut up," said Alice tipsily. "We're fine now, Jamie's just gone to have a bath and put some clean clothes on, and Geoffrey's cooking sausages."

"When will you be setting off home?"

"Oh, two or three weeks," said Alice. "The car broke down. A wonderful man called Mundersleeves has taken it away to do things to its head gasket. But he can do it terribly cheaply because his son had a 2CV and he crashed it and Mr Mundersleeves was just that minute wondering what to do with the engine which is quite OK—"

"What do you mean, weeks? Jamie ought to be at school."

"Oh no," said Alice gaily. "What's going on up here is more important than school."

Daniel had rarely been provoked to violence, but if Alice had been within reach he would have shaken her. Instead he said, "I'm driving back to Norwich tonight. I'll be at Moss Cottage in the morning. We'll talk this over. Be there." And he rang off before he had to hear her voice again.

29

When Geoffrey had left for the evening and Jamie had gone to bed, Alice and Violet sat either side of the fire, each cradling a glass of the pale dandelion wine which Violet made every summer. It had a sharp, dry fragrance like good sherry, and its warmth spread through Alice's weary limbs so that she felt herself sinking deep, helpless, into the old armchair.

"Oh, goodness," she exclaimed suddenly. "This is bliss. Complete bliss."

"Not complete," said the old lady from her higher, harder chair. She bent to knock a log back into her small fireplace with the poker. "I think you will find there are some matters outstanding."

The cloud of hazy bliss suddenly thinned. With a sinking heart, Alice sipped at her wine and recognized the return of the equally sharp and dry version of Violet Lancing. All day, the old lady had supported her, proffered advice with finely calculated diffidence and refrained from even the most tacit criticism. She ought to have known, from fifteen years' acquaintance with Daniel's godmother, that this reticence could not last.

"Jamie seems fine," she said defensively. "Really fine. Better than he has been for weeks."

"Yes," said Violet. "Nor am I for a moment inclined to argue with your idea that he should finish the job, however erratically he may have started it. He'll fall out of love with hard work soon enough, and that'll be a lesson in itself. I meant that you have problems to solve, beyond Jamie."

"You mean Daniel?"

"You have reason to think I mean Daniel?"

"Well, you know, we were living sort of apart."

"Sort of? Norwich and London *are* apart. He has telephoned me once or twice and it became clear how things stand."

"I don't suppose," said Alice, her blissful mood now quite evaporated, "that he mentioned why."

"He did not. I assumed some adultery, or suspicion of adultery, on his part."

"Why assume that?"

"Because of his tone. Hangdog. I am afraid that had it been *your* adultery, Daniel would have told me in quite different tones."

"You didn't think it might be something else?"

"I suspected not. Daniel does not do much else wrong in your household, does he? He has habits of kindliness and family duty. He is a good and loving man. Adultery is the only offence which creeps up on such a man, suddenly, without warning."

Alice looked at the old woman with astonished respect.

"Yes," she said slowly. "You're right. It was a woman. A girl. A fling, I suppose, and it was over, but it made me very angry."

"It would," said Violet dryly. "Wives can be very harsh on men in these circumstances, and who am I to criticize them for being angry?" Who indeed? she thought privately, with a dull ache of guilt half a century old, guilt over Celia. And over Geoffrey, who might have had the son he longed for if Celia had not been so deeply angry for so long. She poked the dying fire again, watching the embers crumble and turn black.

"Remember, though, that it probably made Daniel feel very guilty and unhappy too."

"He sounded more angry than guilty on the phone," said Alice. She was tired now, and not a little cross. She had been feeling warm and soft, sentimentally exalted by Jamie's discovery of his gift; talk of Daniel brought cold, hard, unwieldy lumps of trouble into this softness. "In fact, he's on his way up to Norfolk to have it out with me in the morning. I'm the villain now. He said I was irresponsible."

She was about to signal her crossness and draw the conversation to a close by going markedly to bed, but Violet was too quick for her. The old woman stood up, pushed the fireguard closer to the embers, and said lightly, "In that case, I shall go out for the morning and leave you the field. Charlie can take me on to town when he has dropped Jamie off at work. Geoffrey won't be calling because he spends Tuesday morning with the Venture Scout leader, designing rickety bridges. You can have your discussion in peace."

Upstairs in the tiny spare room under the eaves, Jamie was asleep on the single bed, the curtain open to the stars and a chilly breeze ruffling his black hair. Softly, Alice closed the window a little, fixing it on the last hole of the black iron stay. She swiftly undressed to her T-shirt, eschewing the cold cottage bathroom, and slid beneath the sheet and heavy blankets which Violet had arranged on Geoffrey's ancient canvas camp bed. Jamie had offered to sleep on it, indeed had clearly rather wanted to; but Alice had insisted he have the soft bed for his first night. The camp bed was not comfortable, except perhaps by contrast with a stony battlefield, and it creaked dangerously whenever she moved; but Alice was asleep in minutes, and lay undreaming until the morning.

When she woke, the bedroom was empty. Pulling on the heavy corduroy gardening trousers and ancient matted sweater laid out for her by Violet, she wandered downstairs and found a note on the kitchen table in Violet's precise pre-war italic.

8.20 Jamie and I have breakfasted well and set off with Charlie. I shall lunch with Angela Hawkings and she will give me a lift back for about 3.00. There is tea, coffee, bread, cheese, cold meat and fruit. The fish man will call. Please buy tuna steaks for 4 or of course 5 if Daniel can stay this evening. He also sells excellent cabbages which he will not mention owing to the food laws, but if you ask he will give you one for 30p from the sack on the front seat of the cab.

Alice pushed the note aside and flicked on the electric kettle. She had occasionally been in this kitchen alone before, when the family camped in the garden and used the cottage as a base for Norfolk holidays. She liked its peacefulness, its battered air of shipshape utility. Violet might be old and pious and make dandelion wine, but she did not accumulate clutter. Apart from the commando dagger, a Portuguese statue of St Martin dividing his cloak and a few holy pictures, the cottage was restfully bare of ornaments. The curtains at the kitchen window were plain cream cotton, the sink and wooden drainer kept clear. The few plates were on racks, and the dresser held only six good pieces of willow-pattern china, a jug of change for the milkman, and Geoffrey Gordon's spare pipe. Alice smiled at it; she liked the staid elderly romance, as she saw it, between the old widower and the maiden lady. It was endearing. She liked the idea of a stately, reasoned, unpassionate geriatric courtship.

She would have been quite hurt, and very surprised, if anybody had suggested to her that this view was patronizing.

A stupefied idleness still held her after the stresses of the past few days, and she read the parish magazine for a while, sitting at the kitchen table with her mug and piece of toast. Just as she was finishing a report on the Mothers' Union outing, a thundering knock on the door broke into her reverie. The fish van, she hoped. Daniel, she feared. The knocker crashed against the old door again. Oh yes, definitely Daniel. Damn. She went slowly across the sitting room and opened the door on to the lane. Daniel stood there, a step down but his eyes level with hers. They were not reassuring eyes to meet. She stood aside for him to enter.

"Where's Jamie?"

"He's at work, at a place called Bailey's farm, helping to paint some roundabout horses."

For a moment she wanted to explain the wonder of it, the moment yesterday when she saw their son happy for the first time in weeks, flying past to golden wheezing strains of Verdi, laughing at Rowley in his tattered coat as he leaned outward from the golden pole. She wanted to tell him about the evening talk in the cottage when she learned what Jamie had done, how he had fled through the night unhappy and alone and yet found a place for himself, a beauty to love and a job to do. She wanted his father to know all this and share it.

But somehow, she could not begin to explain. Not when she was so tired, not with those cold angry eyes on her.

"Alice. Jamie is my son as well. I think you owe me an explanation."

"I think," said Alice, firing up, "that *under the circumstances* I owe you exactly nothing. Except to tell you he's safe. And I did that. Before the police, even. I left a message yesterday at Mrs Hammond's."

"Yesterday," said Daniel through gritted teeth, "I was driving down to London to find you, to see what the hell was going on and to talk to the police. And when I get into the house, I find that you have installed this woman—"

"Isn't that meant to be my line?" taunted Alice. "Or are you going to accuse me of wantonly introducing your mistress into your house?"

"What's she doing there?"

"Feeding the cat, I presume," said Alice. "She turned up, looking scrawny and holy – I don't think much of your taste – and she said she wanted to atone for her sins against me. So I got her to bring some muscular Christians down to help me get the car out when it was blocked in at the canal park. And I thought she might as well mind the house."

"I found her there with a *vicar*," said Daniel.

"In flagrante?"

"No, of course – oh, Christ, Alice. You really are a bitch, sometimes."

"Not," said Alice, "often enough."

But when he had gone, slamming the door and almost falling into the gully by the steps, she sat on the deep chair, bent her head over its cat-shredded arm, and wept bitterly for half an hour until the fish man's knock roused her.

Daniel had to ask for Bailey's farm, and got lost several times among the cold, spiky winter lanes. When he arrived, it was drizzling and grey. He smelt no steam, heard no music, saw no roundabout. Satisfied with the functioning of his cranks, Tim had dismantled the gallopers and was helping Ed to load the ride's components into the larger of the two lorries. All Daniel saw was the rundown farm, the motley collection of vehicles, and a cavernous canvas shelter between the barn and the big lorry, from which came sounds of scraping and conversation. The whole effect was, to his eye, distinctly seedy.

He walked towards the noise and, rounding the bonnet of the lorry, saw a small group of people at work. Susan Bailey was rubbing down the undercoat of a pale-grey wooden horse,

Jamie was whitening the eyeball of a pure black one which bore ghostly lines to suggest some future harness, and Rowley was painting the name *Samson* on a red-and-yellow scroll on the neck of a third. The old man had just said something, and Jamie was laughing as he worked. Susan Bailey said, "What, on their faces? Get away."

"S'true," said Rowley. "The old gilders, they used to rub the gold leaf on their cheek and use their old face as a palette, to save waste. You put the brush to your cheek and it comes up lovely, fresh and ready for the wood. The gilders used to have half-gold faces all through the spring. Demigods, my dad called them."

"They must have looked like aliens in *Star Trek*," said Jamie. He finished the eyeball and wiped his brush with an expert hand.

Daniel came into earshot only for this last remark, and to see Jamie levering the lid off a tin of new silver undercoat. He saw a draggled, gipsyish woman with her hair falling out of an untidy black knot, a couple of burly labouring types loading the lorry, and an old tramp with string round his boots talking to Jamie. The scene did not reassure him. His weeks on the university campus in Norwich had accustomed him to clean-cut hardworking students, and he had with some pleasure seen the younger children in the streets with their blazers and uniforms coming to and from the better city schools. A part of him had hoped all along that Alice would see sense and come to Norwich, and let Jamie settle into one of these calm, purposeful, civilized schools. He had not been any happier with Finchamgrove than Jamie was. Its examination league place was tolerably good, but there was a tough disorderliness about it every time he visited, a toleration of rush and shouting and insult. Rackety, assertive children (like Clementine) might well thrive there. Jamie did not. But he could not see that Jamie was thriving here either, untaught and scruffy, sitting among these gypsies and vagabonds fiddling with fairground rides.

He called out, "Jamie!"

"Whozat?" said Rowley.

"My dad," said Jamie, and putting the paintpot aside, he got up and went to him. "Hi, Dad. Did Mum and Godgran tell you where to find me?"

Daniel looked down at his son, his heart tugging, his dismay for a moment forgotten.

"You all right, Jay? You gave us a fright."

"I'm fine. Really. Mum says I can stay here till the Cold Fair, then help out in the booth maybe." Jamie saw his father's face change, and added hastily, "Godgran's going to do some maths with me. She says it's the maths you fall behind with. She's rung my teacher at Fincham and ordered some books."

"Yes, well, Godgran hasn't taught maths for eighteen years. I think we might have to rethink the plan a bit."

Now Jamie's face changed. He glared at his father. "It's settled. I've got to stay at it, or Rowley might not make it in time. Not properly, anyway. Not the detail. It takes two days to paint one mane properly, proper gold, because of the other undercoat. And the tartan and tassels take *ages*, even for Rowley. And six of the shields on the swifts have got smoke damage—"

Daniel began to remonstrate, but Jamie abruptly ceased his explanation and ended flatly, "And besides, Mum said I could." Unspoken between them hung the rest of the sentence: *"And she's in charge of me now because you're not there."*

Jamie turned and walked back, deliberately, to his paints. Daniel watched for a moment, then lamely said, "See you soon," and went back to his car. He had not exchanged a word with Susan, Rowley, Tim, or Ed.

They all watched uneasily until he had driven away, then Tim sauntered over to Jamie and said, "That your dad, then?"

"Yes," said Jamie tightly. "But it doesn't matter. He's left home."

30

Daniel drove back to Moss Cottage, not to knock again on the door but to push through the letterbox a folded slip of paper from his notebook, marked 'Alice'. It said: 'You will be hearing from my lawyer shortly.'

This detour did not prevent him from getting back to Norwich and to the offices of Grouter and Sharp, Solicitors, before their leisurely lunchtime closure began. Dave had pointed out the brass plate to him on one of their journeys through the city to his favoured pub. "Grouter did my divorce. No different from any other bloody lawyers, except they've got a customer car park." Daniel drove into it, not bothering to straighten the car in its parking slot, pulled the handbrake on and strode into the building. A cubbyhole opened to his right, with a little reception desk. No, he did not have an appointment with Mr Grouter, Mr Sharp or Mr Neville. No, he could not wait to make one. This was urgent. Did they want business or didn't they?

The receptionist, flustered, trotted from her desk into an inner office, and after a moment returned looking relieved. Mr Neville could see him. Daniel walked in and sat down opposite the balding young man at the desk.

"I believe this firm did a divorce for my friend David Edicott,' he said. Mr Neville's brow cleared. Ah yes, divorce. That explained the man's manner. They did sometimes come in rather suddenly, divorces. Especially the men, and Mr Neville always preferred dealing with the men. Not only did they tend to have more money to spend on legal advice, but women always seemed to want therapy more than law, and it embarrassed him. They had much to thank that car park for; it was, old Grouter used to say, the free car parking that drew the male impulse clients. The passing trade. Women hesitated more and waited for personal recommendation; often, they didn't have cars anyway.

'Yes,' he said. 'Is it, er, a divorce matter that brings you . . .' He cocked his head with painstaking delicacy to one side.

"No," said Daniel. "Not yet anyway. But I am living apart from my wife, nothing official so far, and I am concerned at the way she is handling my son's education. Do I have any rights?"

"Indeed, indeed," said Mr Neville enthusiastically. "We do belong to the Solicitors' Family Law Association and we would initially urge you to make friendly representations—"

"But failing that?" said Daniel doggedly. "What rights do I have, if reason does not prevail? She's taken him out of school and is not educating him adequately at home. In fact, between you and me, she has put him to work. Can I make her send him back?"

"Ah," said Mr Neville. "Obviously, we would have to know the circumstances, but there is scope for a Prohibited Step Order under the Children Act—"

"Good enough for me," said Daniel. "Go to it."

"He's gone to a *lawyer*," said Alice. "Violet, this is just not reasonable. It's appalling."

They were sitting in the cottage kitchen on Thursday morning, with the sun streaming in through the small panes of the window. Alice's weariness had gone, and she felt alert and combative. The days had passed happily. She walked in the lanes, made friends with neighbouring dogs, browsed in Violet's bookshelves and once rang Yazz – at a time when the answering machine was bound to be on – to leave a brief, guilty message saying that the crisis continued and it might be a week or two before she was ready to come back.

Jamie went off to the Baileys' every morning, apparently by no means out of love with work. He was home by four, full of Rowley's latest stories, and then sat obediently with Violet for an hour doing mathematical investigations. Then, at Alice's instigation, he spent a further hour reading. There was no television in the cottage. When Violet wanted to watch something, she generally went down to the Flats with Geoffrey. From Violet's shelves Alice chose her son *Kidnapped*, which he read with pleasure, then *David Copperfield*. Stories of boys out on their own in the world, she felt, would engage his attention. The three of them ate supper, then Jamie took his book to bed and fell asleep with it on his nose, and Alice read for a while downstairs, or wrote long letters to Clemmie. Violet had not mentioned Daniel again, not since Alice had silently shown her the note pushed through the door.

"He won't go to a lawyer, of course," Alice had said. "Not yet. He doesn't approve of divorce."

But now he had, and not about divorce at all. "Can he do this?" she asked Violet, showing her the letter with the Grouter and Sharp heading.

Violet said, "Probably. It sounds as if this Prohibited Step Order has to be brought in, forbidding you to keep Jamie out of school. So if he got the order, you would have to go back to London or put him in a school here."

"Well, I won't," said Alice. "We'll fight it. Could you convince an inspector, do you think? That he's not missing out?"

"Social Services," said Violet, "would be involved."

A silence hung between them. The one bad moment of the past few days had been a visit from the local police on Tuesday afternoon, with a great many questions about how it came to be that Jamie had been staying with his "grandmother" who was not a grandmother at all, without either parent seeming to know. Social Services had been mentioned then, and Violet had reacted, Alice felt, with uncharacteristic and unreasonable hostility. They expected a visit from some social service official, and did not look forward to it.

"So should I go?" said Alice at last. "Should we give up?"

"You could play their game," said Violet. "Get a doctor's letter saying that he has had some form of breakdown, making him temporarily unfit for school, and that the painting is suitable therapy."

"That's brilliant!" said Alice.

But when it was put to him that evening, Jamie refused point-blank to talk to any doctor, especially what he called a "head doctor". He maintained that he was not nuts and had not had any soppy breakdown. Moreover, if anybody tried to stop him finishing the gallopers, he would run away again, and this time he would be better equipped. "I'm not dropping out for *good*, Mum," he said, with an air of maturity that made Violet, listening from the kitchen, hide a smile. "I just happen to have a job to finish. OK?"

Alice, sensing difficulty and multiple defeats ahead, rang Daniel. Or at least she rang Mrs Hammond, who wrote "Please ring your wife Mrs McDonald" on a scalloped sticky note and put it on his door.

Daniel's annoyance at the way this was put, as if he had a great number of wives to choose from, not all of them called Mrs McDonald, transferred itself to more anger with Alice. He did not ring. He had not yet told Mr Neville to start the processes towards the Order against Alice but he damn well would in the morning, even though Mr Neville had warned him of the "possibly substantial" legal costs involved.

But in the morning he had a letter from Clementine. She had, she informed him, had a note from Mum saying that Jamie was out of school and staying in Norfolk for a bit doing lessons with Godgran. Weird, she said, but there you are, Jamie always was a bit weird. It was better than bunking off school to play Battlezone, anyway, wasn't it? Anyway, more importantly, she was in the first ever BCSE team for an inter-schools one-day event, guess where? At the Norfolk and Norwich Showground! On Saturday! So she trusted that her dad at least would turn up (properly dressed, not like some ratty don) and support her. BCSE's jumpers, she added, were bright yellow with red rings round the cuff, and their silks yellow and green. The horsebox for the four of them was also yellow and green, with a red stripe. He couldn't miss it. Their horses, junior ones anyway, were all coal-black Fell and Dale ponies, fast and hardy and no nonsense about them. Later, obviously, she would get to ride thoroughbreds, but her favoured mount, Dart, couldn't half jump. She signed off "YOUR DARLING CLEMENTINE" with musical staves scribbled around the words.

This letter, read and re-read between the morning's appointments, so cheered Daniel that he forgot to ring Mr Neville until after lunch. He then had lectures and seminars until five. Monday would do.

Alice heard from Clemmie as well and, like Daniel, carried

the letter around with her like a talisman all through Friday. Clem would have got her second, longer letter by now, explaining more about Jamie. She wondered whether to go and watch the event – Jamie had announced his intention of working straight through the weekend, only excepting the maths lessons – but the car was still under the care of Mr Mundersleeves with his cannibalized 2CV engine, and Charlie's taxi account was building up remorselessly. A trip to Norwich was out of the question. She was very conscious of not having an income of her own and depending on whatever Daniel put into the joint account. The habit, or at least the instinct, of financial independence was strengthening in her like a muscle. As if she was preparing for single life again.

Early in the week she had even considered going down to London to start work at Euradio, leaving Jamie with Violet. But he had woken on Tuesday night with some screaming nightmare about Dad, and Battlezone, and a bus that wouldn't stop and that went all the way to Hell. Even if he would not see a doctor, even if he did display a surprising new maturity when he talked about the fair, he was not yet a child she wanted to leave. Not by night. She did not talk to Violet about the nightmare but was suddenly compelled to mention it when she met Geoffrey one afternoon on his way up from the Flats. Obscurely, she felt that these things in a boy of Jamie's age were more fittingly discussed with a man.

Geoffrey was gruffly reassuring, and unusually forthcoming. "Bound to have dreams," he said. "Especially since he was out on his own, at night. Slept rough, remember, that's always a shock the first time. And he must have wondered if he was for it when that big bearded chap Ed stood over him. Toughest lads in my regiment used to wake up screaming after a bad do. Even on the research station, Orford Ness, we had a bit of trouble. Chap called McAdam. Blew off both his legs. Wrote crazy letters."

"Well, Jamie hasn't quite—"

"No. The point is," said the Colonel, "it *wasn't McAdam who had the nightmares*. He just wrote loopy letters, otherwise perfectly cheerful. It was the rest of us. That's what led to—" The old man broke off, stopped walking, and looked sideways at Alice. Then he seemed to make a decision, and beginning to walk rapidly forward again said, "Did you know about me and Violet? In the war?"

"I didn't know you knew each other then."

"Worked together. Ballistics research, godforsaken place called Orford Ness, between the sea and a river in Suffolk. We both had the nightmares after McAdam. She found him. Actually, first thing she found was the leg, what was left of it. Then saw him on the ground and ran in to my hut for help. It was her second week. It's what threw us together. What you need, with nightmares, is someone you can tell about them in the morning. That's why Jamie'll be all right. He's got you here. Same room, that probably helps too."

"Why didn't you and Violet, er . . ." She paused, embarrassed at herself.

"I was married." Alice was finding that she had to hurry to keep up with his long stride. She thought that he was almost certainly right about Jamie, and felt comforted by his plain belief that she should stay near her son for the moment. But this new subject intrigued her in spite of herself. She began again, tentatively.

"Your wife . . .?"

"Died in a fire, nineteen fifty," he said. "I was there too. Had a spell in hospital, had to leave the Army. Violet looked after me for a bit."

Alice continued walking fast alongside him, but this time did not ask the question that hung in the air. Colonel Gordon seemed to come to another decision, and stopped again, poking in a gully with his stick.

"I asked Violet to marry me, in nineteen fifty-one. And in nineteen fifty-two, and several other years, come to that. I was free, she was free. But she wouldn't."

"Why?" It seemed all right to ask it now. A gleam of sun came through the bare branches, the lane was quiet, and Geoffrey, who was still clearing mouldering leaves from the gully with his stick, seemed to want to tell her.

"Because she and I broke my marriage vows, at Orford, all those years before. Violet said that she hadn't respected my marriage when Celia was alive, and she had made Celia pretty unhappy in the process. Because I told Celia, you see. Trying to say sorry, but it backfired. So Violet felt she'd done all that damage, not respecting the marriage, and the least she could do was to respect it now. She said Celia was still my wife, dead or not. So I went to Oman for a bit."

"But that's terrible!" cried Alice. "You could have been so happy! That's just punishing yourself for nothing!"

"She's very religious, as you know," said the Colonel, simply. "It was like her to think that way. To think about making up for a sin by giving up something that wasn't a sin."

"But don't Catholics believe in confession?" demanded Alice. "Washing it all away and starting fresh? Go, and sin no more?"

"Do you know," said the Colonel, with a small gruff bark of laughter, "I never thought of putting it to her that way. Hell, it might have worked!"

They walked on, until almost at the steps of Moss Cottage Alice turned to him again and asked, "Why did you tell me all that, just now?"

"I had a reason," said the Colonel lightly. "A strategy. You're young. You've got a good man and a grand little boy. It's worth fighting for. It's worth keeping the rules, even if someone else doesn't. Celia and I would have been all right if it hadn't been for Violet and me. But there's something else: we'd have been all right even then if Celia hadn't spent the rest of her life angry. We would have had a child, maybe. Or you could even take it another way: Violet and I would have been all right in the end if we'd kept the rules in the first place and trusted to God. See what I mean?"

"I think so," said Alice. "But I don't think it's me you should be telling. Daniel was the one—"

"Aha!" said the Colonel. "Don't go on. Think about it."

Daniel parked his car at the showground's edge and made for the distant lines of horseboxes. This world, which his daughter had slipped into so easily, was still alien to him. All kinds of atavistic instincts from social insecurity to downright class hatred stirred in him as he walked cautiously between the lines of glossy horses tied to lorries. He was not at home among these shrill girls with their hairnets and tight breeches, county ladies in dung-coloured Husky jackets and men with flat hats and Prince Charles accents. Even the tousled, countrified rough-spoken horsemen and -women by the shabbier lorries exuded a swaggering confidence which raised his hackles.

But Clementine was here, and he knew his daughter well enough to accept that it was a sport and not a social world which she had chosen. Indeed, as he approached the garish horsebox marked BCSE – BRITISH COLLEGE FOR SPORTING EXCELLENCE – he felt a spurt of pride in the thoroughness with which she had embraced it. If she would insist on being educated in an elitist Thatcherite success machine, it was at least gratifying that she was doing well there.

Clemmie was wearing jodphur boots and breeches with a nylon puffy jacket he did not recognize, and leading out a stocky black pony with an unruly mane. She plainly knew what she was doing, hissing and clicking to the animal as she manoeuvred it down the ramp, tying it up with a couple of deft flicks of the wrist, and stooping for something in the plastic grooming box at her side. He watched for a moment before she saw him, full of pleasure at her competence. Then, tentatively, since the other children seemed immersed in their tasks, he said, "Clemmie. Hi."

"Oh *hi*, Dad." She threw down the hoof pick and came over to him, hugging him hard but briefly before leading the way back to the pony. "Come and brush his mane, talk to me while I get on."

Gingerly, Daniel applied the proffered brush to the wiry mane of the pony. "Clem, I haven't the faintest idea what to do. Will it step on my foot or something?"

"Probably," said his daughter, picking up a hind leg. "But not while I've got his other leg in the air. So get on with it." She checked the hoof, then looked up at him, laughing. "You really are a misfit. Look at your blue trousers." And indeed, no other trouser within sight was any colour but khaki, brown or beige. "You look like an escaped yachtsman. Is Mum coming?"

"I don't know," said Daniel shortly. "She's at Godgran's."

"I know," said Clemmie. "Amazing, isn't it? It's so brilliant about Jamie." She picked up the other hind leg, but put it down again, seeing the hoof was clear.

"Brilliant?" said Daniel. "Why brilliant?"

"Oh, you know," she was running her hand down a foreleg now, and her voice came up to him muffled by the pony's flanks, "found something. He's on the way. About time, too." She straightened up, grinning. "OK. Go on, brush it!"

Five minutes later, none the wiser about the "brilliant", Daniel watched her trot away. Three hours later, bored stiff by the repetitive spectacle of ponies jumping over fences and trotting in tidy circles, he managed to corner her again near the lorry where she was giving Dart a bucket of water and some hay.

"Sweetheart, I'm sorry, but I really don't understand too much of this. Are you winning?"

She snorted. "Don't strain your tiny mind, Dad. But basically, yes, we are. Are you staying?"

"I ought to work. Do you mind?"

"No, it was great you could come."

"Need anything? Money?"

"Always welcome." He gave her a £20 note which she tucked into her boot. Then she looked at him directly and said, "I'm making the most of this term, you know. I do know that it might not go on."

"Why?" He was taken aback.

"Because," said Clementine, "when this magic roundabout business of his is over, Jamie will presumably have to go back to Finchamgrove. Yes?"

"Y-yes, I suppose so," said her father. "Your mother—"

"Mum will be in Camden, yes? And you'll be in Norwich?"

"Things are difficult, you know that," began Daniel defensively, but Clementine, glancing across at her team mates, hurried on in a lower voice.

"I think that if you're not home, I'd better be. Mum on her own isn't good for Jamie. They're too like each other. He'll go loopy and bunk off school. So I'm coming back after Christmas if you and Mum aren't sorted out. Full stop."

"Clemmie, absolutely not!" said Daniel angrily. "You've found your thing, you must do it. Live your own life. It's your big chance."

"I know," said Clementine bleakly. "But I can't enjoy it if it means kaput for Jamie." She looked at him questioningly. "Can I?"

"It's our responsibility. We're his parents, and yours, and we run the family. You're not an adult yet. You mustn't take all this on yourself, sweetie."

Clementine swung herself lightly up into the saddle and looked down at him with a kind of rueful pity.

"Someone has to. Look, I've thought it over, I can cope. A couple of years on, I might get a chance to start again." Seeing his still mystified air, she said more gently, "Dad, have you talked to Mum about Jamie? Really talked?"

He did not answer.

"Pass my other jacket."

He handed her the quilted jacket, and from its pocket she pulled a creased, folded letter of several pages.

"I think you ought to have this. So that you see the point. Look, Dad, don't worry. We all do what we have to do."

And she rode off, leaving him standing by the horsebox in the raw, damp November cold with the letter in his hand. It was in Alice's handwriting.

He went to a roadside café and ordered a cup of tea. For a moment he read the menu with attention, as if by concentrating on descriptions of Mighty Brekburgers and Sizzling Sausage

Platters he could blot out the letter which lay shimmering on the table under the neon lights. Clemmie's words had astonished him as well as shaming him, and left him uncertain of his ground. He half-hoped, half-feared that the explanation of her attitude would be in the letter. At last, he unfolded it and began to read.

> *Dear Clem,*
>
> *I hope you got my note on Tuesday, about us staying at Godgran's for a bit. If you want to ring here or write, this is where we are, Jamie and me. Dad at usual Norwich address. Not that you'll probably have time, by the sound of things! Did you get anywhere in the 500m trial, after all that? Sunita sounds dopy to me.*

Daniel frowned. He, too, had had a letter from Clemmie before the weekend, including a lively account of some mix-up over the swimming entries and a girl called Sunita. For the first time, it occurred to him that ever since he had moved to Norwich his daughter had had to write her twice-weekly letters home in duplicate. The same stories, the same expressions of valiant optimistic cheerfulness, copied out twice with slightly different slants. What a chore. Poor Clem. God, why did one never think about these things?

> *But I want to tell you some more about Jamie. He got off the train, you know, on the way to Norwich. All alone, in the night. He just says he felt muddled, and it seemed the right thing to do. Anyway, he climbed on some bus which was going from pub to pub with darts teams in, and had no idea where he would end up. When he got off, it was pitch dark, so he walked down a lane and went to sleep inside a big round thing he thought was a barn, only it was a roundabout! A real old-fashioned one, with galloping painted horses. I think you saw one years ago when you were little, at St Giles's fair in Oxford. Remember? We went to the roundabout service the night before the fair, and the organ played hymns.*

Daniel sat, staring unseeingly down at the letter on the plastic table. They had taken the train down to Oxford for supper with Sam. Clemmie must have been about two, because Alice was heavily pregnant with Jamie and could not bear to be in the car. She was beautiful to him in those late stages of pregnancy, despite her physical clumsiness: There was a glow about her, a double radiance of personality as if the baby's soul – as he once sentimentally put it – was adding its shine to hers. Alice had laughed, but then soberly said, "It feels like that. Another star rising."

It was September, and the streets were empty of students. But St Giles was blocked at either end, so people had to park north of it and walk down. The great street fair was set up for its opening the next day. Closed, so they thought; but as they approached James Noyce's traditional roundabout with its bright galloping horses and ostriches, the lights were on and the golden organ at the centre struck up a wheezy rendering of "The Day Thou Gavest Lord Is Ended". A priest stood on the platform, his vestments fluttering, and around him stood a small crowd: showmen in grubby neckerchiefs and sideburns, townspeople, a few early undergraduates, two policemen and a local radio reporter with a heavy black tape recorder. Alice and Daniel had stopped, with Clemmie in Daniel's arms, and stood at the back during the hymn and the prayers. Clemmie's eyes were wide and soft with wonder at the jerky moving figures on the organ and the brightness of the horses in their red and gold and blue liveries. Typical of Alice to assume the child might remember it. But maybe she did. He read on, sipping unsteadily at his tea. He was on the third of the folded pages now.

Anyway, he woke up in the morning feeling rather hungry, and saw some paints near one of the horses which was half finished. He says he didn't dare start painting the horse, but he was so fascinated by the patterns and the colours on the other ones, real fairgroundy stuff, that he tried some out on a plank. He thought he could pay for the paint later, he says. I'm not sure he thought at all! I think he just followed his nose. You know Jamie.

He had just started painting the horse when they found him – the fair people, Ed and Susan Bailey. They thought he was a boy who had come to help this old man, Roly (Rowly??), who is a fairground painter, a very famous one in that world, apparently. So they just gave him food and a caravan to sleep in and didn't ask him anything. So he went on painting, all weekend. I think he must have felt like Princess Scheherezade in your old Arabian Nights book, who had to tell all the stories – keep on painting, and he kept on staying alive and being fed!

The wonderful thing is that he turned out to be really, really good at it. So when Roly turned up, they didn't want to lose him because they're desperate to get the roundabout fixed for a Christmas fair, but of course Susan was terrified that someone would be looking for him, she's got boys of her own. She was determined to find out who he was and give him back, whatever Ed thought. Jamie didn't make it easier, he just said his name was Jack, and that he didn't have a home, or something. You see, he wanted to stay too. Then I arrived, which was sort of by accident. I'd found out where he'd rung me from, by detective work.

Daniel's mouth set grimly for a moment. Alice's irresponsible solo detective work and her subsequent lies to the police were something which he knew he would always find it hard to come to terms with. Yet such was the change in him, these past hours, that he knew he would have to come to terms with whatever Alice was and whatever she did. He could argue and remonstrate, sometimes losing and sometimes winning, but he could not detach himself. The family would have to be healed, whatever private disapproval or humiliation it cost. He read on.

When I got there, the Baileys' big son Tim happened to be testing the organ and the cranks, whatever they are, and the roundabout was going, and Jamie was riding this amazing horse, up and down, flying round, and the old man Roly was laughing, and the organ was playing that tune you love from La Traviata, the drinking song, and Clemmie, they just looked so happy! Jamie looked like he used to, before he started at Fincham and got so crazy about those battle games. I couldn't take him away, could I? You know Jamie as well as anybody does, you've always been able to calm him down ever since he was a baby. I wish you'd write and tell me I'm right to keep him here for now, finishing the horses and feeling proud and capable of anything, and doing quiet lessons with Godgran. I just feel it's right for him. The Cold Fair is only a couple of weeks off anyway. Just into BCSE holidays — we could all go, and see his horses in action!

Anyway, sweetheart, I'm sorry to ramble on. I just needed to tell somebody. You're the most sensible of us all, in a lot of ways. You always seem to know what Jamie needs. If you approve, I'll feel less guilty about it all!

> Lots of love,
> MUM

PS. Don't worry about Catto. She's being fed every day by a nice girl from the Camden Christian Pioneers Mission, or whatever it's called. She's kindly looking after the house with her friends. Maybe they sing her hymns while they dole out the Whiskas!!!

Daniel sat for a long time, looking down at the letter his daughter had given him. *The most sensible of us all*, Alice had said. Indeed she was. *You always seem to know what Jamie needs.* In handing him the letter, Clementine had given Jamie what he needed. She had blown away Mr Neville, Grouter and Sharp and the Prohibited Step Order, and like a defiant little Canute turned back the lapping tide of anger from the family sandcastle. Fences to mend, thought Daniel. He had fences to mend. He folded the letter carefully and put it in his wallet, then walked back out to his car and headed for the Fakenham road.

32

He stood behind the lorry, the green canvas tilt between him and the workers, listening. Lights had been rigged against the early dusk and it was difficult to hear properly over the sound of the blower heater inside; but quite close to Daniel's flap Rowley was talking.

"Hero of Trafalgar, o'course. What, don't you know about Nelson? Died on the deck, saying 'Thank God I have done my duty'. Hero of the nation for two hundred years."

"Well, I knew *that*," said Jamie. "I mean, I knew he was a famous admiral. I suppose that's why it says Great Sea Lord. The red needs a bit of touching up on the bottom half of the Lord, by the way. Shall I do it next? I can't start the black horse till it's dry."

Rowley's reply was indistinguishable from outside, as if he was bending to some task. Jamie went on, abstractedly, clearly at work himself.

"And I knew about Baden-Powell, because of Scouts. A bit, anyway. I recognized the hat. It says 'Hero of Mafeking'. Was Mafeking a battle?" He pronounced it Mayfe-king.

"It's Maf-er-king, you ignorant little bleeder," said Rowley. "Yes, it was a battle. I think. Relief of Mafeking. Miss Lancing did it at school with us, but blowed if I was listening. I suppose you don't know who Isambard Kingdom Brunel is either."

"Great engineer," said Jamie promptly. "It says it here. It's flaking."

"It is that," said Susan Bailey's voice. "The heat must have done more damage up the centre than what we thought."

"Ah, bollocks," said Rowley. "We'll get done. When those last

243 •

three hosses are dry, Jack an' I will get the bad bits rubbed down and painted by Thursday, then we can finish the shields. Edward the Seventh has got a bit missing out of his hat."

"No, what I wanted to ask," said Jamie again, "is why those kings are up there, and why the middle of a roundabout should have an engineer and an admiral and the founder of the Scouts and the other one, the circus one, Lord George Sanger? I can see why you have animals and horses and gold crowns and birds and stuff on a fair, to be cheerful. But why d'you have those history people?"

"Heroes, boy," said Rowley. "Great British kings an' heroes. When they built these gallopers, people liked the idea of heroes 'n' princes. People right up at the top of their own tree. Then you ride the horses, the most beautiful horses there are with the finest harness, and you look up at real gold, and birds and angels and kings and lions, and you whirl round a bit with the music and the lights, and it all turns into a muddle of beautiful strong heroic *proudness*. So you get off at the end of the ride feeling good, right? And pay your sixpence for another turn. Cheaper 'n drink an' drugs, boy! But just as vague! There don't have to be a meaning for putting Lord Nelson up there, just a feeling!"

He cackled, and Jamie's voice rang out in glad laughter. Daniel hesitated, then stepped back from the green flap so that the voices, beginning again, blurred with the shashing of the heater inside the canvas cave. Jamie's cave, where for the moment Jamie belonged. Daniel burned with shame at his earlier haughtiness about the adventure and the company. Alice was right. Clemmie was right. Jamie was right. This curious Victorian interlude was an experience no child could lose by. He, Daniel, had been wrong. Slowly, taking care to make no sound, he walked back to his car out in the lane.

An hour earlier, a self-important puttering sound outside Moss Cottage had heralded the arrival of Mr Mundersleeves at the wheel of Alice's multicoloured car, with his eldest son following on a motorbike and sidecar with Russian lettering down the side. Violet came unhurriedly out on to the cottage steps with an air of the Queen Mother inspecting a drive-past of the armoured division, and called to Alice behind her.

"It's William Mundersleeves, with your car. It appears to be under its own motive power."

"Oh, goodness!" cried Alice, coming out behind her. "That's so wonderful! Mr Mundersleeves, what do I owe you?"

"Well, for the labour, I'm afraid, that's fifty-three pounds," said the man, emerging in his neat overalls and pulling out the protective paper sack on which he had been sitting in the driving seat. It was, Alice noticed, redundant; the sack was cleaner than the seat underneath it had been for years. "And as for the parts, well . . ."

"The parts was from my old car," said the boy on the motorbike. The older mechanic was putting the paper sack carefully into its shiny black sidecar. "I give that car up as a bad job, I did. Got the Cossack now." He slapped its iron rump jovially. "Bought that off a batty lawyer, up in Louth. 'S Russian. Better 'n that Citron!"

"We couldn't charge you much for parts," said Mr Mundersleeves. "A tenner? Sixty-three, in all? That right?" He looked at Alice. "Make it sixty. We don't get involved with that VAT."

Laughing, she wrote out a cheque for sixty-five pounds, leaning on the corrugated bonnet of her car, and gave it to him. "Have a drink!" she said. "I'm just glad to have it back. Charlie was costing a fortune."

"He does that," said Mr Mundersleeves, winking. Raising his hand in solemn salute, he said, "Well then!" and climbed astride the boy's motorbike. They proceeded up the lane in a cloud of blue exhaust smoke. Alice patted her car affectionately.

"Violet, that is a wonderful mechanic. Thank you."

"Charlie found him," said Violet. "I knew his cousin Jack better. He was in my recorder group. He's living in Norwich now, I think. Working for the mustard people."

So Violet rang Charlie to cancel his afternoon run, and Alice drove to Bailey's farm that afternoon to collect Jamie. On the way, she passed a car that looked very like Daniel's, heading for Wetheringham, but thought little of it.

"Godma," said Daniel, pushing the door open. "Godma, it's me."

"We expected you for supper the other night," said Violet mildly. "You rushed off. You must be so busy."

"Don't tease me," said Daniel. "You know perfectly well I stamped off in a rage with Alice. She probably showed you the note about the lawyer."

"She did," agreed Violet, pouring him a cup of rather stewed tea from the brown teapot. "If I may say so, I thought it was very childish."

"It was," said Daniel. "I was furious. I'd been frightened. I wanted Jamie back in the system, everything ordinary."

"It can't be, can it?" said Violet placidly. "If you two are living apart."

"We must stop that," said Daniel. "I see that now."

"So which of you is going to move?"

"If I move, I don't have a job," said Daniel. "Not in London University. I don't know what I'd do."

"Teach in a school? Sixth form?"

"Maybe." He threw himself gloomily into a chair. "You don't think she'd move to Norwich? I really like it. And the schools might be more Jamie's cup of tea than where he is now."

"She has a job in London. Did you know?"

"Yes. Something Yasmin set up. Bloody interfering woman."

"That," said Violet, sitting down opposite him, "is not the kind of thing to say to Alice."

"I know," said Daniel. "Oh God. What am I going to do?"

Jamie erupted into the cottage a few minutes later, tearing off his padded jacket and going straight through to the kitchen to forage for snacks. He did not see Daniel. Alice followed him in and stopped short at the sight of her husband.

"Hi." She sounded wary, but no more.

"I came to say," said Daniel, "that I've stopped all the nonsense with the lawyer."

"Yes, it was nonsense, wasn't it?" said Alice. She still, Daniel noted to his relief, did not sound sharp. "That's good."

"So you can go on here with Jamie. You were right."

"Thanks," said Alice, and she smiled at him, properly, looking into his eyes. "Thanks, Dan. Jamie!"

The boy had come through from the kitchen with an untidy sandwich, and stood there, dropping small pieces of cheese on to the floor where the cat cruised, happily, picking them up. Alice put her arm round him.

"Jamie, did you hear that? Dad says you can finish at Bailey's, finish the job, I mean."

"Yup. Thanks, Dad."

"I came along today," said Daniel. "I peeped through the canvas. I could see how hard you were working, all of you."

Jamie thawed perceptibly. "Yes, we do. Rowley's so brilliant. Ed says he's the best fairground painter there is, because he's fast and he's joyful."

"Do you feel joyful?"

"Yup. But I'm not so fast. I'm better than Susan, though. We can't trust her even with the harness. Only base coats. But her dapples are all right. Nearly as good as the Colonel did with just one arm."

"Dan," said Alice suddenly, "could I have a word? Jamie, you stay here and start your maths with Godgran. We'll go in the garden."

They walked into the darkening garden, Alice leading the way, until she turned and stood under a crooked medlar tree. Daniel held his breath, but her tone was matter-of-fact.

"Dan, are you working tomorrow?"

"I could be not working."

"Only I really need to drive down to London, now the car's back. I've got no clothes, and nor has Jamie really, and it's getting so cold we need warm stuff. And I ought to speak to one or two people. I could be back by tomorrow night late, but it would be brilliant if you could stay here. In my bed. Jamie sleeps on the Colonel's camp bed next to it. He hasn't had any bad dreams for two nights now, but when he does . . ."

"Of course I can stay. But tell me, he has bad dreams?" said Daniel.

"Yes. I think it all went a lot deeper than we knew, for a long time. There's been something going on at school, or at that battle place, because he shouts about ripping up pictures and people bombing him and Mrs Davis, and he wakes up crying and saying he's sorry, he's no good, he ought to die."

Daniel's distress shook him out of his formality with her. "Oh, Allie, no. Since when? Poor little boy!"

"He's fine after a minute or two. I talk to him as if he was five years younger. I talk about the Cold Fair, and how proud we'll all be when the roundabout's done, and how we'll all be there to see it run with his horses. I'm afraid I promised him that you would come too."

"Well, you were right. I will. Whatever."

The "whatever" hung on the air between them, but they walked back together to the cottage in silence. Alice told Jamie the plan, which seemed to please him, and began throwing things into her shoulder bag for the journey. In ten minutes she was gone, trundling down the dark lane in the garish 2CV for the four long hours' drive to London. Daniel did not express his feelings about her car. Somehow, obscurely, he felt he had lost that right. From the front step, he watched her go and then turned back into the cottage where his son was arguing about fractions with his godmother. A great sense of comfort washed over him, as if he had been among labyrinthine winter lanes and at last found a turning with the signpost that he needed. He began, softly, to sing.

33

Jamie did not stir that night in his sleep but was tiptoeing clumsily around the room half-dressed when Daniel awoke in the small bed that smelt so comfortingly of Alice.

"Sorry, Dad. Didn't mean to wake you."

"No, I have to get up. I'll drive you down to Bailey's."

"Charlie usually – oh, I forgot. Mum got the car and cancelled him."

"That's right. When do you have to be there?"

"Well," said Jamie, "if I get there by half past eight I get hot breakfast. Otherwise I only get muesli here."

"Hot it is," said Daniel. "You've got it all worked out, haven't you?"

Companionably, they finished dressing, took turns to do their teeth in the tiny bathroom and crept past Violet's door, through which they could hear the *Today* programme on the radio.

"She doesn't sleep so much, but she hibernates till nine on winter mornings," said Jamie. "Says there's no point getting up when it's so dark, unless she's going out and about with Colonel Gordon."

They drove down together, silently enjoying one another's company, and Daniel returned to Moss Cottage.

"Godma," he said, finding her in her chair with the newspaper and a cup of coffee. "Could you do me a favour? Tell me the names of a couple of good secondary schools between here and Norwich. Not this far up, but towards the City."

Violet seemed unsurprised by the request, and named two good ones and one she deemed "iffy on senior science, but fine for juniors and humanities".

Daniel said admiringly, "You do keep in touch, don't you?"

"Yes," said Violet, fixing him with a stern blue eye. "I do. Good luck. There are a surprising number of *family* houses for rent in Norfolk. Since the property recession."

He could not tell whether she was making this observation because of something in the newspaper. The old woman had turned back to her reading with such close attention that he did not ask. He ate some muesli, thinking enviously of Jamie's hot breakfast, and told her he would be out for the morning. She only said, without looking up, "Good hunting."

Alice woke stiff and aching on Monday morning. The four hours had turned into six, with a wilderness of lorries north of London and crawling traffic through the suburbs. The 2CV was, she reflected, a terrible car on fast roads, so light that the wind of every passing truck made it shake and swerve and bounce. Still, it had got her home, and miraculously there was a parking space close to the front door. She had come into the Camden house at eleven, shuddering with cold and nervous reaction, and made herself a cup of tea in the unnaturally quiet, spotless kitchen. There was no sign of the cat, although a neat row of cat food tins stood on the worktop, an unfamiliar supermarket brand. The house, she thought, felt dead. It was only a week since she had left, nine days since Jamie had, but it felt like a long-abandoned and outgrown place. The bed, too, was cold and dead. She had filled a hot-water bottle, switched on the immersion heater and shivered herself to sleep.

Now she crept out of bed and ran the hot water. Lying in the bath, she mentally ticked off what she must do. Check the post. Jamie's clothes, and more shoes; the same for herself. Letter to Alan; speak to Yazz. Speak to Stevie.

She was halfway through Jamie's packing when the doorbell rang. A familiar waif-like figure stood there.

"I recognized the car," said Lisha nervously. "In the road, I mean. I mean that I knew it was you and not Mr McDonald. Because of the coat on the back seat. I didn't—"

Alice motioned her indoors. "Look, don't keep on going over it," she said. "I'm very grateful that you fed Catto so efficiently, and thank you for bringing the post in and everything."

"You don't have to thank me, because—"

"I know. Because you're doing it to atone for your sins. Yes, fine. Where is the cat, by the way?"

"That's what I came to tell you. It stopped coming for its food. We found it in one of the other gardens. It took ten of us half a day," said Lisha with a trace of pride. Clearly, a mass cat hunt constituted pretty good communal atoning. "It was lying there. We thought it was ill, so we asked Chris what to do and then we all took it to the vet. We decided we would pay, as part of the – you know. Only it didn't cost much, because it wasn't exactly ill."

"What was wrong with it?" said Alice, diverted in spite of herself by the image of Lisha, Father Chris, and her earnest confrères processing round to the vet with a cat borne aloft instead of a censer or a cross.

"It's – she's – had six kittens," said Lisha. "One was stuck, apparently. That's why she felt ill." Disconcertingly, her eyes filled with tears. "The kittens are so beautiful, only one – one was dead."

"Sit down," said Alice, gently. "Sit down, Lisha, It's all right to cry. I'd cry too if I'd gone through what you have, and then ran up against a kitten tragedy." She passed the girl a piece of kitchen paper off the roll on the wall.

"It never even had a chance to grow fur!" Lisha burst out in grief. "The others are getting fur now, and I keep thinking of it dead and bald."

"It's all right to be sad," said Alice. "Cry for the kitten, go on."

"But Chris says," the words came out muffled, "Chris says you shouldn't load the person you're atoning to, shouldn't load them with your own feelings."

"Quite right," said Alice. "But this atoning business does seem to have an awful lot of hard rules."

Lisha looked up, astonished, to see that Alice was laughing. "That's what my parents say. They say religion's all very well if you don't take it too far, and that I'm crazy and ought to live at home. But I only started going to the Mission because of them, I was so upset at what they did to Da— to Mr McDonald. It was so unfair. But I mustn't, not to you—" She began to cry again.

Alice shook her shoulder gently. "Come on. Brace up. Where is the cat, anyway?"

"At the Mission." Lisha gulped, but seemed grateful for the new subject.

"That is a very appropriate place for her, since it's a miracle birth. The people who gave her to Clemmie said she was spayed years ago and really old anyway. They were going abroad. We've had her years and she's never shown a sign of kittens. Perhaps it's the change of cat food that jolted her system into action."

Lisha had composed herself now and dabbed a final time at her eyes with the kitchen paper. "We'll look after the kittens. Till you get back. And I'll still do the papers and things."

"No need. I'm cancelling them. You mind the kittens, and I'll let you know what's happening. Would you be allowed to keep one or two? At the Mission?"

"I'd have to ask," said Lisha, but her eyes glowed. "They're all proper tortoiseshell, with all the colours. One's got a black mask like a bandit."

"Tell Father Chris it's part of the atoning, and that I insist," said Alice. "Now run along. I'm packing."

The interview with Lisha, and the surprising discovery that she no longer bore the girl a shred of malice, buoyed Alice up on her journey to Portland Place. She did not telephone first but appeared at the reception desk at Euradio and asked for Miss Hunter. "Ms Hunter," repeated the receptionist, with a slight stress on the *Miz*, "is in a meeting. Will you wait?"

Alice waited. Half an hour passed, during which she looked around the sleek lobby, lined with awards and with framed ornaments artfully designed to suggest that they, too, were awards. There was a picture of Yasmin, dark and positive, her hair slicked back so that with her curving nose and fierce eyes she put even Alice, who loved her, in mind of a bird of prey. Smart, fast-moving men came in and out, and young women with short black skirts and baggy knitted jumpers over their flat chests darted neatly in and out of the lift. Alice sat and watched them, feeling frumpish and maternal and outlandish in her voluminous – but, she thought defensively, seasonally warm – striped velvet skirt. She was wearing some Venetian glass beads which she had flung on that morning because they reminded her of Clementine spending her last holiday money at a stand outside the Ferrovia in Venice. Glancing at the receptionist's skinny torso in a plain cream knitted silk sweater, she surreptitiously took the beads off and dropped them in her too-messy, too-large leather bag.

When at last she was sent up in the mirrored lift, she found Yasmin glowingly pleased to see her.

"Alice! Thank God you've turned up! Have you seen Alan yet? No? Tell you what, we'll go out for an early lunch then I'll take you in to the newsroom ten minutes before their one-fifteen meeting, and Roddy will run you through everything. You can do Personnel and Contracts tomorrow."

"No," said Alice. This was going to be harder than she thought. "No, Yazz, I came to tell you that I can't."

"What do you mean?"

The silence was so charged that Alice stumbled over her next words. "I can't – come and work. I'm sorry. It's all too complicated. I shouldn't have come after the job. I have written to Alan. I would have rung him, only I thought I should see you."

"Alice," said Yasmin, "every day this week I have been to Alan's office and made excuses for you. Every day for a week Alan has threatened to withdraw the offer. He's said you're clearly irresponsible, discourteous, and unprofessional. Every day this week I have had to bloody well talk him out of it. And now you say you don't want the job anyway."

"I know," said Alice miserably. "I just am sorry, that's all. But I couldn't leave Jamie, and I don't see that I will this side of Christmas, and he's in Norfolk, and I don't know where I'm going to be. In the long term."

Yasmin got up from her desk and paced, helpless with anger, round the big office she had fought to occupy. Alan was not her immediate superior but technically an equal; however, news assistants were his responsibility and she had needed to put some pressure of persuasion on him to welcome Alice so warmly. Alan had quite enjoyed the game; Alan, she thought bitterly, enjoyed all sorts of power games, and if there was a sexual frisson there, so much the better. Living with him for eleven years had prepared her for most of his savage little ploys, but it was some time since any of them had disturbed her like the past week's taunts. "Your little friend the house-mouse . . . love the way you girls stick together – divorcing, is she?" And finally, on Friday afternoon when she had to admit yet again, in front of everybody at the one-fifteen meeting, that Alice was not in the building, he had said, "Yazzie, love, wouldn't it be less *trouble* just to set your *friend* up in a little flat somewhere?"

Yasmin had suffered, all right. Alice, on the other hand, appeared beautiful and calm and unexpectedly radiant, even in those dreadful clothes that looked as if they were bought second-hand from a travelling folk band.

"So, just like that, you're turning it down. After stringing us along for a week. Alice, do you have any fucking idea what I had to do to get you this job?"

"You didn't have to."

"I must have been sodding well mad to. I suppose you're going to live in Norfolk now, are you?"

"I think so. Dan's job is there."

"Your job is here. You know you'd be earning as much as him within a year or so. More, probably."

"Yes, but, the main thing is, I don't belong to all this. I belong to a family. I think it has to stay together."

"Oh, think about it, Allie." Yasmin's rage was ebbing now, her care for Alice forcing its way back to the surface. "You'll give up your home, and your friends, and go to live in some godforsaken *suburb* of *Norwich*. You won't get any job that uses your mind, you won't be anybody, you'll be the scrimping, saving wife of a dead-end redbrick don."

Alice raised her hand as if in self-defence and opened her mouth to say something, but Yasmin swept on.

"A dead-end redbrick don who shags around. Don't think it'll stop. He's at that sort of age. Alice, I was only trying to *rescue* you."

"I don't have a choice," said Alice. "Even if it was true about the shagging around, which I'm not convinced of. While the children still need both of us, both of us ought to be there."

"I was only trying to rescue you from a rubbish life," said Yasmin again, stabbing a pen viciously into her thick padded blotter. Alice looked up sharply. It was an odd emphasis: why should Yazz, who never wasted words, say twice that she had no motive beyond rescue? Why go on about it, unless it wasn't entirely true? This, she uneasily saw, went further than mere annoyance about work. Yasmin wanted her to stay in London, apart from Daniel, a single working woman like herself. Company, reinforcement. Maybe she always had wanted that. Wanted Alice's family out of the way.

"Yazz," she said carefully, "I'm sorry if I've screwed things up for you at work, and I have apologized in a letter to Alan. But I have to do what I have to do. I've got responsibilities. I have to judge for myself whether I should live with Daniel."

She paused, looking with troubled affection at Yazz standing behind the desk, tense and accusing and more than ever like a bird of prey. Then slowly, deliberately, Alice added, "I'm not yours to rescue."

Yasmin's face closed, her lids drooping, her eyes angry slits. "Alice McDonald," she said with slow, soft hatred, "I've been a bit wrong about you, haven't I? You're a coward, you're a doormat, you're a sentimental waste of space. I wish I had never bloody well set eyes on you."

"Funny," said Alice, getting up and hefting her muddled leather bag. "You're the second person who's said that to me in a week."

But things were easier, surprisingly easy and affectionate, when with her heart pounding uncomfortably she went into GardenGrow to make her peace with Stevie. He sprang from behind a display of vegetarian cheeses and bay leaves to embrace her, and in the dark doorway from the inner regions Simon stood, silhouetted, going through an exaggerated mime of obeisance and delight while Stevie spoke.

"Allie, gorgeous Alice, I have rung, and rung, and called and peered through the windows. I have thought of pushing roses one by one through your letterbox, only they might have faded and been bad luck. Where have you *been*? Is Jamie all right? We thought he must be when they let Simon go, but we didn't *know*!"

"Jamie is better than fine," said Alice. "And I am sorrier than sorry, I really am, about Simon."

"It was only one night," said Simon, flicking back his forelock. "And actually, once your sweet Detective Sergeant Clough moved in, they were terribly nice. And I do have some horrid friends of friends, and I think I helped the coppers a bit. Not about murders, you understand, just horridness down the 'Dilly arcades."

"He did," said Stevie. "He was a star. So sweet, not vengeful at all, were you, pet? You reminded me of that picture of Saint Sebastian smiling though pierced with arrows."

"Wasn't that Saint Stephen?"

"No, he was stoned."

"Weren't we all."

"Did you know," said Stevie, "that Saint Sebastian didn't die of the arrows? He was nursed back to health by a widow called Irene. My nan used to tell me."

"No! Really? Irene? *Fab*."

The two men, Alice realized gratefully, were carrying on like this because she was so near to tears. But her laughter turned into sobbing nonetheless, and there was a woman customer standing uncertainly in the shop doorway poised to flee, so Stevie nodded Simon to serve her and led Alice through the door to the storeroom and the living room beyond. As they went, she could hear Simon chirruping to the customer, "No, you're so right, tofu's rather last-Wednesday-fortnight, but the oat cutlets are *sensational*."

Alone with Stevie, she said, "What happened?"

"He got questioned and held till they got your phone call on Monday morning. But they were going to let him go anyway, they knew it was nonsense. Sergeant Clough talked to the Gay Liaison Squad or whatever it's called. Simon was super all the way. Very calm."

"He wasn't as furious with me as you were?"

"To my shame, no. He was sweet. Worried about Jamie, too."

"I do love Simon," said Alice.

"Me too. And Allie," he dropped his voice and moved his lined face nearer to her with an exaggeratedly grotesque expression, the one he used for his much appreciated rendering of *Have some Madeira, m'dear*, "the good bit is that he's gone a wee bit thoughtful about his little weekends of adventure. The charm is fading rather."

"Adolescence over?" said Alice.

"I think so. At last. Now, tell me about Jamie. Where? Why? Why is he 'better than fine'? And are you going to be sensible and move back in with hunky Dan the Philosophy Man?"

34

Daniel closed the door of the redbrick house and slipped the keys in his pocket for the agent. It was a damp, raw, misty day now tending to dusk, but in his mind's eye he saw daffodils along the drive, blossom on the apple and pear trees and, best of all, boats passing on the river. The house had no river frontage – it would not have been up for rent so cheaply if it had – and if there were to be a dinghy it would have to be dragged across the main road on its trolley and down a farm footpath. But it could be done, with a light boat. Jamie would like that. He would like the school too: ten minutes away on the bus, with pictures and batiks and collages and irreverent poems on every available inch of wall and a headmaster with a broad Norfolk accent, a sharp mind, and the county's informal motto "Do Different" framed on the wall of his office. Mr Henshaw had been charmed by the story of Jamie's escapade and confided that he was having an educational outing to the Cold Fair for years 8 to 13.

"Victorian engineering. Recreational uses of industrial revolution technology. Whatever you like. Do you think this Rowley would come and do a talk?"

"I think it might be full of expletives," said Daniel.

"Good," said Mr Henshaw. "They might listen, then."

Driving away from the village, Daniel severely told himself to count no chickens. Alice had a London job. It would be a hard and serious thing for her to give that up and find herself a role in this wet, beguiling, lonely Broadland wilderness. He must not use Jamie's welfare as a bargaining counter. He must be prepared to offer his own return to Camden, if she wanted it. He might get teaching work at one of the former polytechnics, or in a sixth form. But at least he now had a shape of life to offer in Norfolk. For a year or two, anyway. On the outskirts of the city, he dropped the keys back in to the estate agents. The girls behind the counter watched him go.

"Handsome," said one. "Mr Darcy, eh, Ginny?" For a version of *Pride and Prejudice* had lately swept the nation for the second time of showing and Jane Austen's prideful hero had become synonymous with brooding romance.

"Yeah," said the other. "That house in't Pemberley, though. Ever so damp, Mr Roake said. And creepy."

"Well, they like that," said her colleague sagely. "London people. They call that character."

Daniel was late picking up Jamie and found him in the farm cottage, eating a slab of Susan's lardy cake. He brought it into the car and continued eating as they drove off.

"Jamie, do you like Finchamgrove?" asked his father.

"No," said a muffled voice through the greasy cake. "I hate it."

"Would you like to go to another school?"

"Not a sporting excellence one," said Jamie more distinctly. "Forget that. Clemmie can hack it, I can't, no way. Could I go to art school?"

"Not yet," said Daniel. "But if everything changed, if we didn't live in Camden for a bit but out here somewhere and you went to school near Norwich?"

"Day school?"

"Yes. Comprehensive."

"Great," said Jamie, and dived into another mouthful of lardy cake. Daniel let the subject drop.

Violet Lancing rose from her knees, laid the rosary down in front of the icon of Our Lady, and turned composedly to greet the Colonel who had been in the room some time, quietly turning the pages of an ancient catechism from her shelves.

"Sorry, Geoffrey. Today is a momentous day. Prayer was necessary."

"You're sorting those two out, aren't you?" he said admiringly, laying the catechism down.

"I am doing nothing," said Violet primly. "I am not interfering. God is doing it."

"Good old God," said the Colonel heartily. "Incidentally, you know confession? Absolution? All that?"

"Yes?"

"Well, when you're absolved, right, the sin's all gone? You don't have to keep on atoning for it? You start fresh?"

"Yes. In a sense. But ethically you must of course return any gain your sin brought to you."

"But you aren't honour bound to be miserable for ever because you are a sinner?"

"That," said Violet, "would itself be a sin against the Holy Ghost."

"Good old God," said the Colonel again. "Tea?"

Daniel and Jamie came home before the teapot was cold. The old couple were sitting in their usual chairs but something different hung in the air between them.

"Can I?" asked the Colonel, looking at Violet. She nodded. "News, chaps. Miss Lancing has done me the honour to accept a proposal of marriage."

"What?" said Jamie. "But you're—" Daniel shot him a warning look.

"Old. Yes indeed," said Violet. "Ancient. But nonetheless, engaged to be married."

Jamie, exalted from a good day's work, could not contain his curiosity and ignored Daniel. "But you could have got married years ago," he said. "My mum said you knew each other *fifty years* ago."

"More," said the Colonel. "And to tell you the truth, young man, which you might as well know because you'll have women of your own to handle one day, I asked your Godgran several times in the nineteen fifties and she said no."

"Did you keep on asking?"

"He did not," said Violet. "In fact, today's proposal is the first since nineteen fifty-six. Forty years without a proposal, imagine!"

Daniel could not, seeing the degree of levity with which the old fiancés were willing to treat their situation, resist joining in the questioning.

"Might I ask what brought on the, er, resumption of hostilities?" he asked.

Violet glanced at the Colonel. "Shall we just say, Geoffrey," she put her hand on his, "that it was in the air?"

Alice left Camden at five, the back seat and the boot full of clothes, wellingtons and books and a basket of cheese and exotic ham from GardenGrow as a present from Stevie to "this *heroic* great-aunt or whatever she is who's putting you all up and saving the day". The little car struggled up the North London hills in a mounting flurry of sleet which turned into snow when she reached the M11. She wished she had taken the gentler eastern route, past Chelmsford and Colchester; lorries flung up great sheets of dirty water and rattling ice particles, swamping her little car. Cold water dripped in through the gaps at the top of the doors and the torn patches in the canopy. She delved into the bucket bag at her side and pulled out a woolly hat of Jamie's, jamming it on her head with one hand as she drove, hunched and tense, up the merciless motorway.

She almost wept with relief as she turned off it. But the darker roads leading into Norfolk filled her with a new trepidation: it was cold, so cold, and the snow was beginning to lie deep on the verges. Suppose the damn car packed up again? Mr Mundersleeves' repairs had no claim to be anything but a jury rig; he would probably have been horrified to know that Alice was driving to and from London, even at thirty-five miles an hour. She wished she had a companion. Or a mobile phone. Anything to alleviate the threatening loneliness. She focused on the haven of Moss Cottage, pretending it was round the next corner. The day had been a hard, emotional one. As she closed the door on the Camden house, she had a strong sense of closing a chapter in all their lives. It had left her exhausted. She wondered whether to stop in some small town while there still were towns and check into a pub for the night, but was too drawn by the vision of the cottage, of warmth and lamplight, of Jamie and Godgran and the Colonel.

And Daniel. Unless he had driven back to Norwich, anticipating her return, Daniel would be there. She put her foot down and coaxed the little car up to 45 mph, rattling and bouncing along the highway.

Hours later, north of Fakenham, at last she relaxed. Not far now. Cruising along in its fifth gear at 40 mph, melting snow running down the insides of the doors, the little car was gallantly getting her home. Funny that it should feel like home, more like home than Camden. Odd, she thought hazily, how fast the focus of home could change, the needle swing.

Approaching a sharp bend under the trees, Alice put her hand on the worn pommel of the gear stick. The old plastic globe broke in half under the pressure of her palm. Startled but quick to react, she gripped the bare steel rod instead and pushed her foot down on the clutch to change down into second gear. The clutch went down under her foot normally enough but abruptly lost tension and flopped uselessly to the floor. The gear lever would not move. By now her foot was on the brake and the light little car was going into a long bumpy skid. Too late, Alice got her left hand back on to the wheel. Nothing could have steered the car. Nor stopped it from continuing its skid, head on into the still darkness of the ditch. Something hit her forehead and Alice's world went black.

By ten o'clock Daniel was nervous; by half past, with Jamie despatched to bed, he was pacing around Violet's living room, an activity for which he was patently too big and the room too small.

"She should be here by now. God, it's snowing hard. She'd either have got here or stopped and rung up. Is the phone working? We're not cut off?"

"No," said Violet, lifting the telephone for the tenth or eleventh time that evening to check the dialling tone. "No, it's on. Are you sure she would have rung?"

"Yes, yes, yes," said Daniel. "She's not unreliable that way, never at all." With a stab of shame, he remembered the night in the pub with Dave, the comradely agreement between them that all women were devious and unreliable even over children. "She would have rung, Godma."

At eleven, he rang the police. Violet still sat by the fire, her book open on her lap, as if she suspected that her Whistler's Mother tranquillity might help him. It did, to some extent. Waiting on the line, tapping his feet, breathing hard through his teeth, he looked at her and felt momentarily safer. Anchored.

The police offered no clue. Yes, there had been accidents. You expected it, this weather. No Citroën 2CVs, though, not on the M11. Nor the A12. Nor on any of the Cambridgeshire or Norfolk side roads, not so far. Oh yes, hang on – a green one, involved in an RTA at Great Yarmouth, by the bridge. No? Well then, sir, nothing yet. Daresay she's just coming on a bit slowly, it's the best way, this weather.

Daniel put the phone down and said to Violet, "I'm going

out. Going to drive down your roads a little way. It's the most dangerous bit, with all those bends. I won't be long. Will you be up? If I ring to see if she's home?"

"Yes," said Violet. "I might say a prayer."

"Do that," said Daniel. "You know what I think about all that, but my mum would have insisted on saying one, so you might as well."

He put on his heavy coat and scarf, borrowed a moth-eaten fur hat of Geoffrey's which hung in the kitchen lobby, and crunched out into the snowy lane. The snow was falling thick and fast now, piling up in the narrow lane; it occurred to him that neither he nor Alice would necessarily be able to get a car into Wetheringham later, but they could always leave the cars on the main road, which rarely blocked. Maybe she was already walking in. He drove carefully through the snow, his wheels spinning occasionally, and began the journey down past Bailey's farm crossroad, and southward towards Fakenham.

Alice came round slowly, conscious at first of extreme cold and of something that cut savagely into her neck. Her seatbelt. Fumbling beside her for the catch, she pushed the button and, to her surprise, fell forward on to the steering wheel, catching her chin a sharp blow. The car was nose down, ridiculously so; the piled clothes on the back seat had risen up and begun to climb over into the front. There was a goat's milk cheese resting on the windscreen. The smashed windscreen. An accident. She had crashed the car, for the first time in her life! But she was alive, albeit aching. Carefully she moved her hands, then her whole arms, shrugged her shoulders, and tested her feet and legs. No problems. The clutch felt funny, flat on the floor. It was the clutch – and the gear lever – that had done the mischief. Perhaps dear Mr Mundersleeves had some more bits left over from his son's car which would patch things up.

The sound of her own manic giggle at the thought of the mechanic and his son brought Alice suddenly back to waking reality. She was – oh, God, somewhere. Ten or eleven miles from Moss Cottage. She remembered thinking how blessedly close it was, just before the crash. It was snowing hard outside and the ditch in which her bonnet rested was filling up with whiteness. It would fill the car soon, or bury it. She must get out. But outside it was cold. And which way would a telephone be? She remembered the night eight days before when she had walked one of these damned roads, looking for Jamie's telephone box, and gagged with sudden fright. Her eyes filled with tears. Not again, not another walk through the winter night, afraid and alone.

"Dan," she whispered. "Oh Dan, come on, I need you." There was an engine, coming closer. A car. That was something. They could take her to a phone, tell Dan, get a hotel, anything. Just not, please not, whiz past and leave her alone out here in the snow. They wouldn't, would they? Not in Norfolk? People in the country looked after one another, didn't they? Or maybe not, these days. She opened the bent door with difficulty and dragged herself out. The engine was getting closer, the driver might not see her. In her long black coat, Alice struggled desperately in the deep ditchful of snow, climbing at last to its edge and kneeling there, arms flailing, trying to be visible in the dazzling headlights which were almost on her.

Daniel slowed down, seeing some black arms waving. Could be branches, could be a walker. The headlights picked out a kneeling, waving form emerging from a mound of snow at the roadside. He stopped, as near to the edge as he dared, and wrenched the door open.

"Help!" said the form.

"Alice?"

"Yes!"

He ran to her, knelt in the snow and held her. For a while neither said anything, nor moved. Then gently he pulled her upright and helped her to his car.

"Sit there. I'll move the kit across." And Alice sat in the front of his car, shaking with relief as in the headlights' beam she watched him working, bringing successive loads of clothes, boots, books and cheeses carefully across the wilderness towards her. And stopping, each trip, to put a hand on her shoulder and ask again, "All right? Sure? I won't be long. I love you."

At midnight, Violet put down her rosary again and smiled at the impassive golden picture of the Virgin. "Thank you," she murmured. And she went upstairs to prepare tranquilly for bed. There was just enough human doubt left in her to keep her awake until she heard them half an hour later, two pairs of footsteps and some giggling whispers. She closed her eyes, pleased. One of them could sleep on the sofa. Or perhaps – the old woman's smile broadened as she lay there with her crêped eyelids closed, her arms folded on her breast the way she had learned long ago from the nuns – perhaps they could *both* sleep on the sofa.

Dear Clemmie,

The hot news is that Catto has – wait for it, wait for it – had kittens. Five alive, one died. Remarkable, considering that the Hudsons swore to us that she was spayed in 1985! Even odder, it seems they're all full tortoiseshell with all the colours. One has a mask like a bandit.

The other hot news is that Dad has found a brilliant house, near the Broads. Great big Victorian brick thing, with a lot of terrible falling-down sheds. We drove down to see it today and it certainly looks pretty in the snow. Probably because the falling-down sheds look better that way. You can see the river from your bedroom, and Jamie is wild to have a boat he can play Coot Club in. Dad can get to work in half an hour and there's a day school for Jamie ten minutes' bus ride down the road. Dad says the headmaster is great, and it wins a lot of national prizes for art. We can rent the house for the moment, two years anyway, which means we don't have to sell Camden. We'll find a tenant for it, quite easily I should think. The nice girl who feeds the cat can show people round after Christmas, when we've moved.

Clementine put her mother's letter down on the breakfast table and looked around at her companions. Sunita, Clare, and Sharon were reading their own post but Diana, her closest friend, said, "Well? News from the broken home?"

"Yup. Not broken any more. Reconstituted, in sunny Norfolk."

"That's good. Is it?"

"Double yup." Clemmie raised both thumbs and grinned.

"Were you really going to pack in BCSE and go back to London if they split?" asked Diana curiously. "To look after your brother?"

"Well," said Clemmie, "like I said, that's what I told my dad."

"Would you have done it? Even now you're in the event team?"

Clemmie hunched one shoulder, twisted her face into a horrid rictus, and quavered in reedy rustic tones, "Nay, niver ask that, child! Niver ask! My secret mun go to my grave wi' me."

The class, under a peculiarly imaginative English teacher, had been reading *Cold Comfort Farm*, and it had entered deeply into their daily conversation. Dropping her impression of Judith Starkadder, Clemmie glanced down at the letter again and said, "More hot news. My cat's had kittens. Five. All tortoiseshell, proper tortie with all the colours, and one's got a mask like a bandit."

The other girls broke off from reading their letters and gave the matter their full attention.

"Oh, brilliant!"

"Can I have one?"

"Shall we ask to have a House one here?"

Clemmie dispensed notional kittens, benevolently.

Dear Olivia,

Thank you for your news. I am delighted the Bishop has told the senior laity to take a firmer line about these terrible women. To recruit hoteliers is an excellent scheme. It will save you personally weighing in against these predatory Hausfrauen, which must be very tiring and tedious. People always believe that a nun, or indeed any virtuous woman, can know little of the imperatives of sex. You and I know the fallacy in that.

My dear, I am to marry Geoffrey. I see now that I was arrogant to refuse him as I did year after year. I was not responsible for Celia's death, and he risked his life to prevent it. We should have taken the joy we were offered, and it was wrong of me to cling to the guilt which had been washed away by our willing Lord, years before.

Almost as wrong, I am thinking, as the ridiculous rift between my godson Daniel and his impetuous wife, of which I wrote last week. That is now quite resolved. The pleasing thing is that although their resolution was romantic enough (a rescue in the snow, very Barbara Cartland) it was plain beforehand that each of them had accepted the duty to reunite, independent of any surge of emotion. But emotion there has been; and I suspect that the time we have all shared with that young family has been the catalyst for Geoffrey and myself. One does become ossified, at our age. The comfort of friendship seems too great to risk.

I think I always meant to make this marriage. Perhaps if Geoffrey had not gone away in 1960, perhaps if he had come back from Oman a decade earlier than he did, he would have asked again and I would have given a different answer. We were already getting old when he came to Wetheringham, an elderly schoolmarm and a retired Colonel; how could it be a courtship? But now here we are, with a combined age of 156, to be married on Christmas Eve. The absurdity of doing any such thing at our age does not escape me. But oh, Ollie, nor does the joy of it!

The old nun, her face shrivelled and bleached to parchment by years of African sun, smiled down at her letter and gave inward thanks for the pleasure of reading good news from home in the coolness of the evening. Tomorrow she would write her own letter, full of dry enduring love, to the sister she would never see again.

There were hundreds, thousands even, at the Cold Fair. The park had a gentle slope to it which in Norfolk passed for a hill. On the summit of that just perceptible hill, at the heart of the fair, stood Bailey's gallopers. Steam rose comfortably from the central chimney, and as the dusk fell, the ride stood bright against the dull frosty air, the year's last defiance of the winter and the dark.

Whirling or standing, there was every piece of light and gilding, all the myriad images and shapes of bird and beast, hero, prince and treasure that Victorian yearning had brought into being and a long, unrecorded craft tradition had maintained. Around it, the other rides and games picked up the style, proclaiming in overcurled lettering *British and Best, Original and Remarkable, Jolly and Joyful, Hot Dogs £2.00 Only the Freshest*. Beyond those again, the trade and charity stalls did a roaring trade in Christmas presents from high craft to low trash, and on the fringes a group of car boot stalwarts had set out their trestles and planks.

Alice and Daniel wandered through the fair hand in hand. Violet and the Colonel had spent an hour here and gone on to pass the night with Norwich friends; Clemmie had attached herself instantly and effortlessly to the Baileys and was running a popcorn stall with brisk efficiency. Jamie was where he had asked to be, beside the gaudy pay desk at the heart of the gallopers, helping Tim with the engine and organ and taking money from riders.

Rowley was nowhere to be seen. Alice had hoped to talk to him at the fair, to thank him for all he had given to Jamie. She had a private vision of herself becoming his friend, almost patron; feeding him the odd meal as Violet did, hearing his stories, sharing him with her friends, having him paint some amusing fairground patterns up her banisters. But Susan Bailey, harassedly minding the small children's roundabout, was surprised when Alice asked about him. Everybody knew, she said, that Rowley never came to fairs while they were running. "He gets it all ready, helps build up if he's sober. Then he takes his money and goes. Always the same. I'm afraid he goes off and drinks for a while on his own. But we'll see him again in February, we always do. He needs the work by then, and we need him to get ready for the season. So we feed him up a bit."

Susan turned to take some money from a draggled mother whose children jumped impatiently at her side, and Alice felt a sudden unfamiliar wave of shame. She saw that she had wanted to catch Rowley and make him a quaint little social lion for her own benefit. Jamie had been odd about it when she talked of "having him round for a few meals"; clearly, Jamie knew better than she did. So she just asked Susan, "Is he all right? Living all winter in that little caravan?"

Susan began to answer, but Ed Bailey appeared behind her, with a bag of cash strapped to his belt, and moved to put his arm round his wife's shoulders in a brief cuddle. "He always has been all right, girl. So far, so good. Rowley is Rowley, thass all. No point trying to change him now."

"No point at all." Alice smiled, and walked on through the fair a few paces behind Daniel, who as if drawn by a magnet kept heading for the gallopers and his son. She thrust a hand deep into her coat pocket and felt the shape of a letter. She had found it in Camden yesterday before she and Clemmie took the train up to Norwich. Oh, the ease and speed of that train! Her car, she resolved, would never again stray outside a twenty-mile radius of wherever home might be. Even though Jamie had promised to paint it up like a galloper.

The paper of the letter was thick, crisp and expensive; the writing dashing and familiar, the message short.

Dear Alice,

   OK, I give in. Never again will I try to drive the mother hen off its nest. I did try to change you, and only half of it was for your sake. A pointless exercise either way. But I don't really wish that I had never set eyes on you. Good luck.

Love
Yazz

She had underlined *love*. Not heavily, but Alice knew what such gestures cost her, and treasured the tiny pen mark accordingly. There was a postscript.

   PS. I presume even the unworldly Aquarian wives of obscure redbrick dons need some sort of job. If you ring 01703 66699 (Eastward Opera) and ask for Martin Lisle, he will tell you about the new regional touring company. They got the first Lottery grant not tied strictly to buildings. It came through last week. He is expecting a call. He has got some deals with our highbrow European radio partners and no doubt hopes for more.

Alice knew the letter by heart. Tomorrow, perhaps, she would ring Martin Lisle from Mrs Hammond's. Mrs Hammond was very obliging about her private telephone, indeed about everything since she had started staying there. She really could not see what Daniel so disliked about the woman. But it would be nice to move to their own place by the river after Christmas in Camden.

They reached the gallopers just as the horses began to slow their plunging pace. Jamie waved from the booth, then came out to help a small child off a ginger horse. On its neck was its name: *Aida*. Behind it, a quartet of horses galloped neck and neck, mouths open and eyes rolling, and the names on their necks had been Susan Bailey's thank you present to Jamie in the last long hectic days of preparation. They might, thought Alice, gallop on together with these names through another century, or for as long as there were showmen to run them and Rowleys to paint them. Slowly they began to move again, and she looked at them with love. The first three scrolled names were *Danny*, *Alice*, *Clem*. "No room for all your long name, bumface," Jamie had rudely said.

But the blackest and wildest of all, with savage eyes and

dazzling white teeth and a royal coat of arms on its breast, was *Jack*. "Well," Ed Bailey said judicially when Daniel raised his eyebrows about this at the unveiling. "If a boy can't choose his own name . . ."

Casting Off
LIBBY PURVES

What makes a wife and mother, pillar of the community and partner in a cosy tea-shop (The Bun in the Oven) suddenly run away to sea, alone?

Joanna Gurney hardly knows herself. But as she moves along the rocky, dangerous coast of Britain, evading police and press, Joanna meets other cast-off and washed-up individuals in 1990s Britain, and finds that she can also make a voyage into her own past. And, in the end, find her solution.

'Ms Purves has the gift of tongues – a born novelist'
Fay Weldon

'Humour, humanity and relish for the enjoyably mundane'
The Times

'A feel-good novel . . . hilarious . . . humorous . . . fabulously incisive'
Independent

'Well-told and enjoyable . . . [the voice] is that of someone genuinely interested in the varieties of human experience, amused but not mocking, understanding but not judgmental'
Sunday Telegraph

'A glorious romp . . . with a healthy dose of satire on media manners and a generous injection of knockabout comedy into the bargain'
Country Living

∫

SCEPTRE